He playfully
lace, her soft skin excited by his touch. She reached
behind her back, allowing the covering to fall. His hands
moved lightly down her slender back as he unbuttoned
her skirt. He gazed into the caressing eyes of this goddess
standing before him and wondered how it was that he
stood in her presence. Her hair flowed down around her
soft shoulders, just barely covering her angelic skin. She
tilted her head as she looked past his eyes and straight
into his soul; her lips curved into a slight smile as her
unspoken passion burned through him. For the first time
in her life, she was happy and fulfilled.

Without words, slowly and deliberately, she
unbuttoned his shirt. He wrapped his arms around her
and pulled her closer. Her head fell back as his lips gently
touched her neck. Lucas had never been with a woman
like this, and heaven could not have been closer at that
moment, he thought.

Savannah gasped with sweet surrender as they
became one, folding onto her bed. A touch, delicate and
tender, she was warm and soft. Tomorrow would bring
no regret. Tonight, there would be no moments of shame.
They released their passionate desires, holding no
secrets. They surrendered into each other's arms without
regret as time passed two lost souls into the morning
light.

Praise for Steven LaBree

"I enjoyed the story."

~ Sam Keen

"Steven writes with incredible emotion."

~ Jeanne Krause

"What a story! I loved it! Your words and descriptions are masterful."

~ Borbala Branch

A Heart Lies Within Us

by

Steven LaBree

A Heart Lies Within Us

Cover Art by *Kim Mendoza*

The Wild Rose Press, Inc.
PO Box 708
Adams Basin, NY 14410-0708
Visit us at www.thewildrosepress.com

Publishing History
First Edition, 2022
Trade Paperback ISBN 978-1-5092-4331-0
Digital ISBN 978-1-5092-4332-7

Published in the United States of America

Dedication

To the only woman, I have ever truly loved

Chapter 1

In the letter my father gave me it said, "Just after I turned eighteen, just before I left home, I killed a man. I told myself it was an accident, but no one in town would have believed me—not with my reputation, nor his.

There was no way I was going to hang for his death, so I chucked the lantern down the hallway toward the back of the house and watched for a moment as yellow flames raged across the wooden floor and climbed the walls. At the time, the whole thing made perfect sense. I figured before anyone would notice the fire, gather help, and haul in water, there would be nothing but a heap of ashes and smoke, and I'd be long gone.

If you were to ask me to pinpoint the day my life changed, I'd say it was my tenth birthday, August of 1918, the same day my father died.

Eight years later, I buried my mother, the darkness taking her as the wind carries off the flicker of a candle. She said she loved me, but at that point in my life, after I'd learned the truth, I didn't know what to think, and since I couldn't ask her, I guess I had to figure it out for myself.

Being poor didn't begin to describe us. Mother worked, but Finley owned the house, the land, and just about everything else, and at the time, I thought he was a kind man. After she died, I found a tin box full of the lies that my mother had kept hidden under her bed; all the things you don't want anyone to know. All the secrets kept hidden while you are alive. All the things that can destroy any sense of faith or respectability or unconditional love. But because of my curiosity, I opened the box and released the Pandora curse that filled all the evil things of her life, exposing the lie she lived, the truth of my father, and Finley and what he did. If I had never known what happened, how just one man destroyed my family, how he murdered my father, perhaps my life would have been different. Then I think of where I would be today. If I'd never left that town, I would have never met Savannah or your mother, and our lives would have never touched. I suppose that hope rebounds within each life of tragedy and brings us to the right path of our existence, providing us with our purpose.

Still, this made me realize everyone lies, and, in the end, everyone gets what they deserve. Finley, without a doubt, got his.

Since the only thing mother had left me was a whole lot of nothing left to lose, I did what I had to do and walked out the front door as flames began to spread through the tiny house. In retrospect, it was in that moment that I understood, death is sometimes the perfect substitute for life.

My years have taught me that lies, even ones you tell yourself, hide nothing, and if you lie long enough, the deceit becomes the truth you will carry within your heart until it kills you.

I could go on about the other crap; voices through thin walls, over the shoulder looks, deceit from someone you should be able to trust, or the conflict she'd held within her heart that, I believe, killed mother faster than any cancer, but I'll save that for later. I have covered most of my life in the journals on my desk, and they are yours to use as you wish. It's my hope you will learn from the mistakes I've made and the undeserved absolution I've received which showed me that love, although rarely perfect, is a gift that you can only receive when you open your heart to the truth.

It's a sure thing, that you are confused, so it's my hope you will see, through these journals, how we all ended up in this particular place. The last thing I expected after all these years was to find my son."

Chapter 2

I folded that letter, placed it between the pages of my journal, and turned off the lamp. I tried to sleep, but my restless mind thought only of how quickly life could change course.

My wife, children and I had arrived in Brantôme earlier in the week. We were there to visit my father as we often did and enjoyed the area where he and Savannah had retired. We did not intend to bury him on this trip, but as Lucas Colby would've told you, you can never predict the destination of your journey.

I awoke sometime later, knowing it would be hours before the sun would rise. The hearth fire at the far end of the bedroom created a ginger glow across the elaborate ceiling as shadows danced above my bed, entertaining my tired eyes. A soft radiance in an otherwise dark room reflected the surroundings as sleep escaped me. I examined the intricate artwork thinking of the gift found within the hands of the aging master, skills lost through the ages, along with the art, hope, and romance. I was restless and with a slight headache.

My wife slept, and I watched her and thought of how fortunate I was to have found my love so easily when some men try all their lives, searching for the perfect love. She clutched the bedsheet in her slender hand and pulled it closer to her chin. I slid my cover down and lifted myself from the bed.

I stood and raised the sash at the window, hoping to relieve the stale air in the warm room. A light breeze drifted across a marbled sill, and silk curtains billowed as cool air chattered the wooden blinds. Looking through the black of the morning, I closed my eyes, inhaled the taste of morning dew and thought, darkness has a scent all its own.

I stared into the distance, and soon, it seemed night faded as the sun peeked over distant hilltops. I watched as the sky transitioned from starry black to shades of red, orange, yellow, and blended into the cerulean heaven.

The sound of rushing water beyond the surrounding stonewalls drew my attention. It splashed against the water wheel and delivered a souvenir memory reminding me of perhaps how life itself works: lifting, pulling, and turning while the ever-changing tide of the river ebbs without thought to patience or circumstance. Turning away from the window, deciding to go downstairs, I recalled how he was always the first to rise.

The hinges of the oak door creaked as I pulled it open. My wife, in her slumber, shuffled and pulled the bedsheet closer to her face. In the quiet of dawn, passing the library, I recalled the endless joy and laughter created from his engaging stories that always ran deep into the twilight hours as we sat near the warmth of the fireplace. Time advanced quickly and without notice as it does when one is enjoying occasions occupying mind and spirit.

The aroma of fresh coffee, which had welcomed me each morning, was absent. A cold pot sat alone in a kitchen lit only by sunlight streaming through the paned window. Typically, I would've found my father sitting on the portico overlooking the banks of the river, as if in anticipation of a guest long overdue from a journey. I knew he longed for Savannah, missing her every moment of the day and night. He often mentioned how he would give everything he had built or created for one more day in her arms.

I started the coffee and returned upstairs, peeking in on my wife. Still sleeping soundly in the quiet of the morning, I walked to his library where he wrote his stories. I sat at his desk and called to mind our last conversation.

I had entered his bedroom after a soft knock on the door. He was pensive through the evening, and I wanted to ensure his comfort before we retired. He'd appeared to be asleep upon large pillows against an immense and ornate headboard. His hands folded across his stomach. He opened his eyes as I approached and turned his head.

"Running a bit late this morning, are we?" I had asked.

"A bit. I'm a little more tired than usual."

"Well, we have no plans for the day, so just rest, and when you are ready, ring me downstairs. I'll bring you coffee." I stood, and his hand touched mine.

"We had a good time last night, didn't we?"

"Yes. It was a lovely evening, and the children enjoyed it as well."

"Do you have a moment?" he asked, and I knew there was only one answer.

"Of course. What is it you would like?"

"I want to tell you a story."

"You've told us many stories," I said. "Yet, there is still another?"

His expression changed, and his eyes wandered to a place in the past, beyond my view.

"I had a dream last night . . . about Savannah. She reminded me of something I hadn't told you. Not that I haven't wanted to, it's just that—"

"I can't imagine what it would be," I said. "You have shared so many stories."

"True, but this story is different. It's the story you don't know; how all of this ends."

The lines on his face, like a map of life, told a tale few have lived, and I knew it was my time to be quiet.

"Take this advice with you if I teach you nothing else," he said. "Never let deceit stay within your heart and allow a lie to come between you and the one you love. What you hold inside your heart will define you. It will define your life."

His eyes glistened, like emeralds in a treasured life, showing happiness and yet some regret as he continued.

"After leaving my past, I lived my life believing everything I did had a purpose. Before those times, before I met Savannah, the world bowed to me. I had wealth, power, and everything a man could want. I was that man before Savannah. Now, I am not. What the world saw in me was only the shell of the man. What Savannah saw in me was the man I could be. I refused to listen to her, broke the rules, made my own, and treated people who loved me without compassion. I have paid for those deeds many times."

I realized this was his confession, truths from a man believing his time would soon pass. I felt a tinge of discomfort knowing of secrets not shared but understood. Perception is an odd companion. As you grow up, innocence allows you to believe so many things as truths only. In time, you discover things are not as they seem.

My mother and I had shared many talks; her love for Lucas was evident. Together, the gazes shared between them, something in their eyes one rarely sees in a relationship, told of a secret only they knew. Now, I was beginning to understand.

"There is no reason why you should share this with me, Lucas," I said to him.

"There are many reasons," he said. "Some of which you know nothing of." He continued as if this conversation must persist without close. "Over the past few years, we have talked of a great many things. There is still so much you don't know about my life, Savannah, and even your mother."

Trying to evade the unavoidable conclusion, I said, "We have time. We have today, tomorrow, and even next week before we leave."

"It's nice to think so, but I am an old man and afraid tomorrow may not come." He paused for a moment and then said, "I have mostly finished my journal, and I would like for you to have it."

He raised his arm and pointed to five brown leather notebooks neatly stacked on the corner of his desk. I stepped across the room to look over the books.

"Sit down," he said. "No need to stand."

His chair held me like embracing arms as if coming home from a long passage. I felt oddly at ease, as if I belonged behind this desk. My eyes scanned the mahogany desktop covered with mementos, traveled recollections of his life. His typewriter was at my right, the keys worn and faded, a picture of Savannah capturing her spectacular beauty, a picture of him and my mother from more recent times, and a hand-carved wooden tray holding a Conway Stewart pen.

"Your mother bought that pen for me," he said.

"It's beautiful."

"I've written a few stories with it."

"I bet you have." I placed the pen back into the tray.

"When she gave me the pen, she had placed a note in the box. It simply said, 'Lucas, Write your story.' So, I did, and the results are the journals before you. All my sins, all my confessions. All you need to know about our lives together and how we ended up here."

I turned the pages of the first journal; it reflected a life not experienced by many. I understood this was to be his gift of eternity.

"This is your life?"

"You could say that."

I read the first few pages of his journal as heard the latch on the bedroom door. Maryann, my wife, stood in the doorway.

"Good morning, men," she said as she entered the room. "Am I interrupting?"

Lucas smiled. "Good morning, Maryann. No. No interruptions. I was just giving Luke something to read."

She walked to the desk and stood behind me. "What are you reading?"

"Lucas wrote these journals," I said as she scanned the pages.

"This is wonderful, Lucas," she said after a few minutes of reading over my shoulder. "Will this be your next novel?"

The warmth of her hand touched my shoulder as heard the casting tone of her voice breach the silence, whispering my name. The need for words evaporating as I saw the glisten in her eyes telling me the end of another story. I knew on that day, this was the gift handed down through family; my duty to take his journals and share the story of my father, his life, his journey, and his truth. The last chapter breaking my heart.

Chapter 3

The journals of my father explained that in a quirk of fate somewhere around 1903, Martha, my grandmother, from whom my father inherited his writing curiosities, wrote a letter. It said that "staying in Thurmond, West Virginia would've spelled an early death," and yet, she and my grandfather died before the age of forty.

Recent from shaking off the innocence of youth, William Colby, my grandfather, expressed determination to make a new life, unwavering in his conviction to be a good father to carry the family name to a better future.

Martha's letters said the Colby clan made Thurmond home for over a century, and everyone knew only two ways to survive the hills of West Virginia. The honest way, carving an existence from the coalmines—the families joked of your first toy: a chunk of black gold dug from deep within Capital Mountain—or the dishonest but lucrative making of moonshine.

William didn't want their children to follow the death walk of a coalminer's life or the unlawful dangers of running white lightning on moonlit nights through the Appalachian mountainside. He and Martha shared dreams and long talks while planning their future as the evening sun fell beneath the tall ridge leaving a hint of twilight for hours.

"I hear Ohio is full of land that's rich with crops of corn, hay, and barley. It would be good work, Martha, and safe," William said.

"I'd like that, but what about our kinfolk here?"

"Them that ain't dead's making shine in the hills. Coal mining is dangerous, but that stuff'll kill you. And if the law gets you, that there's a whole bigger trouble yet."

Moving to a better place offered the chance to find a better life not consumed by the darkness and dust of a coal miner's existence. More importantly, Martha could see the dangers of moonshine and the effect on the families of Thurmond. She just didn't know those problems would follow them to Ohio.

I've never met any of my relatives. Both great-grandfathers died in the Red Ash Mine collapse and forty-six other miners, all of them friends or relatives. Not much later, there were six more mining accidents—the last one killing many relatives, and then death knocked once again, taking my great-grandmother.

William made his way while working the mines. Intelligent, strong, and tall, he worked hard and saved his money. With the last days of winter closing in, the snow melted from the lower elevations. Father hitched a small, covered spring wagon to the back of the family mule and gathered Martha and the few possessions they owned, heading north toward Ohio.

Martha said the narrow mountain trails of West Virginia cut along the steep sides of the gorge. Deep ruts formed in the hard-packed ground making for a rough ride, and the steepness of the mountain trails proved a challenge to the old mule. During weeks of travel, my grandfather would stop and find work along the way.

Each morning, the rutted path continued. In the distance of grassy fields, stumps from timber long since felled looked like sentinels guarding their path. Back home, their field of vision blocked by high mountains and thickets of the forest was unlike the open land stretching across a quiet countryside with small hills and narrow valleys. Their path turned west, pointing them toward Anstead.

Growing weary of the long days, Martha asked, "Will this never end?"

William, sensitive to the needs of an expecting wife, held her close, keeping a hand on the reins. His mind ignored Martha's scripture, but he comforted her fears. "Soon, my good wife. Soon we will reach our destination."

The journey ahead seemed without end until they came upon the small town of Mapleton.

William guided the small wagon through the town's narrow street. They smiled and waved politely at the local folks walking the paths outside the small stores. They passed a small dress shop, a church, a barber, and a blacksmith shop. William stopped the wagon and tied the mule to a post outside a small supply store.

He pushed the door open, and the bell hanging from the door jamb chattered. The proprietor—a small man with large sideburns and an even more prominent mustache—stood at the rear of the store. William could see him balanced on a small stool; his clothes covered with a long apron.

Busy stocking shelves with bagged goods, he glanced over his shoulder and said, "Howdy, stranger. What can I do for you?"

William smiled. "Need some supplies, a place to

stay for a bit, and hopefully some work. I hear there is plenty work on the farms around these parts for a man willing to put his back into it."

"I see," said the owner as he approached and extended a friendly hand. "Name's Jenkins." William noticed the grip was firm and his hands calloused. "That your wife in the wagon?" Jenkins asked while looking over William's shoulders and through the front window of the store. "Looks like she's in a way."

"In a way?" William asked, puzzled. "She's having a baby if that's what you're sayin'. Due in a few months, we think."

"In that case, sir, your travel should be limited."

"Yes, sir, I agree, but I need to find some work before we can settle in."

"Not a problem, young man. It just so happens that I can put you to work right here if you like. Ain't much, but it will get you by until the little one comes."

"That'll work, I suppose, and we could use some time off that wagon."

"Well then, welcome! This town is truly nice. If you like, I have a small room available above the store."

"That sure is nice of you, thanks."

"Nothing to brag about, son. I can use a hand around here if you're much to working the retail trade," Jenkins said.

"Can't see why not, and I think Martha would appreciate us stopping for a while and stretching our legs."

Chapter 4

My grandparents found that life in the small-town promising. Martha spent her time helping when she could, and in the evenings, they enjoyed time with the folks living in town. During the day, while William worked, Mrs. Jenkins and Martha would knit under the store's porch.

"Are you two looking for a boy or a girl?" Mrs. Jenkins asked.

Martha smiled and rubbed her swelling belly. "Doesn't matter, but I think William would love to have a son."

"By the way you're carrying, looks to me like he will get his wish," Mrs. Jenkins agreed.

Martha shifted in her seat, trying to be comfortable. "I hope he gets his wish soon. I don't know how much longer I can handle all this hot weather."

Martha and William's new son was born within the week. Lucas Colby was healthy and full of life.

A few weeks had passed as Theodius Finley rode into town with a need to replenish his supply wagons. He and his crew were returning from a long haul delivering his corn to the neighboring towns.

He stepped onto the store's porch; Martha sat on a rocking chair with Lucas bundled in her arms. He tipped his hat as he passed, and she smiled.

As he entered the store, he eyed William working

behind the counter.

"Damn Jenkins. They build 'em big in Mapleton," he declared.

"Not from here," Jenkins replied without looking up from his account books.

"That so," said Finley. He sauntered over to where William stocked the shelves with the canned goods and stuck his thumbs in the upper armpit of his vest. He rocked back on his heels and affirmed in his booming voice as if he expected the world to bow before him, "I'm Theo Finley." William smiled at Finley while keeping on task.

Finley directed his conversation to no one in particular and boasted of his land holdings across Ohio. "I am the largest landowner in this part of the State. So much, the Governor wanted to name the town after me, but I told 'em no. I am but a humble servant of this glorious State, not in need of special treatment or honor."

William rolled his eyes and continued working while listening to Finley's rhetoric, and from time to time, Jenkins looked up and shook his head in wonder at the arrogant chattering.

Finley approached William once again. "Listen up, son. I own some land, a big farm, up in Independence, and I'm looking for someone like you to help me manage my men in the fields."

"Do you now, Mr. Finley," William said.

"Sure do, and it's a big one. Not too far from here, as a matter of fact. Anyhow, I'm looking for someone that could help with running my boys. They're a good group but need some direction. Do you have any experience in handling crews?"

William stood and glanced over to his boss, and

Jenkins gave a look of approval. "I ran some crews back home in the mines," he said.

Finley, interested, asked William if he would move west and work on his farm.

William agreed it could be what he was looking for, and he promised Finley he would give it some serious thought.

"Good, good," Finley said. "How about I expect you at my farm in two weeks. That enough time for you, Jenkins?"

William ended the day speaking with Jenkins about Finley's offer. Jenkins said, "He's a boastful man, but he will make good on his promise. Besides, he can give you more than I will ever be able to offer you."

The following morning, William hitched the wagon and readied their supplies for travel. He filled the rear of the wagon with two sacks of cornmeal, three pounds of salted beef, flour, and a bag of dried beans.

Chapter 5

The journey was not as treacherous as the mountain trails of West Virginia, and the well-worn trail was smooth and level. William estimated their travel would last seven days.

It was a strange world to William and Martha—accustomed to the high mountains and deep hollers of West Virginia—the landscape of Ohio was rolling of hills and open, allowing one to gaze for miles without obstruction. Martha missed the soft cast of the Blue Ridge, the gentle haze covering the morning dew, the faint smell of the surrounding woods, and their family. She took comfort in their journey by quoting scripture from her Bible as they traveled.

Days passed, and their journey brought them to a split rail cedar fence along the side of the carriage path. Extending as far as the eye could see, the fence followed the sloping elevation of the land. Rows of corn and rolling acres filled with wheat and barley lined the path. As the sun crested at midday and the heat shimmered across the fields, William slowed their wagon upon arriving at an open gate marked with a sign stating, FINLEY FARMS.

William directed his wagon off the main road and onto the property. A tree-lined path of oaks and maples shadowed the ground beneath them as they traveled the pathway toward the house. As the main house came into sight, William stopped the wagon. A multi-floored mansion stood in his view.

Six fluted columns stood sentry stretching toward the sky, supporting a second-story balcony. A cross-patterned trellis bonded each column, and a low-lying neatly trimmed golden rod hedge with bright yellow flowers lined the front of the house.

William moved closer to the front of the home, stepped off the wagon, slapped his hands against his clothing to remove the loose dust, removed his hat, and smoothed his hair. He walked up the five red brick steps leading to the porch extending the length of the house and another ten strides to stand below a large, solitary lantern hanging above his head, marking the two massive black doors. He knocked, then turned to see Martha smiling at him. After a few moments, a small man with a slight build, dressed in fancy clothes, answered the door.

"I am here to see Mr. Finley," William said.

The man, whom William took as a butler, said, "I gather you are William Colby?"

William smiled, and the man asked him into the house. Stepping through the doorway, he stood on polished dark wood floors before dual staircases—one left and one right—with intricate, hand-carved balusters following the curved walls leading to rooms on the next level. Looking up, he saw what he believed to be the largest chandelier in the world hanging high from the ceiling, sparkling like the sun. Ahead in his view, two brass figures of horses faced each other while reared on their haunches. To his left, a room extended to a bay window overlooking a garden. Hand-painted artwork lined the walls, and the furniture—elaborate and detailed—showed the comfort of wealth and position. To his right, he saw a library full of books neatly shelved ceiling to floor, a large desk with hand-carved figures, and inlaid ivory sat stately in front of a window that reached to the ceiling. Theodius Finley sat in an oversized high-backed leather chair in his library, smoking a large cigar. He stood at William's introduction.

"Glad to see you made it," he said, extending his hand. "I hope you didn't have much trouble finding the place."

"No, it was just as you said, Mr. Finley."

"Well, good. I have set up one of the houses for you and Mrs. Colby. You will find it just down the main road a bit—about a mile and a half."

"Thanks. We appreciate it."

"Not a problem. You will find the house in order, as well as the furnishings. I think you will be comfortable. Why don't you head on down there and rest for the evening? Be back here at six in the morning, and we will get you working."

The two chatted for a while longer, and William thanked Finley for the job and the hospitality.

They arrived at their new house and saw an uncluttered home painted white with green shutters, a front porch, and a barn. The property was large, and a big oak tree stood shadowing the front porch extending across the front of the tiny home. They decided that a small barn erected on the right of the property would be perfect for their wagon and a cow for milk.

"There's plenty of room for a garden and chickens," Martha said.

"Sure is, and you can be sure you and your garden

will be the talk of the town," William told her.

William opened the door and stepped inside. Martha followed close with Lucas in her arms. She could see the layers of dust settled on the furniture, but she knew this home was ready for a family. Down the hall were two bedrooms and a large kitchen located on the right as they walked in.

"It has a beautiful brick fireplace, William."

"Yes, it does," William said while walking toward the back of the house.

Martha stepped into the kitchen, and from the window, she could see the barn and most of the yard where Lucas would play. She sat at the oak table inside the kitchen and said a prayer of thanks. Though she whispered reverently, William could hear her from the other room.

"Oh, Father in heaven. Thank you for your guidance and bringing us to the safe haven of goodness."

The following morning came early, and William was ready for a new beginning. Standing at the front door of their new home, he kissed Martha and rubbed the head of young Lucas.

"I'll be back home as soon as I can," he told Martha.

"Do try and be home on time, William."

"I will, but you know it's my first day, so no telling what will come up."

"Yes, I know, but don't forget, we have Bible study tonight."

"I know. I will be here with you and Lucas."

William stepped onto the front porch and noticed a wagon headed toward the house. Finley held the reins.

"Good morning," Finley said as the wagon rolled to

a stop.

"Good morning." With his southern upbringing, William was quick to introduce his wife. "This is Mr. Finley. Mr. Finley, this is my wife, Martha."

Finley climbed down from the wagon and took her slender hand, lifting it to his lips. He touched his lips to her pale skin and said, "It is my pleasure to make your acquaintance."

"We are glad to be here and thankful for your kind consideration," Martha said. "William speaks of you with high regard."

William could see Finley's interest in Martha's beauty, but he'd seen this before with other men. Martha smiled as Finley stared, eyes frozen to hers. He said, "I am happy to see both of you're here, and if you need anything at all, be sure to see me personally."

He turned to William and suggested they move along and get to the farm. "I'll need to introduce you to the crew and get you situated with the foreman. His name is Ethan Moss. He's a good man, trustworthy. I think you'll like him."

They climbed into the buck wagon and headed toward the main road. Turning out toward the farm, Finley said, "Lovely wife you have there, Colby."

"Thank you, sir."

"Yep. She's a pretty thing. I would keep a close eye on her."

William smiled. "Thanks for the advice Mr. Finley, but I think she'll be okay. She's a good Christian woman, strong, and has a mind of her own. It is not easy to sway my wife."

Uneasy with Finley's comments, William wished his new boss' words would stop running through his head, but they repeated as they rode in silence to the farm. Competition from others was easy, but William could see the determination in Finley's eyes.

As they approached the buildings, a large group of men gathered just outside the barn area. Pulling up, Finley yelled out, "You boys better get your asses moving. The day's not long, and dark will be here before you know it."

Ethan Moss walked from the barn and wiped his hands with a red cloth handkerchief, meeting them at the wagon. He smiled at William with a giant grin and friendly, weather-worn face.

"Ethan. Meet William Colby. He's the one I been telling you about."

Ethan extended his hand and welcomed him to Finley Farms. "We have a lot of work here, so let me get you with the men."

William's determination and hard work moved him up the chain of command, and before the season was out, he managed his farm crew as they toiled in the bright sun bucking hay, corn, barley, and other crops grown.

****

As the year moved on, Theodius Finley became a common sight around the Colby residence, ensuring his presence was known to Martha. Finley provided small gifts, always with the intent of enjoyment by all. He assigned men to clean the yard and tend the gardens. "We need to be sure your man is working and not being bothered by things around the house," he always told Martha.

Finley also ensured William's absence by assigning delivery for the crops pulled from the fertile land.

It was a three-day trip from the farm to Cleveland,

and time away from family does things to a man. With the fields cleared and the work done, Theodius Finley allowed the men certain pleasures. Celebrations became common at the end of the week, as did games of chance and stilled whiskey.

William enjoyed his new life, and he discovered Friday night with the boys was more fun than staying home with Martha's partiality for Bible study. As time moved forward, William moved away from family life and further into the arms of another. This harlot of the night did not arrive in the shape of a beautiful woman. She came in the form of a bottle filled with fun. It was a chance to escape the realities of his world.

Chapter 6

My father was a prolific writer with a capacity to craft words like an artist paints a picture; brush strokes, colors and creations of images forming in your mind. In his journal he wrote:

In August of 1918, my tenth birthday, Mother had promised me a special breakfast. It had been a bad crop and a dry summer, with most folks moving from town to town in search of work and a better life. There wasn't much to offer anyone, and I can tell you, we were barely surviving. I'd always speculated why God hadn't done something to improve these conditions, considering the amount of time she'd pray each day. But then again, as a ten-year-old, my thoughts wandered quite often between the wonders of God and then off to some other irrelevant activity. Mother believed the spirit of God occupied every living soul, and it was His hand guiding her and me and the rest of this damned world through life. On this morning, He, according to her beliefs, gave us an orange-blushed sky. It spread across wilting corn stalks in the fields surrounding our house.

I stood at my bedroom window and looked through holes of a tattered, hand-sewn curtain while my mother walked through the yard, which was nothing but powdered dirt. She stopped to pick up the morning paper, and something caught her attention. I didn't know it then, but soon, we would share in her discovery of the headline story: the body of a man found inside the Finley Emporium during the night. These simple words were to become the impetus of change in her life, setting into motion my undeniable future.

Dark clouds hung low in the distance and began to hide the sunrise, promising a coming storm. The distant thunder rumbled across the sky as mother raised her head and realized her time was short.

This day was the dead of August. Still, a cool wind brushed my face, and the smell of the rain was in the air. She paused for a moment, then bowed her head, and I can only imagine she prayed for God to bring water to our thirsty land.

She prayed, tucked the paper under her arm in a fold, and hurried toward the hen house to gather eggs for breakfast.

She hustled back across the property, returning to the steps leading to the porch. The screened door slammed shut as she came into the kitchen and called to me. Grabbing my overalls from the bedpost, I pulled them over my skinny ass and dashed down the hallway as fast as my gangly legs could carry me. I wrapped my arms around her legs and buried my face in her dress.

"Good morning, Lucas," she said. "You're awful chipper this morning. Is there something going on I should know about?"

She spoke with a teasing voice as if joking, and she knew I knew something was up. I played along just to hear her talk; words as thick and sweet as pure honey, ending with each expression lifting as if they were the wisp of a soft white cloud twisting up toward the sky on a summer wind. I could listen to her for hours.

She rubbed her slender hands across my head,

smoothed my tousled curls, and leaned over. Her hair, black as a raven's wing, covered me like a warm blanket, and she kissed my forehead with lips as soft as cotton.

"Happy birthday, baby," she said. "You're growing up so fast."

I knew she loved me, and she believed this would be a day of celebration in a life of quiet solitude within the confines of a home with little laughter.

Standing as tall as my toes would allow, I peered over the stovetop and asked, "Is them pancakes?"

"Sure are, sweetie," she said. "Now, you just go and sit. I'll be bringing you your breakfast shortly."

I took my seat at the kitchen table and licked my lips in grand anticipation of my favorite breakfast while viewing every detail before me. At the center, a small pitcher of maple syrup the color of rich amber. Next to my hand, a glass of fresh milk, a fork, and a knife atop a neatly folded napkin. The morning newspaper sat on the corner of the table just within my reach. Mother considered every detail on this morning, and she knew the paper's headline would be cause for my attention.

She gave me a sideways glance, viewing me out of the corner of her eye as mothers did when they don't want you to know they are watching. I paid little mind to her; my stomach called louder than the newspaper. With the napkin tucked into my collar, sunlight streaked through the open window and across the table, landing directly on the newspaper as if guided by spiritual hands. Looking back, I'm sure her self-righteous thoughts brought her to believe God hand-delivered this beacon of light at the precise moment to change my point of focus.

As if poked with a stick, I reached for the paper and asked, "What happened?"

"A man went and broke into Mr. Finley's store during the night," she said as if she didn't expect me to see the headline.

Her practiced response, set to reflect her intolerance of the deed. It wasn't unusual for her to set things up as stories to teach me a lesson—parables, she called them. She would say, "That's how Jesus taught His disciples."

Of course, with my impeccable manners, taught respectfully through hours of Bible study as dictated from a mother with expectations no less than perfect, I asked, "May I read the story?"

"You ain't gonna know much of the words, but go right ahead, baby," she said.

She knew I was too young to understand everything. Nonetheless, this news, however unfortunate, would become her courier—a gift, so she could teach me once again of the demons facing me if I chose to wander from the straight path of life.

"Ma, Mr. Finley says here in the paper this man was all liquored up. What's that mean?"

She took my hand and said, "What this means, this story, is the damn fool was drunk from the whiskey he found in the store."

I giggled under my breath, trying to hide my grin as she immediately caught herself using a word of drastic nature. Embarrassed at her outburst, she apologized and begged God's forgiveness, as I paid little mind to her flailing request reading more of the story.

"It says he shot himself, Ma!" I said. I didn't understand how any man could decide to kill himself. Was it anger or hopelessness causing such pain?

Now more content than ever, knowing she could make her point answered, she said, "Mr. Finley kept a shotgun tucked under the counter, and this man found it. This is why you should stay away from drinking, Lucas. Liquor is the devil's drink, and this fool was so drunk, his eyes was crossed."

Satisfied with her pronouncement, she boasted to herself in glory, her point proven without a doubt.

"That's enough," she said as she removed the newspaper from my grip. "Your breakfast is ready."

Reluctantly, I released the paper as she slid a plate of hot pancakes before me.

As any young boy would be, I was curious and wanted to know more, but she seemed replete with satisfaction.

"Drinking is the work of the devil," she would recur as a constant reminder of the sins and temptations ahead of me.

This lesson became a faded reflection; my mind focused on the tower of pancakes.

Refocusing her thoughts as if looking at a mirror seeing the legacy of my father in me, she said, "You're so much like him. You carry his handsome face, his lanky walk, his intelligence and charm." Then she stopped talking, bowed her head as I'd seen a hundred times, and prayed.

As I finished my breakfast, a loud knock shook the front door. From my chair in the kitchen, I saw Theodius Finley. He dressed as if for a Sunday morning. He blocked the sunlight with his large frame. His mustache hid his lips, and the wide brim of his hat threw a dark circle across the room. Wide lapels defined his broad chest and his boots, highly polished, came to a point. Mother jumped from the table upon hearing the knock, leaving me more curious.

He would often visit with her, but he was not expected this morning and never this early. The expression on his face was solemn, and it was apparent he'd arrived with intent.

"Good morning Mr. Finley," she said, stepping onto the porch.

"Morning, Mrs. Colby." A golden chain hanging from his vest pocket glistened in the sunlight as he stepped off the porch and into the morning sun.

Standing quietly in the hallway leading to the front door, I strained to hear the hushed and somber utterances taking place in the yard just beyond the doorway. I could only listen to parts of the words of their conversation: "Finley's" and "Sorry." Bits of their talking drifted across the porch and into the kitchen, where I waited for her return.

She sat on the front step, a vacant expression on her face, her head down, eyes staring at the ground beneath her. Tears in her eyes reflected emptiness caused by a conversation held on this day of supposed celebration. Finley handed her a white handkerchief and motioned toward the house with his hat in his hand. Her hands tightly clasped between her legs, she shifted her body and glanced back at the doorway. She softly shook her head and responded, "No."

I heard them say goodbyes and Finley offering his services as Mother stepped back into the house, trying to appear as if nothing happened. Her face gave way to truth: her eyelids pink from tears shed, and her high-cheeked face downcast and pallid.

"Ma, you okay?" I asked.

"Yes, honey, I'll be fine." She folded onto the worn couch in the sitting room, emotionally exhausted from the morning events, and called for me to join her. She extended her slender arm and rubbed the cushion beside her. "We need to talk," she said.

I sat next to her, like many times before while reading scripture on Sunday afternoons. She was hiding something, but I couldn't imagine what it could be and decided to take things at face value.

She brushed my hair away from my forehead and looked deeply into my eyes. "Emerald green, like your father, and your hair is so brown and wavy. You remind me so much of him," she said.

She pulled me close, praying under her breath, then she pushed me away, placing her hands squarely on my shoulders, and looked straight into my eyes.

"Mr. Finley came by with some bad news," she said.

I could see the monogram of "TF" sewn into the corner of the handkerchief she held to her slender nose.

"What happened?" I had the feeling of impending doom brought on by her solemn expression.

"It's your father, baby," she said, trying to regain her composure. "Mr. Finley stopped by to tell me your father won't be coming home. He got himself killed."

"But Ma," I cried out. "You said he was supposed to be coming home and be with us."

I had honestly believed, as any young boy would, my father would arrive one day in celebration of his being a war hero—of that, I held no doubt. In my mind, the school band marched in celebration, proud of my father's heroism as a soldier fighting the wrongs of the world. I imagined flags and fireworks and banners hung from the tallest buildings. I would sit on my father's shoulders, showing everyone how proud I was as we sat atop the back seat of a beautiful shiny automobile on a bright and clear morning. The crowd would cheer and clap as we passed, my father and I would wave and smile, I would be happy on that morning, and we would be a family again.

I felt the tears well up in my eyes, my lips curling down, and my nose warm, heat rising in my face. Mother pulled me close to her bosom, gently rubbing my head with her long, slender hand.

To be honest, looking back, I don't know what bothered me most—my father not coming home or not being in the parade.

"I know, baby, I know," she said. "But I'm telling you what's so. Your father is in heaven now, and God will watch over him and see he is taken care of. They will celebrate his return, and he will watch over us from heavens high above."

She prayed for her husband's soul, asking God to let him enter the Kingdom of Heaven. "I know he didn't do right all the time, Lord," she said. "But the fault did not lie within him."

Sitting on the couch with her as she prayed, I didn't know what I should feel. I knew my father by name only, along with the sparse array of pictures set carefully on the fireplace mantel. To me, my father was a man told by my mother but never held in my recollection. I felt sad for her, but the emotions were no more for my father than for the man in the newspaper — a curious disposition, but not one of love or affection. Still, I could see her pain, and I held her hand as we sat on the couch, and she wept.

Chapter 7

In stark contrast against a cerulean sky, squared in a cleared patch of dirt and brown grass, amidst fields of corn, at the end of a long dusty road, Independence Baptist church served as home to the Sunday gatherings of undeserving townspeople. The white clapboard building had a steep roof, topped by a pointed column that stretched toward the heavens to show the only way to salvation.

Three days beyond my birthday celebration, I watched my father arrive without the fanfare expected toward a war hero. I stood alone in front of the church, dry grass beneath my feet, and watched two men sitting in the cab of a faded black flatbed truck driving toward the church.

One man on the bed of the truck leaned against the back of the cab, his hat pulled down tight, arms rested on bent up knees. His head bobbed rhythmically as the truck maneuvered the dips in the road. The truck carried an object covered by a black tarp tied to the bed rails. The sun-baked earth and the tandem wheels left a clouded trail of gray dust as evidence of travel.

The engine grumbled, and brakes screeched as the truck came to a stop near the church's back door. The dust from the road covered the tires and the inside the wheel wells, settling along the flat surfaces and crevices around the truck's body.

The driver reached his burly arm through the open window and slapped his meaty hand on the top of the truck cab. The man sitting on the empty bed looked up as the driver motioned toward the church.

The driver remained inside the cab, and the man sitting on the truck's bed stood, showing a tall, thin build. He adjusted his hat, hopped off the tailgate onto the ground, and walked to the church, disappearing through the side doors and into the darkness.

Preacher Dan returned with the tall man from the back of the truck after a few moments, and the driver opened the door and stepped out.

The driver wiped his right hand on his pants and offered it to Preacher Dan. After exchanging words, the driver and the tall man removed the canvas tarp revealing a casket. Other men approached and helped move the coffin to the church, their expressions dour. I watched, dry-eyed and without compassion, my mind holding a yearning curiosity while sorting ambiguous thoughts. I knew my father died alone on a battlefield, but I didn't understand why. As the silent box passed me, the feelings within my heart were as dry as the heat rising from the earth.

The men stepped from the church, and I watched the driver hand Preacher Dan some papers. The preacher signed them and returned them to the driver. They shook hands and talked while exchanging watchful glances toward me. The driver walked to the flatbed, started the engine, and blue smoke billowed from the tailpipe. The tall man climbed onto the bed, and the driver pushed the truck into gear with a grinding sound and drove the dusty road leading back to the long main road in front of the church.

The leaves and branches on the trees lining the property caught the gray dust left stirred and abandoned by the passing truck. Quiet settled on the church grounds as the truck became a small dot on the horizon of the long road.

Inside the church, the preacher's wife pounded the ivory keys of the church piano with the hands of a farmer's wife. Poorly tuned notes wafted through the thick summer heat as Abigail Peterson crooned a hymnal in preparation for Sunday services, drawing my attention away from the diminishing speck on the horizon. I considered the sharp tone of my classmate's voice to carry a tone more reminiscent of screeching owls rather than the voice of an angel's saving grace. To my pleasure, the practiced recital soon stopped, and Abigail Peterson, complete with pigtails, a floral dress, knee-high socks, and white shoes, bounced down the steps of the church, stopping only long enough to stick her tongue out at me.

I responded in kind and walked to a large oak tree standing on the property line of the church grounds next to the field of corn. It stood five feet high, barely reaching the top of my head leaning against the massive trunk, my arms outstretched over raised knees. I didn't miss my father, and the thought weighed heavy on my mind.

The caretaker for the church approached from across the grounds. I saw him coming and stood to greet him. John Watson kneeled on one knee, matching my height.

"Hey Lucas, you doin' okay?"

I stepped from the tree, stuck my hands deep inside my pockets, and said, "I guess so, Mr. Watson. I was just out here wonderin' about stuff."

"Thinking about your father, I suppose."

I shuffled at the dirt beneath my feet for a moment. "Should I be sad? I mean, with my father'n all that."

John Watson looked out over the fields surrounding the church, took off his hat, and wiped his sweaty brow with a bandana from the back pocket of his overalls. "I would think it would be a personal choice, Lucas. I'm guessing you don't remember much about your father, so you're feeling sad for someone you've never known probably wouldn't feel just right."

"I only know what Ma told me," I said, "and we have pictures, but I don't ever remember him at our house. She said he died a long way from here, and I should be proud of him. Suppose I am, but I still don't miss him so much."

Mr. Watson said, "Guess you can't miss something you never had."

Chapter 8

The night before the funeral, my mother placed my only dress clothes on the chair in my bedroom while I slept. Early in the following day, she sat at my bedside watching me sleep. I opened my eyes, and she was smiling.

"Good morning, baby. It's time to get up."

I yawned and stretched my arms. "It's still early."

"Yes, it is," she agreed. "I made you some breakfast, and we need to head on to the church soon."

Still tired, I rose from the bed and ate a small breakfast while sitting at the table in silence. After breakfast, I dressed in my best white shirt and a pair of black pants.

It was a short walk from the house of Colby to the final resting place of my father, and although it was early, the sun heated the day through a cloudless sky. She held her Bible under her arm, and with her other hand, she touched me on my shoulder.

Preacher Dan stood at the front door of the church as we walked up the dusty road. After polite greetings, we stepped inside the church and stood in the foyer.

Mother motioned toward a chair and said, "Sit here for a moment, baby." She and the preacher went into his office.

I looked around the room, curious. A picture of Jesus hung above a small table with an empty basket sitting askew. Someone had placed a bouquet on another table near the sanctuary, and the door was open far enough for me to see inside. I stepped inside, then stopped, bathed only in the light from side windows. The pews lined a path to the front of the church, and there I saw the casket.

I stepped toward the plain wooden box, never seeing a coffin before, and wondered about many things: the color of his hair, the shape of his eyes, the feel of his hands, and the sound of his voice. I touched the surface of the coffin and walked its length stopping near the end, then I sat on the long bench and didn't know what to do. Mother called out, and I walked back to the front of the church.

"You okay, baby?" she asked as if I were lost or into something I shouldn't have been, which was probably more likely. I said, "Yes. I'm okay."

Why don't you sit in my office, Lucas?" asked the preacher. "I have a nice book you can look at until we are ready."

I sat on a couch in the preacher's office and looked out the window. Soon, a small assembly of people gathered quietly inside the church sitting on the long wooden pews. One of the men came into the preacher's office and took me to the bench where my mother sat.

There were soft murmurs outside her earshot. Sanctimonious eyes darted through the gathering of townspeople as they shared the gossip, secrets held by those knowing the truths unstated to the ears of an innocent child.

Inside the sanctuary walls, the sealed box presented the only testament to the existence of William Colby. She told me there wasn't enough of my father to bring back from wherever he was when he died.

Placed within a simple wooden frame, a photograph of my father sat on the casket. I looked at this picture and thought it must have been from happier times. He was smiling.

Preacher Dan stood elevated on the stage, most of his portly stature hidden behind a podium, vocalizing my father's life. His jowls shook as his voice echoed from faded church walls while speaking of death and resurrection.

I listened to the rhetoric with the boredom of a young child as my thoughts wandered to the late nights of constant Bible study with my mother and how she would tell me of the sins of man and how no one was worthy in the eyes of God. I thought about the hours spent on my knees in prayer and the constant reminder from my mother of how sin could creep into my life and destroy me.

I watched my mother and held her hand while sitting quietly in the front row, staring at the box before me. She wiped tears from the corners of her eyes with a white handkerchief, and I felt her body tremble as she inhaled the stale air of the church.

Preacher Dan prayed once more, then stepped down. He approached us and whispered words near her ear while holding her hand. Mother thanked him and nodded. Four men stood to carry my father to his final destination on the grounds of the church. We followed without words.

In the pounding heat, the earth's scent rose through the air bringing the smell of fresh, dry dirt as the morning sun approached its apex. A light breeze touched the leaves of the giant oak tree, its branches creating a canopy over the congregation, providing dappled shadows over the black hole where my father would rest for eternity.

My hair stuck to my forehead, and I felt the beads of sweat slip down my back. I licked my lips, wishing to quench my thirst on this summer day.

I watched men and women dressed in shades of black, undoubtedly wishing this would end, as the speckled sunlight reflected off their faces, the shade providing a coolness few deserved. As I stood there, I wondered if they kept these clothes for only these occasions.

During our walk home from church, mother explained the pine box from Uncle Sam was all we could afford. I didn't know an Uncle Sam but thought he must have been a kind man to help us. It seemed there were uncles at my house, but I never knew one named Sam.

As the months passed, Martha seemed to prefer the solitude of her thoughts and didn't often speak of her husband. She continued to draw further and further away, reluctant to speak of the past. I believed, in the end, my father was afraid, as most men would be when finding there was no hope for tomorrow and no time left for goodbye. I also believed my mother held hope in her heart. I felt that without hope, there isn't much of a reason to live.

I would have preferred to have a father, and I believed a mother would rather have a husband. She would tell me, sometimes fate controls what you want, but God will give you what you need if you take the time to listen for His voice.

Some nights, I'd hear her voice, muffled through thin walls, as I tried to sleep. She would talk as if my father were in the room with her. I prayed each night, asking God to stop her pain. Each morning, I would sit at the kitchen table waiting for her to rise until I would hear her footsteps shuffling toward the kitchen, and she would stand in the doorway and rest on the frame, catching her breath.

I asked, "You okay?"

She always responded, "Yes, baby, I will be fine." She would never let me see the pain she was in, but I knew by the look in her eyes and the way her shoulders slumped. Her reiterated answer echoed the loneliness in her voice as she balanced her thinning frame against the support of the doorway. I could see the pain consuming her, eyes swollen, distant stares looking nowhere in particular.

"Ma, did he love us?" I asked.

Chapter 9

Finley continued to visit us a few times each week. Some days, I would awake, and he would already be there, drinking coffee with my mother at the kitchen table. Other days, he would arrive in the afternoon, and he and my mother would walk the long road running along the front of the house. Other times, they would sit on the front porch and talk about things adults speak of when children shouldn't listen. I never paid much mind to their exchange of adult talk until one afternoon, I was sitting in the kitchen, and I heard one of their conversations without their knowledge.

"Why don't you and the boy come live in my house, Martha?"

"I would never consider that type of arrangement. Besides, Lucas and I do fine right here."

I watched from around the corner as she stood and leaned against the railing surrounding the porch. Looking across the dry grass and the sprouting corn stalks adjacent to the house, she continued, "I can't imagine what the people of this town would say if they knew about all this."

"They would say that old man Finley ain't so bad after all, with helping that Colby widow and all that."

"Is that how you think of me? That Colby widow?"

"No, Martha. I don't. I just want to take care of you and the boy."

"You're not serious, Theo."

"If I asked you to marry, would you think me serious?"

She turned toward Finley. "Marry?"

"Yes, Martha. Marry me and let me make you an honest woman."

"I think you need to change the subject."

"Martha. Please. You're not doing so good here, and it seems to me having all of us together would be so much easier."

"You know I can't marry you, Theo. You know I won't do that."

"What are you going to do, then? Working at the hospital just brings bad memories, and besides, it doesn't pay enough to keep you two in good health."

"We will be fine, Theo. Besides, you know as well as I do, Lucas won't leave here, and he certainly won't live in your house with you thinking you're his father. This is the only house he has ever lived in. We'll be fine. Don't worry."

Their conversation continued into the darkness of the evening. I walked out the back door and into the barn. I rested on the pile of hay and stared up, thinking how I couldn't imagine Theo Finley marrying mother, and I could less imagine living in his house. I wish I'd been smart enough then to understand the ways a man thinks when he wants a woman. So many things would have been different.

Even then, as a child, something gnawed at my gut about Finley. There was no trusting him, and my soul said he was up to something.

Soon, I heard the car start and pull onto the road. Mother called to me, telling of supper.

****

As the years passed, what little memory I held of my father became a simple recollection of thought. Other than the pain seen within mother's eyes, I seldom reflected on how it could have been, and I never missed him as I thought I would. As her motion became predictable and her shoulders slumped, her walk became tired. I was now nearly sixteen years old and the man of the house. I had to rely on my judgment as her health dwindled and she became old before her time. Each afternoon, before the sunset and supper, we sat, and she read scripture from her Bible of rugged pages and a cover worn from her grip.

She prayed each night for God to show me the straight path, instill a sense of goodness in my soul, but unknowingly, I chose a direction closer to my father's lessons.

As I discovered liquor's effect on a man, I honed my skills with a woman in the back of a hay wagon on those moonless nights in Ohio. My restless soul and sinful ways pushed the limits of my mother's sanity and created pain and sorrow as she watched me arrive in the early morning hours, unable to deter my crooked path. It was a harsh and forbidding life as a child became a man, left alone and without the control of a father. A boy needs a man to kick his ass and show him his direction. I grew up having my way and believed a woman just couldn't control a man.

Chapter 10

Mother worked at Northeastern Sanitarium, a small state hospital on the edge of town near our house. The castellated gothic citadel with massive towers and buttresses stood alone like a sentinel on a hillside overwhelming the sky as it posed, ominously overlooking the town below. Soaring windows, like empty black eyes, reflected the iniquity of the souls locked away and forgotten, eyes looking down in shame toward the town and the people. I recall days of roaming the endless lengths of the corridors. I witnessed the desolation presented by faded walls, peeling paint, and pipes running overhead that would moan and creak; unavailing silhouettes of human frailty set upon indolent expressions peering through locked and barred windows. Mother's job as a nurse's aide was tiresome and complex. She worked long hours. Her paltry income was hardly enough to cover food for the table.

The hospital, home to the invalid, the insane, and the afflicted, was a place that held nothing more than sadness for her heart and the guilt of her secrets lying just beyond her reach. She worked late almost every day and would arrive home tired from serving patients demanding more assistance than she could provide.

By the time I finished school, her health had declined, and she didn't do much more than stay in bed. At her young age, her raven-colored hair had grayed the color of a sullen winter day just before the snowfalls, withering from luxurious waves of attraction to nothing more than thin strands without life. Her frame was thin and frail against translucent skin, and her dresses, once filled by a beautiful, full woman, now hung on her shoulders like worn drapery shading the sunlight from a closed window.

Visits from the doctor became more commonplace, visits from Finley became a rare sight, and she spent more time in pain than out. Morning became night, and the darkness fell onto another day without remark as I sat with her at her bedside. Holding my hand, she whispered a Bible verse I'd heard so many times.

"But there is nothing covered up that will not be revealed, and hidden that will not be known," she said, her eyes hollow.

I ignored her ramblings as paranoia, ramblings caused by the morphine injected by Doc Phillips. I didn't understand the pain she suffered or why this should be happening, but she said I would understand one day.

Looking back, perhaps she thought this was punishment for her deceit, the lies of her life causing this sickness.

Throughout the night, I listened to her confused thoughts as she tossed and turned. I placed cold compresses on her forehead, and she prayed in her sleep, quoting scripture. "Whoever is naive, let him turn in here," she said while reaching into the air as if to touch the sky. Her eyes open, staring beyond me, she grabbed me by the arm, looking at me as a stranger would look upon someone suspicious.

In the darkness of a fallen moon, her voice barely above a whisper quoted scripture once again. She said,

"Stolen water is sweet, and bread eaten in secret is pleasant." The hours passed as she mumbled of days past, calling out to her husband.

In lucid moments, she'd begin to tell me of my father but would then fall quiet and look away. Each day, her pain grew worse as I watched over her while sitting in the chair by her bed.

Powerless, I watched her labored breathing as her emaciated chest heaved up and down, her eyes looking as if sinking into her head, dark and empty, her hair wispy, falling over her forehead. Once radiant and full, her complexion was now pallid and thin – her cheekbones protruding as if they would soon tear through her ashen skin.

In late September, as I dozed in the chair next to her bed, she arched her back and cried out once more, the pain seizing her withered body. Startled, I jumped toward her and clasped her hand within mine. I brushed my other hand across her forehead. Deep from within, with eyes staring through me, she whispered, "Lucas, I'm so sorry."

Chapter 11

A September sky peeked through muddled ribbons of gray blur suspended above the church steeple on Sunday morning. I sat on the church's back steps, gazing toward the distance and into the heavens, solemn and dreary. I was thinking about what was to become of my life now that everything I'd loved was gone.

My friend, John Watson, stood at the doorway, giving me a moment to gather my thoughts.

"Seems like all the folks that's comin' have arrived. We'd better get started," he said.

I stood, dried my eyes, straightened my coat and tie, then climbed the steps to the church; the same church, the same seat, and the same soft murmurs waited outside my earshot. The eyes of the self-righteous followed my moves, watching me and holding secrets yet known, at least to me.

Together, they sat as one in judgment, all too quick to cast damnation toward a life of struggle, of things unsaid and unknown, and complications not understood by simple minds.

Preacher Dan, still the symbol of strength for the small town, spoke only as he could speak. Words of kindness and sorrow for a young man left on the precipice of a life unsettled, facing an uncertainty I had not realized.

Only Abigail Peterson held enough kindness in her

heart to stop, hold my hand, speak a kind word, and give me hope for tomorrow.

Four men carried my mother's casket to the oak tree, standing next to my father. I looked upon my father's grave with little remembrance as each person passed me with few words. I watched in silence as her casket lowered to the obscurity of earth, ending a life of pain, then stood alone as each person walked away, leaving me to my thoughts.

I tossed a hand full of dirt into the darkness and said goodbye for the last time.

My walk back to the house was slow and quiet, giving me time to think of the future, but the only thought I had was of sorting out the few belongings I could call my own and hoping to find something of remembrance—a keepsake of good and of love. I knew of nothing left to keep me on the farm, and the town held nothing for me other than a cold limestone marking the remnants of a past no longer mine.

As night fell, I consumed a half bottle of whiskey I had kept hidden in my room and laid back, allowing the demons to destroy me. I sat alone in a drunken stupor and thought of my future, knowing this day would come. Still, I didn't have a plan. I had considered staying on, finding work, and perhaps living with my past as it was.

Without family, without love, there wasn't much to hold on to, no reason to stay. I blew across the flame on the small lantern, watching the casting smoke of the wick curl up and dissipate into vapor. Sleep would do me well.

Chapter 12

The morning sun brought little relief from a night spent in restless thought and indecision. My head hurt from too much whiskey; still, I pulled back my bed covers, repeating a ritual practiced each morning of my life. This day held little for my comfort; coffee did not boil on the stove, and my mother did not call to remind me of school or chores or the events ahead of me on this day. I passed through the house, room by room, finding nothing of significance. At the end of the hallway, I approached my mother's doorway, and I noticed my heart beating against my chest, reliving the recent events. I stopped, my hand holding the glass doorknob, uncertain of any need to enter.

With a twist of curiosity more than a requirement, I pressed forward. To this day, I regret that decision.

The sunlight streamed between curtains drawn against the window frame. The stale air pulled at my throat as I searched for dampness to swallow. Mother's room stood unadorned, pale walls holding a single crucifix above her headboard, her Bible on a nightstand, her last struggle evidenced from disheveled bed sheets. The violence of her death left the room in disorder, her bed skewed. In the corner, a solitary chair stood.

I stood in the doorway and rethought the last moments of her life. I recalled her rambling of scripture about *nothing covered up that will not be revealed.*

Mother had always used her scripture to teach me the lessons of life, and it was at that moment I knew she meant to tell me something before she died; it was the reason for her rambling.

I crossed the room and sat on the chair across from her bed. It was as if she had called to me from the heavens. My head hung low toward the floor, my arms relaxed and held atop my legs. In my view, a small tin box peeked from beneath the covers of the bed. I assumed that, at one time, she had pushed the box far under her bed, now exposing its secrets and revealed to my eyes as if her hand moved it forward. I leaned over, grasped the rusted box, and opened it while kneeling on the floor at the side of the bed. I thought nothing at first; old photos of my parents, love letters from before their marriage, a note from my father to my mother. I reached into the tin box once again and found another letter wrapped within a newspaper clipping. Unfolding the brittle paper, it revealed the secrets hidden for all these years. My eyes fell on faded print; memories of a day long ago flooded my mind. I stared at the words. My surrounding view became dark and unfocused. I did not clearly understand what I held in my hands. My mind raced, my breath shortened, and I felt dizzy as the mystery of unanswered questions unfolded before me.

Memories filled my mind as tears filled my eyes. I brushed my fingers across the aged words in this letter as if the action would explain the slander in my possession.

Addressed to my mother, I discovered a letter from the hospital concerning my father, William James Colby. The letter stated my father's condition was delusional, and he had paranoid schizophrenia. The doctors concluded the overuse of liquor was the cause of an unstable mental illness. Considering this disposition, the court agreed that he should remain in the facility's custody for additional psychological evaluations. The recommended treatment would consist of sedatives, antipsychotic medication, and shock therapy.

I continued to sift through the contents of the tin box, thoughts and memories racing through my mind as I felt my heart pounding in my ears, blood rushing through my veins. I found more papers—more truth. I pulled other papers—a newspaper clipping. The headline read; *MAN FOUND DEAD*. I looked at the date—August 1918—and I remembered, with vivid detail, this story on my tenth birthday.

Sitting there on the floor next to my mother's bed, I recalled the knock on the screen door on that morning we were to celebrate my birthday. I clearly remembered Theo Finley blocking the sunlight, standing on our front porch, the conversation, and my mother's face as he spoke.

I pulled another official document from the box. This time, a death certificate from the county morgue completed the storytelling of my father's death by his hand. The official cause said death by suicide.

My thoughts wandered. I tried to make sense of past events. They came into focus; late-night conversations I heard drifting through the walls from mother's room; the emptiness in her soul, the loneliness in her eyes; sad eyes without love or hope, and the lies she held in her heart. I could not understand why my mother would carry such lies to her grave. Too many unanswered questions. Too many lies posted throughout my life. "Life ain't worth living without somebody to love," she had always said. The truth was cancer didn't kill Martha Colby.

Loneliness and lies scared her heart—something I could not stop.

Alone, I pondered the words and lies my mother had hidden from me all these years. I thought back over all things said and began to understand what I had denied myself for so long. It was evident, plain, and always there. I came to understand what she meant while she muttered in her sleep: confessions of a mind left on its own without fear of prosecution—affirmation before judgment, forgiveness before death. I finally understood how she survived and, more importantly, how she afforded our house, my clothes, and the things belonging to us. It was not that we had a lot, but we had more than one could expect on her pay as a nurse. The secrets held within my mother's heart had become apparent, and I understood the muffled voices through thin walls, along with the self-righteous looks from the people that would pass me on the streets in town. Finley had set it up, and he was behind all of this.

My father was just the pawn, and Finley was the King that had set up everything. Just as King David had committed adultery with Bathsheba after sending Uriah to war, Finley sent my father away. He took advantage of his weakness for liquor, using that failing to destroy his life. Then, after having my father locked away, he pretended to come to her rescue. Soon, I believe Finley tired of having my father lurking in memory, my mother's hope of recovery, believing that my father would come home one day and we would be a family. It was my belief that Finley let him escape knowing the first thing my father would do was hunt Finley down and demand retribution. However, Finley was more intelligent than that and had set it up, waiting for him on that night. He murdered my father, and, in my mother's grief, he became her comfort and then took my mother for himself. I believe she must have had her suspicions, so she made up the war story wanting me to believe my father was a hero. The guilt she carried had to have been tremendous. She didn't understand this man in her innocence, and the bastard never revealed himself as the cheat and liar he was. Instead, he became the benefactor, her protector. The only sin my mother had ever committed was she trusted people. She believed everyone was inherently good. But I knew better. People will always lie to you, and people always have secrets. I knew Finley had secrets, and I knew he had murdered my father.

The passing weeks did not bring closure as each day flowed into the next, ending without direction as if a thick fog settled across the plains, refusing to move on.

Each night, I tossed and turned in my bed. Inveterate scripture echoed in my thoughts as if my mother reached out from her grave, repeating scripture foretelling my future. My mother's dutiful reminders pounded in my mind like distant drums. In my heart, I knew she wanted the best for her only child. I understood, in her heart, she carried the weight of the world while trying to protect me. I recalled my days at the hospital, waiting as my mother worked, my father's hope held abandoned behind the spiritless walls kept silent by steel doors.

Soon after I buried my mother, one afternoon, Abigail Peterson's mother stopped by. Mother worked with her at the asylum. Abigail knew of my father all these years, and she confessed that my mother had asked her to hold the secret between them and keep it hidden from me. It seemed the entire town knew about my father, my mother, and Finley. Still, she said my mother would sit with my father each afternoon before coming home, which gave me some comfort knowing she still loved him.

"Not that he would have known her from the window he stared through each day," she said. "Them medicines the doctors gave kept his mind empty as that field he stared across."

I believed this was my mother's time of confession and her asking my father to forgive her. With what I discovered after her death; it was the only reasonable explanation.

As difficult as it must have been for her, she found time to sit with him, to talk, tell him of his only son. Sadly, she believed that Finley took care of my father's health and worked with the doctors. She never realized my father's mind worked fine, and it was the medication blocking his path to salvation.

In some ways, I consider what I found in that old tin box a good fortune. Mother meticulously wrote our history, lives, and everything she could tell me while she was here. I have treasured those letters over the years, being they are the only things left from my past. Those memories gave me hope.

Chapter 13

Lucas Colby's life, considering the turbulence he experienced, began in relative obscurity. After he had buried my grandmother, found the letters and clippings, he concluded: Theo Finley had started the downhill spiral leading him to the inevitable meeting between them. He'd poetically described the morning of the tragic and fateful event, beginning with, "the sun crept across the horizon." My father, even as a young man, showed the talent of a fine writer.

In his journal, he wrote:

'Finley pounded on my front door, which jolted me from bed, and I wondered what urgent situation created such an early arrival on a Sunday morning. Two weeks had passed since my mother's death, and after I discovered the letters, I had not slept well."

"Good morning, Lucas," he said as I opened the door. "Looks like I woke you up on this cold morning."

"Yeah, looks like. What do you want, Finley?"

"Mind if I come in and sit while we talk?"

"Don't make no mind to me. You can do as you wish. This is your house, I suppose, and I don't know what else you can do to screw up my life."

Finley owned most of the land around these parts. He also owned this house, so I figured that's why he came by—to collect rent.

He stomped his boots on the porch floor, removed

his hat, and stepped across the threshold. I shut the door.

Without invitation, he sat in a quilt-covered chair near the fireplace. This action aggravated me even more. It was where my mother loved to sit, by the fireplace, as she read from her Bible.

I sat on the couch across from him and watched as he unintentionally displayed the air of presumption reserved only for those having the affluence to sustain their attitudes. I didn't have the money of a beggar, and that would be on a good day.

If he was collecting, I figured he'd be leaving empty-handed—not that I cared one way or the other, as long as he went away and let me be.

He smoothed his mustache with his fingers, and he cleared his throat. "You know. Your mother was a good woman," he said.

I didn't know what to expect of this unsought visitation but thought about how I could make him pay for what he'd done to my family. His word was law in this town, and I knew men like him believed they could do as they wished.

Mother was dead, I didn't have anyone else, and it was his house. Still, I wasn't about to take any crap from him. I let him speak for a bit until I tired of his rhetoric and interrupted the conversation.

"Is there a reason why you are telling me all of this, Finley?"

"Well, I just wanted to let you know, even though you don't have any family here, you're welcome to stay on. I could always use an extra hand around the fields and seeing you haven't anyone to take care of you, you're going to need to support yourself somehow."

"An extra hand? I don't think I need your kind of

help."

"You think so, boy? It appears you're already living hand to mouth."

"That's not what I meant, and you know it," I said.

"Let's not be difficult, boy. You know, your mother always told me you were stubborn, but she said I needed to care for you if she died. I have no problem with having you work on my farm."

I couldn't have imagined working for Finley, not after what he'd done to my life. Mother had no idea as to what this man had done. He'd hoodwinked her for years, and still, she trusted him. I knew different, and I wished I'd known about everything before she died. I would've told her, although she probably wouldn't have believed me. Funny thing about folks and lying—it seems they have a hard time believing anyone else telling the truth. Still, even though it wouldn't have benefited me somehow, here was my chance, at least, to make him uncomfortable.

"What exactly would you have me do?" I said.

I knew exactly what I wanted to do—to him, that is. I had found the box of letters my mother kept hidden under her bed. Mother had tried to protect me and raised me to believe my father died a war hero—that was just one of the lies. Growing up with all this and seeing those letters, I can tell you I put it all together. I knew what had happened. Proving it to a point where everyone would've believed me, however, would be something else altogether.

He rambled on about all kinds of nonsense, finally got to the point. "I think you could do just about anything you set your mind to, young man. I can start you over in dairy and then move on from there. Come to think of it, that's how your father started."

"Why would you do this for me?"

"No reason, I suppose," Finley answered. "I just thought you could use some help. That's all."

I figured it was about time to test the waters. He didn't know what I knew, but I did, and I was about to drop it on his head.

"Maybe it's because you want to keep me close? Perhaps keep me quiet?"

Well, that made an impression on him. He lowered one eyebrow, cocked his head, and pursed his lips. I guess he was acting as if he didn't have a clue as to my reference because he said, "I have no idea what you mean. I'm just offering help."

I thought that was weak and decided to challenge him some more. "Like you helped my mother? Like you helped put my father away? Is that how you kept her quiet all these years, Finley? Taking care of her?"

I think, at this point in the conversation, he thought I was beginning to figure out I knew what he did to my father. How he tricked my mother and then played the hero. It wasn't hard to figure out. He held a fondness toward my mother since the first day they met. My father knew, and I think he did everything he could to stop any of Finley's advances. Still, Finley was smart and played on my dad's weakness with liquor—I knew about that from her letters— then he paid off the doctors and locked my father up in the sanitarium. It was all there if you just paid attention. And he knew I had him because he started with all these excuses. Granted, I was bigger, younger, and faster than him. Still, you didn't cross a man like Finley, and if I could get him out of my life, the sooner, the better. I figured I'd pack up the few things I had and would just leave this town and never look back. I was ready to drop it, I had had enough, but he just kept talking and pressing my nerve, every one of his words cutting through my brain like a plow cutting through the earth. I held my hand up, letting him know I'd had enough.

I guess he figured he talked himself to innocence because then he uncrossed his legs and sat up in the chair, adjusted his bolo tie, smoothed his collar, and said, "Son, you have to understand. I had nothing to do with your father. Your mother couldn't handle his drinking, and he was just out of hand. He needed medical attention, and she couldn't do it herself."

It was as if he thought these actions would forgive him for what he'd done, but the more he talked, the more anger built inside me. I tried to control my temper and did my best to contain my burning rage.

I sat up onto the edge of the couch, and he could see I was getting agitated. I said, "You gave him work to keep him away. You made sure he wasn't around to be a father or a husband. You worked him hard, just to keep him away from home. You gave your men liquor, telling them to have some fun since they were far from home. You set it all up so perfectly, didn't you, Finley?" I asked, knowing the answer.

"That's not the truth. I gave your father a job, but I didn't put that bottle in his hands. I didn't lock him away."

I knew men like Finley. They believed if they paid someone else to do the dirty work, their hands would be clean. Their conscience is clear. I also knew he was becoming more uncomfortable, so I said, "I see. You just made sure he wasn't around."

He paused for a moment and reflected. I could see his attitude change, and I knew either he would leave, or he just might be thinking about killing me. He could have. He could've killed me right there, and no one would've known. He could've left me dead on the floor for the rats or worse. There wasn't anyone else coming after me, looking around to see if I was still there. He knew I didn't have anyone, so who would miss me? I began to think I might have just bit off more than I could chew. Then I saw his mood change and that arrogant attitude of his return.

"Well, there ain't a whole lot you can do about it now, is there, boy?"

I couldn't believe he confessed right there and without one cent of remorse. Here I was, standing in front of the man that destroyed my life, killed my father, and undoubtedly had a hand in my mother's pain. My mind reeled with what I wanted to do to him, but in my heart, I knew there was nothing left. I thought that was it, and I was about to open the front door and tell him just to get the hell out, and then I would leave, until he said, "But you have to understand something, Lucas. Your mother and I had a special relationship."

I took a deep breath, and I could feel my fist curling, but I knew I needed to control my temper.

"A special relationship?" I repeated. To think of this man holding my mother made my skin crawl. I knew that anything she'd done, she did for me, or at least she thought it was the best thing for me. Sure, she lied about things, but she had to, I would suppose. He could have been a gentleman and lied to me too, but that wasn't Finley. I knew the guilt she carried, knowing her only option was to succumb to the demands of this pig so she could eek a simple life for me, was enough to drive her crazy. I understand now that she tried to protect me.

Without a husband, a woman's choices had limitations in those days, and Finley was there with open arms. Desperate people do desperate things, and my mother, as strong as she was, was so weak in many ways.

Sadly, she believed my father died at his hand, driven there by demons and wrongdoing, as she called it. It's probably better that way. Finley had kept his deeds hidden from her heart, but not from me. I knew what this man could do, and I knew what he did to my life.

I leaned over, placing my face close to his, and I could feel his breath. "You bastard!" I said. "You fooled her all these years, but you're not going to fool me."

"One day, when you're a man, you'll see. You'll understand."

He spoke as if it were his right to ruin our lives, his privilege. He owned everything in the county, so why not my family as well?

"You made sure you were here to take care of things—your special relationship, as you call it. The truth is, my father was looking for you on the night he went to your store, isn't it, Finley?"

"I told you what happened."

"Yes, you did. You set it up, Finley," I yelled. "You allowed his escape. You let him know, somehow, you would be at your store waiting for him. And you waited, and you blew his head off with your shotgun: you, Finley. You murdered my father. And if I had my way, I'd see you hang for what you did to my father and mother."

"Lucas," he said. "Sometimes, you just to let things go. Realize it's beyond your control."

He knew I understood I couldn't kill him. That would be too easy, and besides, I'd never get away with it. I knew he was afraid of me. I could tell from his eyes. He was like most men. They puff their chests and pound their fists, but when it comes down to it, they're afraid. I know my father had to be scared on that night in Finley's store. Any man would be frightened knowing tomorrow may not come.

"What are you going to do, Finley? Kill me, too?"

"I don't want no trouble, boy, but I am prepared to defend myself."

I could hear the fear coming from his voice; that shake you get when your heart is beating so hard, you can hear it in your words. He was scared, and he was losing control. It made me feel good.

I turned my back to him, daring him mainly, but prepared for whatever would come next; on that day, I welcomed death without fear.

As I thought he would, Finley reached into his vest pocket, pulled his derringer, and pointed it toward me. I heard the click as he pulled the hammer into position.

"Now what, boy?" he bellowed.

The truth was, Finley didn't understand, nor did I expect him to. I had no fear of dying. I knew the facts behind the lies of my youth and understood what surviving meant. I had no one to love, no one to love me. I was alone with only lies held within my heart. Everything I knew or had known over my short eighteen years were fabrications made under the guise of love. Everyone was dead, and I was the only one left. Where would I go?

After all this time, what I did understand was what my father learned—the reason he went after Finley. You can't take everything from a man, strip him of his dignity, and then expect him to let you walk away. My father understood this. I can only guess sometime during his incarceration, he figured it out between the haze of the drugs and lucid moments. Sadly, his mind was in no condition to challenge anyone. But now, as fate would have it, it was my turn and my opportunity to revenge my parents, my stolen childhood, and my life.

"Now what?" I said without looking back. "I'm not afraid of you or your little pistol, Finley."

I could only imagine his mind spinning with the situation as to what to do. He was used to being in charge, and now, I was in control. I felt the heat rise in my body. I wished he'd come at me, and I would kill him where he stood, in retribution of my father's death and my mother's pain. That's what I hoped for; shoot him with his gun and watch him suffer in pain. It would be slow, a shot to his knee first and watch him fall as if begging. He would beg for sure, beg for his miserable life. Weak men always beg.

Then I thought of my mother. *Forgive him. Let him be,* she would've said. It didn't matter. He just stood there pointing that stupid gun at the back of my head as if it meant something.

I spun around, catching him off guard, and my fist hit him square on the jaw. I could tell by the look on his face he didn't expect me to do that. He stumbled back, and I guess I must have hit him harder than I had planned. His arms fell limp at his side, his knees buckled, and he slammed against the corner of the fireplace mantle. He slumped to the floor, and I stared at his head as thick, dark blood, the color of night, oozed from beneath his head.

As I said, I didn't mean to kill him. Not that I hadn't thought about it, but it was his fault. I believe a man prepares his destiny, each living to his consequence, and so went the life of Theo Finley.

I walked to the front window and stood there watching the snow falling. Everything was quiet, and I could see a full circle of the sun behind a grayed opaque horizon. I looked back at what had just happened, understanding—realizing—no one would believe me. My words against the most powerful man in the county would undoubtedly have meant a noose around my neck.

There was nothing left, nowhere to turn, and I was alone in a house holding too many secrets, surrounded by a town where I didn't fit. All that I once believed was now lost—buried within the borders of my heart. The lies became my truth, fitting neatly into a small tin box.

In a calmness never felt in my years, I pulled the lantern from the mantle, struck a match, and lit the wick.

I walked through the dark hallway, and I returned to my bedroom, gathering the few belongings I could call my own: a pair of pants, two shirts, and a Swiss Army Knife given to me many years before by John Watson, the caretaker for the church. For a moment, the memory rose in my head, and I thought, with kind reminiscence, of the only decent man in my life. I placed the knife in my pants pocket and dressed warmly for the cold winter day ahead, long underwear under my pants, a thick shirt of cotton, calf-high boots, and a heavy leather coat lined with the coarse hair of shorn sheep.

I walked each room of the house expecting to find something left for my own, but nothing of value remained.

In the kitchen, I pulled a small bag of cornmeal, a salted ham, a bag of dried beans from the mostly barren cupboards, and a small pan that hung on the wall, placed them within my bindle, and wrapped my only possessions tight with a length of rope. I felt my pants pocket once again for the outline of my knife. I flipped the bindle across my shoulder, placed my hat squarely on my head, and pulled the collar of my coat around my neck.

I took one last look at Finley, crumpled in front of the fireplace, and that's when I chucked the lantern down the hallway like an overthrown horseshoe.

I pushed through the front doorway, passed under the winter-stripped oak tree and onto the gravel road. I could hear the glass from the windows explode behind me, the roar of the fire as it stretched through the openings, and then the crack of the dry wood as the fire burned through the supports of the house and the roof began to give way.

The bitter wind slapped my face and stung my cheeks as I moved toward an unknown future and realized, as I passed the cemetery holding the backwash of my indoctrination:

Lies held within your heart never save you, and your heart always lies to those you love.

Chapter 14

The unblemished trail pointed northeast. Leftover pumpkins from the fall harvest were sheltered under a soft, white blanket as crested tops of fence posts told the boundaries of the path beneath his boots. The bare branches of towering oaks and maples ran the border of the wide path. They outstretched across the sky like jagged black lightning.

Lucas pulled his woolen hat tight over his head and dug his reddened hands deep into his pockets, searching for warmth, but the winters in Ohio are brutal and uncaring, like most of the people he knew as a child.

Soon, the snow turned to small flurries and danced on lighter winds, although the cold of this day still cut through his coat like the sharpened edge of a butcher's knife. The steady rhythm of his boots crunched the frozen snow beneath the ever-increasing wetness of his socks and became his solitary companion. While walking alone, a man's mind tends to wander, and it seemed he had plenty of time to think of how he had ended up at this moment in his life.

The first thought to float across his head was Finley. These thoughts made him think of the house, then he recalled the flames as they shot through the windows and the walls began to crumble.

Soon, the wind changed direction, blowing from the north, and snow began to fall in large, heavy flakes. He heard the muffled sounds of a truck as it approached from behind. With reluctance but little choice, given the freezing temperature, he pulled one hand from his pocket and lifted his arm, raising his thumb in the hope of kindness.

A flatbed truck, filled with the last of the fall harvest, drove beyond Lucas and pulled to the side of the road. He quickened his pace and approached the passenger side. The driver, a man of a happy disposition and the crooked grin of a jack o' lantern sat behind the large steering wheel. He was aged and with a large white beard covering most of his barreled chest. His hands were large and calloused from years of heavy work on farms across the northeast.

"Where you headed, boy?" the driver yelled above the clacking noise of the truck engine.

"Anywhere but here," Lucas said.

Lucas opened the truck door, threw his bindle onto the floorboard, and climbed onto the front seat. The cab of the truck was warm and felt better than the snow-covered road ahead. The driver pulled back onto the road, and each gearbox shift took Lucas further from his past.

The old man shifted the truck into third gear, breaking the silence. "Name's Bardy. Tom Bardy. I'm heading back to Cleveland. You plan on going that far?"

"Cleveland is fine and as good a place as any to get a new start, I suppose." He paused for a moment. "My name is Lucas Colby."

Lucas replayed Bardy's words in his head. He hadn't thought about where he was going—only that he was leaving—leaving the only home he'd ever known.

As the sun crossed over the buried lies of his life,

those words, left home, sounded odd to his ears. The truth he concluded was, there never was something or someplace he could call home.

Chapter 15

"You know how to drive a truck, Lucas Colby?"

"I have lived my entire life on a farm. I can drive anything."

"Good. We can share the driving if you don't mind. We'll make sufficient time as long as this old truck holds out, and we can drive through the night."

"Sounds fine with me," Lucas said.

"Did you happen to see the house on fire?" Bardy asked. "I wanted to stop, but I got a schedule to keep, and it looked like some fellers already trying to put it out."

"Yup. Saw the fire. Nobody lives there. Not anymore."

Trying to avoid any conversation concerning the detail of his life or the fight he'd had with Theo Finley this morning, Lucas asked, "What are you carrying in the back? It ain't a casket, is it?" He couldn't remove the image of Finley's bleeding head jammed against the foot of the fireplace or how all he'd done was react to Finley's pulling out that stupid little derringer and waving it in his face.

Bardy looked over at Lucas. "Nope. Just Pumpkins. Dead pumpkins, I suppose you could say. It's the last crop for the season, and I'm bringing it up to Cleveland for the Halloween crowd. Them city kids love to carve 'em up and stick 'em on the stoop."

Bardy hummed an old hymnal while he stared at the

road ahead, a melody familiar to Lucas. After a few miles, he said, "Hey, listen. Seeing you're not heading anywhere in particular, how'd you like to work with me for a while? I could use some help with winter coming on like it is."

Lucas thought about Bardy's offer for a moment and thought again that his belly would be as empty as his pockets if he said no. "Sure. I can help for a bit, but I'll have to be moving on soon." He also knew he could stay where he wanted if he wanted, and nothing held him— not man, not family, not heart.

As the day progressed, the drive became long and tiresome. Night fell, and Lucas took the wheel while Bardy dozed; his head leaned forward and swayed to the potholes in the road. Dawn peeked through the clouds as they turned into their final road and arrived outside of Cleveland at the Farmer's Market.

"Looks like we beat 'em all here," Bardy said.

"Can't imagine anyone being here this early," Lucas said. "I think I'll doze a bit before they get here."

"Yup. Go ahead. I'll check the office to make sure all is good."

Bardy stepped out of the truck and walked up the steps to the office. There was no one around, so he sat on the ledge of the dock to wait. An hour passed, and a man arrived. Bardy walked over to meet him. Lucas watched as they shook hands, and Bardy motioned for Lucas.

"Let's put 'em right here," Bardy said.

Lucas helped unload the truck, and afterward, they drove into the city.

"I know a place in town that puts up lodgers. We can stay there for the night," Bardy said.

Lucas drove the truck to the junction of Harrison

Street and Cleveland Avenue. He looked upon the large brick buildings and storefronts as a foreign land to his eyes and unlike the simple life he knew. Tall buildings, paved roads, cars, and trucks lined the avenue alongside horses and buggies. Within a block, Lucas could see more stores than he could ever use; a tailor, a dressmaker, a dime store, a place called White Way Drug Store advertising tonics to resolve most any ache or pain that might ail you.

A large Victorian house stood just off the main street. Bardy pointed over. "This is it."

The house, ragged and torn, appeared abandoned. The weathered stairs moaned under the weight of the men. Bardy knocked on the door and stepped back. After a few moments, the door opened with a creaking, and an older woman stood before them. She smiled a toothless smile when she saw Bardy standing on the porch. "Can't believe you're still making the trip, Tom. Ain't seen ya in three months. Figured ya up 'n died." The older woman looked over at Lucas. "Looks like you brought some company, a handsome one. Y'all come on in the parlor."

Bardy stepped across the threshold, and Lucas followed. They sat in a parlor just off the main hallway, left of the stairway leading to the rooms.

"Just made some tea," the old woman announced. "How 'bout I pour ya some?"

Bardy smiled. "That sounds good. How about you, Lucas?" Lucas smiled and politely declined.

Bardy helped the old woman place the tray containing the teapot and cups on the small table in front of the couch.

"This here is Lucas. We met a ways up the road." Lucas stood, and the older woman extended her hand.

"Lucas. This is my sister, Eloise."

After some conversation, she led the men to their rooms.

Lucas tossed his bindle onto the bed and looked out the window. He decided to look around the town. Walking through the hallway, he stopped and knocked on Bardy's door. There was no answer, and Lucas figured he was asleep. As he passed the parlor, he heard Eloise humming a tune and working in the kitchen. Outside, he crossed the street and walked past Cyrus Lowery's Curio Depot. He stopped and looked at the array of curious-looking stuffed alligators, turtles, and a couple of real dogs. The people standing around smiled at him as he passed.

He knew jobs were scarce, and he didn't need to stay in Ohio. He looked down the street and noticed a placard sign on the walkway reading: *See the World. Join the Army.* It made him think of his father. The Armed Services Recruiting Office stood before him, and with that, he believed his future.

He walked into the building and saw a procession of young boys standing along the back wall wearing nothing but their underwear while waiting for their exams and the chance to pick up a rifle and fight. They were quiet and orderly, shifting their weight from one barefoot to the other while they waited to hear their name called. The stale air, hot and without circulation, smelled of men. He stepped up to a desk, the color of gunmetal. The man behind the desk, dressed in an Army uniform, appeared haggard and without patience. He was busy talking on the telephone, his neck arched over with the phone stuck between his head and shoulder while his hands were shuffling papers and file folders about the desk. He raised his eyes and looked up at Lucas without stopping. Lucas announced, "My name is Lucas Colby, and I want to join up."

Without hesitation, he handed Lucas a clipboard with a form attached and a pen. He said, "Fill this out. Strip down to your skivvies, throw your clothes in a locker, and get in line with the rest of them. You'll get your turn."

Lucas followed the sign and walked through a small passageway. He saw a row of lockers painted a dull green and opened the doors until he found an empty one. He stripped down to his underwear and stuffed his clothes into the small locker. He returned to the line of young boys and took his place behind the last one. At his height, he could see over the heads of most recruits. The line was long and he shifted foot to foot watching the nurse as she made her way down the line asking each boy for the form attached to the clipboard.

During the physical, the doctor ran Lucas through basic tests. Lucas had never needed a doctor. The only Doc familiar to him was Doc Phillips. After the first exam, Lucas sat alone in a dreary room with faded green walls, few windows, and no window covering. He watched the snowfall and believed it was going to be a cold winter. A small table held instruments of trade, and a well-worn chair stood in the corner. The nurse arrived and ordered Lucas to follow her to another room. She pointed to a steel table in the middle of the room. With fewer windows and facing another building, Lucas could not see the ground outside.

She said in a firm voice, "I need you to lie down on the table so the doctor can run some tests."

Lucas thought as she attached a series of wires and

suction cups to his chest, the metal table was as cold as her demeanor. He stared at the gray ceiling above him. A single light hung from a frayed cord. In the corners of the walls, high in the ceiling, he could see old cobwebs wafting from the breeze caused by a four-bladed fan hanging from the ceiling. The large fan wobbled and squeaked as it slowly spun around, stirring the stale air. He turned his eyes to the nurse, and he could see her name, Katie Johnson, RN, on her nameplate, perfectly pinned to the right side of her spotless, white uniform.

Lucas could tell by the tone of her voice she was a professional and knew what she was doing. She reached across him and said, "Your being alone and without parents to consent for you and confirm your medical history, the doctor will need to make sure you're healthy."

Lucas tried to break through her ascetic disposition. "Trust me! I'm the healthiest buck in this joint! I'm strong as an ox, can drink all night, and be up at dawn and ready to go again!"

She responded as if the blood in the veins of her slender arms was about to freeze. "Shut up, cowboy, and be still."

The wires crossed his chest like a map of a highway. Lucas asked, this time a little less foolhardy, "So you think I'll pass this test?"

She smiled. "You look like you can handle most anything, you know, a man your size and all." With her long, painted fingernails, she tapped on his chest and added, "But you'll need to behave yourself!"

Not one to give up, he asked, "Tell me, Katie, how would you like to go dancing with me tonight?"

She crossed her arms in front of her and looked at

Lucas. "You don't give up, do you?"

He could see he touched a nerve. "I know what I like," he said.

She leaned over and whispered close to his ear, "The Doc is my husband, so you need to be quiet." She then glanced around the room and said, "He works late all the time, but I'll be out of here by five o'clock."

Smug in his conquest, Lucas smiled and placed his hands behind his head as she walked away.

Moments later, the doctor arrived. He was a tall, thin man of grave deportment. His receding hairline exposed his wrinkled brow and his skin, limpid and bare. He began pushing buttons on a machine next to the table.

"What are you doing, Doc?" Lucas asked.

"It's just a test to see if your heart is working, young man. The other doctor thought he heard something during your examination. It is probably nothing to worry about, mind you. Just be quiet for a minute while the test runs, and I can then read the results."

The doctor pushed a button on the machine, and it made a slight humming sound. A long slip of paper with marks on it came out of the small opening. The doctor reached over, pulled the strip of paper from the machine, and held it up toward the ceiling as if reading a scroll found hidden long ago.

"What does it say?" Lucas asked as he sat upon the table.

The doctor pulled his stethoscope from around his neck and placed the cold silver end on Lucas' muscular chest. "Inhale deeply, and then let it out slowly," he instructed.

Each time Lucas would exhale, the doctor would move the cold metal piece to a new area of his chest.

After a few moves around the front and back of Lucas, the doctor stepped back with a worried look on his face. "Sorry, kid, I wish I had better news."

"What do you mean by better news, Doc?"

"You have what is called a murmur in your heart," the doctor told Lucas.

"A murmur?"

"It's an extra or unusual sound heard during your heartbeat. It could be serious, or it could be nothing, and you may grow out of it. You are still a young man, so I don't think you need to start planning for a funeral right away."

Lucas sat up. "I don't understand, Doc. I feel fine! I am as strong as a bull, and I have always worked hard. I grew up on a farm! I milked cows, fed chickens, and even worked the fields. How can I have a bad heart?"

The doctor leaned against the metal table. "It's not that you have a bad heart. It is a heart murmur, which means you could have a problem later. You could, and probably will be, just fine, but the Army can't take a chance of your having a problem while at war in the middle of some foreign land."

"Die at war? In some foreign land?" Lucas said, releasing a loud laugh. "Now that would be something, doc!"

Without a response, the doctor told Lucas he could get up and get dressed. "Good luck with your future, son. Don't let this bother you. I am sure you will be just fine."

As the doctor wrote some notes on the paper, he said, "You're probably not going to die soon, and you could live to be a hundred years old. It all depends on how you choose to live. Right now, the Army wants healthy men, and your health isn't perfect."

It seemed each time Lucas knew what he wanted to do, something would block his way. He was again at a crossroad, and the only thing he knew was, he was broke and alone. Before leaving Independence, Lucas scraped up some money by selling everything he could get his hands on, and even that wasn't enough for a decent meal.

He returned to the boarding house. In his room, he stretched out across the mattress and stared at the ceiling. He knew this was not what he wanted. He pulled a small flask from his bindle and took a swig of whiskey. It burned his throat. He wrapped his belongings once again and walked down the streets of Cleveland. He sat on the curb of this godforsaken town with his face buried in his hands.

In the distance, he heard a whistle as a train approached the Cleveland Union Terminal. As if someone shouted in his ear, telling him to run as fast as he could, he jumped from the curb and ran toward the sounding shrill. His heart pounded and felt as if it were going to jump through his chest. The train moved quickly down the tracks. He managed to catch the last car and tossed his bindle through the open cargo door as he reached for the handrail. He grabbed the rail on the side of the boxcar and hoisted himself up onto the floor. Covered with a layer of hay, it smelled of cattle and urine.

Without knowing his destination, Lucas settled into the boxcar. He leaned against the back wall and curled into a ball, making himself small. His chest heaved in short gasps for air; his heart pounded in his ears.

The gentle sway of the train became a rhythmic pattern, slowly rocking back and forth. Lucas fell back on the scratchy brown hay as the train sped through an uncertain night. He believed the train headed north and into his future—a future of uncertainty, but his future, nonetheless. This would be a future, Lucas believed, he would control.

The cold evening air blew in through the open door. Lucas could see the landscape change from brick and mortar to small hills. A panorama came into view within a short time, and he watched the sun as it fell beneath the horizon, the clouds like ragged gray cloths against the orange sky. Everything dimmed, faded, and lost shape as darkness came. The train wheels sounded their ta-tok, ta-tok, ta-tok along the tracks, and he fell asleep. He dreamt about his mother, how his life could have been if his father had lived, how they could have been a family.

Chapter 16

The blaring reverberation of the train horn announced the arrival, heralding a new beginning. Lucas jolted awake and stuck his head out the door as the train slowed. He saw a sign posted on the side of the red-bricked building as the wheels squealed against the cold metal tracks entering the station. Before the train stopped, he jumped and hit the ground hard.

Lucas walked into the city and found his way without direction from others he passed. The buildings were tall, and there were so many people, he thought. It seemed the paved roads and cars went on forever, and everyone walked as if they were late getting to someplace. The afternoon moved into the evening as he came upon Washington Square Park, and in the twilight, he saw a large archway. The shelter would offer little comfort from the cold night wind, but it was all Lucas would have. Sleep was slow in coming, and it was not a restful night.

Morning came early as the traffic around him began to stir. The noise of the city was not like the quiet of the country. He stood up, his body stiff from sleeping on the hard ground, tied his bindle, and walked away. Looking back, he could see the archway was a monument to George Washington. Lucas read the inscription aloud: *Let us raise a standard to which the wise and honest can repair. The event is in the hand of God."* He thought it ironic.

Lucas traversed northward through the park. He passed McDougal Street and continued across Comelia and Jones, asking for work at each store. With a long day ahead, he could see it would be full of misgiving. He worked his path down the busy streets carrying nothing more than pocket change in well-worn pants and hope within his wearied heart. He watched for any business with an open door, finding the same rejecting answer. Any work would have been fine, but every turn brought another refusal. He considered his decision as a mistake when something caught his attention. As if someone called his name, he glanced up. Ahead of him, he saw a street sign. It read Barrow Street, and it was just a feeling.

At the corner, he turned left and followed his beckoned path across Bleeker Street. He continued to ask for work at every door, finding the same answer. He was beginning to lose all hope. Tired, his stomach empty, he sat on the curb at Bedford Avenue and reviewed his options. As he pondered, two police officers approached.

"Hey, buddy. Let's move it along."

Lucas stood. "Will be doing just that, sirs."

"Make it quick. We don't like vagrants around here."

"I'm looking for work, sir. I'm not a vagrant."

"Yeah, well, we'll be back by here soon, and if we catch sight of you, you'll have a nice place to stay tonight."

As Lucas explained, he looked beyond his view, over the shoulders of the police officers, and noticed a narrow alley and a foot-worn stone pathway. Lucas believed this was his destination. He couldn't explain it in his mind, but somehow, he knew this was where his search would end. The wind flapped a small handwritten sign tacked onto the arched doorway leading to the stark building. He ran across the street, yanked the sign off the door, and could not believe good fortune found its way to him as he read the note—Need a Job? - See Charlie Inside.

In his heart, he knew this would be his final query. With new confidence, he pulled open the large door and walked into the building. The door slammed behind him, giving him a start. It was warm inside, and the lighting was dim in the old building. Making his way through the room, across a dance floor, the stale aroma of old liquor, cheap perfume, and cigarette smoke invaded his nostrils as the smells floated heavy across the room. His eyes adjusted to the empty darkness, and he wondered if anyone ever put a mop to the floor. A man sat at a table in the corner. The tip of the cigarette he smoked glowed in the darkened room.

Lucas said, in his strongest voice, "I'm looking for Charlie."

"Over here, kid, I'm Charlie. You lookin' for a job?" The voice was gruff and startled Lucas. He moved cautiously toward the table.

Unlike the men Lucas had seen on the street, dressed in fancy clothes with tight-necked collars and ties wearing fancy hats, Charles Leland wore a floppy hat, an open shirt, and a loose tie around his thin neck.

"What's your name, kid?" he asked.

"Lucas Colby, sir," he said as he noticed the dog at Charlie's feet.

He peered at Lucas over the top of his eyeglasses. "You're a big one, Lucas Colby. Have a seat, let's talk. Don't worry about the dog. He doesn't bite unless I tell him."

Charlie lit another cigarette, crossed his legs, and leaned back on his chair. "You know what this place is?" he said with a wave of his hand.

Lucas looked around, saw an open area of the floor, a small stage with musical instruments, chairs, a small piano, and pictures on the walls; some of the women in a provocative pose, and countryside scenery done in oil paints, lamps hung low across tables scattered across the room.

"It looks like a place to dance," Lucas responded, quite unsure of the purpose of the building.

"Yeah. That's it. A dance hall, and that's all," Charlie told him, and he laughed like someone getting one up on someone else. "Lookie here. It's starting to get busy around here, so I need some to help clean the place up, bring in ice, and do the dishes, stuff like that. You can do this?"

"Yeah. I can do the work. No problem," Lucas answered.

"I used to work the Wild West Show in my younger days in the last of the Old West," Charlie said as he shifted in his seat. "I then moved to Chicago and waited tables. You ever worked in the union, kid?"

"Uh, no, sir. Never have."

"Yeah, well, that's okay. I used to be part of the American Workers Union in Chicago, but it got so tough that I split town. As a matter of fact, the authorities started arresting all the big cheeses, so I hightailed it and ended up here."

"So, how did you end up with this place?"

"That was crazy, let me tell you. When I got here, prohibition was in full swing—still is, the dumb bastards.

Anyhow, New York is full of these gangsters, goons, bootleggers, and crooked cops, but what I saw was an opportunity. This business is tough, but it pays well, so I knew it would be a good deal. I bought this old building and cleaned it up. Upfront, it looks like any old dance hall, but if you know your way to the back, well, that's something we'll talk about later. Anyhow, once the word spread, which doesn't take long around here, it was business as usual." Charlie pushed his hat above his forehead, and with a firm look from cynical eyes, he asked, "Think you can make it here, kid?"

Lucas told him, "Sure I can—and I can take care of this place as you want."

Charlie leaned back on the chair. "You married, kid?

"I don't even have a girlfriend."

"Hell! I'm on my third!" Charlie said. "My first wife died on me; my second wife never came home after an argument we had one night. I haven't heard from her in the past two years. Then I found number three, Harriet. She's a tough one, and I think she'll be around a while."

Lucas watched as Charlie took a long drag off his Lucky. He released the smoke, blowing it through his nose. "Over the years, the cops busted me. I was shot twice and robbed once. I've been in a few fights, which you can't help, being in this business." He laughed and rubbed his tobacco-stained finger across his crooked nose. "That's how I got this!"

He stood, told Lucas to follow him, and said, "No matter what happened to me, I always came out on top." Charlie motioned to Lucas. "Let's take a walk, kid."

Lucas followed Charlie up a flight of stairs leading to rooms. Charlie stopped at one of the doorways and explained, "This room is for my AW brotherhood so they could get together and discuss business. The other rooms are for overnight guests or what have you." They turned and walked down the stairs and toward the back of the building. "This," Charlie said as they walked up to the bar, "is where the action is." He walked further to the rear of the building and showed Lucas a trick staircase. "I use this to trip up the cops. I also made the bar entrance look like picture walls, and here is a trapdoor to hide the booze." He smiled at Lucas as if he was a proud papa gloating over his children.

He stopped and looked at Lucas from head to toe. "How old are you, kid?"

"I'm twenty years old," Lucas lied.

"Yeah, well, you'll look a lot older after working here a while."

Charlie pointed across the room. "Most of my customers come in the front door, you know, like they're looking to dance. Some of the customers know the back door."

Lucas asked, "What do we do if we get raided?"

Charlie said, "I'll get to it in a minute." Lucas decided it was best to keep his mouth shut and his eyes opened as Charlie continued talking. "The girls working at night are here to get these chumps to buy more drinks and dance and then buy more drinks. Got that?"

"Yeah, got that, Charlie."

"Anyways, they sit upfront here and escort the gentlemen to the back so they can buy the booze . . . or they go upstairs to them rooms I showed you."

Lucas nodded and decided to keep quiet. He expected a city filled with new and different things, but this wasn't on his list.

"We get a fair share of dames coming in from time

to time as well," Charlie added, "so don't expect all guys. Some girls are chippies, and the men like that, but you need to watch yourself. They come here for the men, and the men coming in here have money. A kid like you ain't got no reason to be paying for it, and if ya keep ya nose clean and show me you can handle the place, you might have a future. Hell, you might make it to twenty-one."

Lucas was puzzled and didn't understand Charlie's references; however, he thought it best to leave it alone for the time being. Charlie continued, "Anyhow. My point is, nice girls don't usually hang around bars unless they have something on their minds."

Lucas was more confused by the minute and finally said, "I have to ask you. What are Chippies?"

Charlie grinned at Lucas. "You ain't never heard that word, eh kid?" He removed his hat, rubbed his hand across his forehead, and thought for a moment. "Let me say this. Sometimes, a woman needs to support herself because there ain't no steady man in her life. There could be lotsa reasons why, but the fact is, they got something, and lotsa men are willing to pay for it—and besides, they need to eat like the rest of us. There ain't nothing wrong with that, and I have the place to make it happen. Also, it makes for a tidy profit for ol' Charlie here. That making sense to you, kid?"

Lucas thought for a moment and responded, "Gotcha, Charlie."

"Anyhow. Let's talk about the cops that come in here trying to bust up the joint," Charlie continued. "I can tell you this. I ain't gonna give the bastards my hard-earned money for nothing. So here it is. Occasionally, they bust in and act as if they were going to close the place down, but they never do. Crooked as snakes, I tell ya!"

Charlie and Lucas walked back to the front and sat at a table. "Hell, some of them are my best customers—I play along, they bust in, I know they're coming. Everybody runs out the back, and the cops have the place to themselves."

Lucas looked around with nervous anticipation. This place was a long way from the small country life he knew—then he thought, probably not far enough away. Of all the abilities he held within his emotional arsenal, there was one in particular that served him well: the ability to read people—an instinct he learned early in life; an instinct that would serve him well in the days to come. He could see beneath Charlie's crusty portrayal and malevolent persona. He knew Charlie Leland could be trusted.

"So, here's how it works," Charlie said. "I need someone to work behind the bartender, and most of the time, it would be me. You put the ice up here from the back, clean the dishes, and make sure you keep the place clean. This ain't a place for the faint of heart, and there will be some tough days, but judging by your size and attitude, a tough guy like you should be able to handle this place," Charlie paused and lit another Lucky. "So, ya want the job, kid?"

Lucas tried to control his excitement. "Hell yeah... I mean, yes, sir."

Charlie laughed. "Okay, kid. Be back here at six o'clock sharp." He pulled a couple of dollars from his pocket, folded them into the large hand of Lucas, and said, "Consider this an advance on your pay, and grab yourself something to eat, kid."

Chapter 17

"Put this on, and I'll get you started, kid," Charlie said as he stepped behind the bar. "You know, kid, I was thinking. You told me you just got into town. Do you got family?"

"No," Lucas replied. "You could say I'm on my own."

"You ain't running from nothing, are you?" Charlie asked.

"Nope. Just trying to live my life the best I know how."

"You have a place to stay?"

"I haven't thought about it." Lucas felt dumb saying this, but it was true. His excitement overtook his good sense. "I guess I'd better find a place to live."

"You're greener than I thought, kid. Tell you what. I got an extra room downstairs, in the back of the building. You can stay until you get situated."

Charlie then turned and walked to the bar at the back of the building. "The first thing you need to know is the code," he said over his shoulder.

"The code?" So much happened during his interview, Lucas didn't recall the earlier conversation.

"Yeah! Like I told ya. I refuse to give them cops or anybody else any of my money or my good booze. Do you know what I mean? And I don't want my customers hurt."

"So, how does it work, Mr. Leland?"

"Jumping Jesus, kid! I see we need to go over the rules."

Lucas took a step back, lowered his head, and stared at the floor. "Sorry, sir," he said quietly.

Charlie raised his hands in exasperation. "Okay. Rule number one: Name's Charlie. You call me Charlie or Boss. Number two: take a stand and show me you got hutzpah. Number three: do what I tell you when I tell you. Rule number four is, see the phone under the bar? When that phone rings, you answer it. If someone on the other end says, 'Is this 86 and Bedford?', you hit the bell hanging above the bar and tell everyone to get the hell out through the backdoor. You then make sure you hide all the booze under the trapdoor I showed you." He pointed his finger at Lucas and asked, "Got it?"

"Sure, boss! I got it! But I thought you said spies or something was looking out, so there shouldn't be a problem."

Charlie looked over at Lucas, took a long drag off his Lucky. "It's the something you got to worry about, kid, and that's how it goes. And yeah, I got spies all over. Who do you think is calling?" Charlie poked Lucas' chest. "Learn this if nothing else. You can't trust nobody, so for chrissake, make sure you keep your eyes open, and no screwing around!"

Charlie walked off and then stopped. "You look like you got a question."

Lucas, embarrassed, said, "Yeah, boss. I do."

"Spit it out, kid."

"Rule number two. What's hoots pah?

Charlie laughed once again. "I forget you're a country boy. Here, I'll spell it, c-h-u-t-z-p-a-h. I say it like hutzpah, which is how most people say it. It means gall, brazen nerve, incredible guts, and maybe some arrogance thrown in. In other words, kid, you gotta have stones to make it in this business. You understand stones, right?" Charlie handed Lucas a mop and a bucket. "Clean up the floor in here, and when you're done, start on the dance floor. After you're done with mopping, grab the other bucket, bring some ice in from the back, and then wipe down the counter. Don't screw around, though. We'll probably have company shortly."

By the time Lucas finished the floors, the water was as black as the night sky. Two men wearing dark business suits came in through the back door before he could clean up and put the buckets in the closet.

One of them was large, and the other was short but fat. Both had solemn looks on their faces, and Lucas thought they didn't look like they wanted to dance. They took one look at Lucas and stopped.

The short one said, "Who the hell are you?"

A voice from a darkened corner of the bar said, "Relax fellas. He's my new employee." Charlie stepped up and introduced Lucas.

"This is Joey and Vinnie. Two of my regulars," Charlie said.

"Nice to meet you," said Lucas.

Vinnie chuckled, looked over at Charlie, and said, "You got yourself a green one, don't ya, Charlie?

Charlie handled the men in stride, responding, "Lucas, pull the bottle with the red label from under the bar and give me three glasses. I think the boys need a drink."

That night, Lucas learned the purpose of a speakeasy.

Chapter 18

At the end of his first month with Charlie, Lucas locked up for the night. He climbed the stairs to his room and stretched out on his bed. There was a flask of whiskey on the nightstand. His mind, haunted by his past, kept him awake as the sun crested the horizon. He stood and walked to the window of his tiny room and looked out at the street below. The street was busy with people walking, stores opening, and horns blowing, and he thought about how far he'd come. The view was nothing like that of Independence, and he was glad. After a few months, a few raids, and some good times, Lucas found he liked working at Charlie's. There were the regular customers, and then a couple of new ones now and again. When the cops raided the place, Charlie set them up with the chippies and gave them all the cheap booze they wanted. With that, Charlie was free to do as he pleased.

As Lucas and Charlie cleaned up after the night's entertainment, Charlie asked Lucas what he wanted to do with his life. "You know, the bar business ain't no good for a smart kid like you."

"Yeah, I've been thinking about the future, Charlie, but I like it here. You know, working with you and all that."

Charlie wiped his brow and tossed the towel over his shoulder. "Listen up, kid. You got what they call potential. I think you need to come up with something that will take advantage of your ability. Look at it this way. If I was to tell you to pick anything in the world you wanted to do, what would you say? Don't worry about money, success, and all that stuff. Just tell me what you want to do?"

Lucas thought for a moment. He considered all the things his mother taught him. Of all the things Martha was to Lucas, she was his mother, and she loved him despite her deceptions. She had always said, "You're a smart boy, and one day, you are going to make a difference." She knew life would be hard for a boy without a father, and she knew she wouldn't live forever, and Lucas needed to grow up strong.

"So, what do you want to do with your life, kid?" Charlie edged.

Lucas looked at Charlie. "Ya know, Charlie. I've been thinking about just that. Ma wanted me to go to college. She said I could make it and I should go. She said I should be a writer because I always made notes and then read them back. I think that's one of the things I learned from her, the writing part. She always wrote things, letters and notes in a journal I found after she died. I told her more schooling would be great, but I couldn't see how we could afford any of it. We barely had money to live on, and after she died, there wasn't much I could do."

Charlie leaned back and shifted his hat. "College? I didn't expect you would say college. I mean, not that there is anything wrong with college, and honestly, I think it would do you good."

Lucas smiled. "My mother always said I had the gift of words."

Charlie chuckled. "She was right about the words, kid. I never met anyone like you before. You can talk your way in or out of about anything. That's what will make you a good bartender."

"You know, Charlie. Right now, I think I'll just keep working here and see how it goes."

"I have an idea, Lucas," Charlie said. "How about you look into what it takes to get in the college here, and I'll help you out."

"You would do that for me?"

"Well. I would do it for you and me. My way of thinking is, if you got a college education, we might be able to make this place something other than a booze joint."

Chapter 19

As the economy declined, it seemed more men found out about Charlie's place. Fortunately for Charlie, liquor was their escape, and a good time with a beautiful woman fit right into the formula. By now, Lucas was a bartender and was doing well financially. Bonnie Walker, the favorite chippie, sat at the bar. She crossed her legs, and the split in her dress showed plenty. She tapped a cigarette from the pack in front of her. A man sitting next to her was quick with a match. She smiled and held the man's hand while blowing the flame out.

Lucas watched as she worked the room with the other men. When things were quiet, she would sit near Lucas and talk about the night, the men, and her future.

"You know it's going to be slow tonight," she said.

"Maybe it will pick up," Lucas answered.

"Not tonight. I got a feeling about it."

Bonnie carried a unique talent. Not only picking men and getting them to spend their money, but she always seemed to know how the night would end before it started, and she knew tonight would bring nothing but conversation.

"Where you from, Lucas?"

"Ohio."

"That's a long way from home."

"If you want to call it that."

"A long way?"

"No," he said, "I meant home."

Charlie came in from the street and called to Lucas, interrupting the conversation.

"I need to see you for a minute."

Lucas followed Charlie into the back office.

"Listen, kid. I need you to go out to my car and bring in the box in the trunk. Bring it in here. But don't stop and talk with anyone."

"Okay, Charlie."

"Now listen. The box is heavy, so I need you to lift it carefully. Understand?"

"Yeah. I got it, Charlie."

"Come right back in here, don't talk to nobody."

Lucas took the car keys and did as he was told, carrying the large, heavy cardboard box inside.

"Put it over there," Charlie said. He pointed to a long table as Lucas entered the room.

"What the hell is in here, Charlie?"

"What I been talking to you about, kid. It's what makes us men."

Charlie took a knife and slid the blade along the taped edges. Lucas couldn't believe what he saw.

"Jesus, Charlie! How much is in there?"

"Quiet kid. Don't let the whole world know."

"Yeah. Sorry. But Charlie, I've never seen this much money."

Charlie smiled. "I'll betcha haven't. Listen, sometimes I do some business outside with the booze. It brings me some good cash to run the place. But we need to keep these things on the quiet, and that's sorta what I wanted to talk to you about."

"Sure, Charlie. Whatever you want."

"Okay. Here it is. I got a feeling the government

can't keep us from selling booze forever. My gut tells me there's change coming. But, until they make booze legal, we can make a lot of money. You keep your nose on the lookout, run the chippies, keep the men buying and gambling, and this stuff will keep rolling in. And you can be sure that I'll take care of you."

"Don't worry, Charlie. I got your back."

"Good. Next week, I want to hire more girls and maybe expand the upstairs rooms with more tables. This way, we can keep the cash flowing."

"Okay, Charlie. Got it."

"One more thing, kid. I saw you talking with Bonnie."

"Yeah. It's okay. We're just talking because it's slow."

"Ain't nothing going on?"

"No, Charlie. Not with me and her. You told me long ago to leave the chippies alone, and that's what I do. I talk to them, you know, to make sure things are okay. Besides, there's plenty of women coming around this place without me having to take a whore."

"Yeah. Well, you just watch yourself. I like Bonnie, but she ain't one to mess with."

A couple of years passed as Lucas and Charlie grew the business, and it came to bring in more money than they thought possible. Lucas was now managing the backroom, running the bar, the chippies, and the money continued to flow. He found this wasn't a job for the faint of heart, but he grew up big, standing six foot four with broad shoulders, a nasty attitude, and tougher than most men. He knew how to take care of himself, bad heart or not.

Lucas also found the company of women wasn't bad

either. He didn't know if it was the bad guy image, the speakeasy, or just every girl in town wanted to be with the bartender on a lonely late night. There were nights when he would go home with a handful of napkins stashed in his pocket after lonely women would write their phone numbers. Lucas would end up with one of them at his place, too drunk to find their way home but easily into his arms. Like trophies, he kept the napkins piled high on his dresser. "You can never tell when you might need the company of a warm and tender body on a cold night," he would say to Charlie.

Chapter 20

In 1933, Charlie found out he was right about the bar business; the government decided liquor was legal, and the speakeasy became the new hangout. Charlie and Lucas enjoyed great success, built a new bar up front, replaced all the furniture, and hired more people. To celebrate, each afternoon, Charlie and Lucas would drink a beer with a couple of shots in the quiet afternoon before the crowd arrived.

"You're a good kid, Lucas, and you have done a great job running this place," Charlie said.

"Thanks for giving me a job, Charlie. I think the truth of it is, if it hadn't been for this, I don't know where I would be."

"We've had some good times and some tough ones, eh Lucas?"

"Well, you said it would be tough. You said I needed guts to be in this business."

"How's college, kid?"

"It's good, Charlie. Hard, but good."

"Have you found a girlfriend yet?"

"No. Not me. I have no plans on settling down, Charlie. Not any time soon. What do I need a regular girl for, anyhow? Because of this place, and you, I have more money than I need, and a nice place, a great car, nice clothes, and women anytime I want."

"I know. But don't let this business go to your head.

Women can be dangerous, and they can take you for everything you've made. I know it ain't easy finding the right girl. Lord knows it took me three tries, but Harriet is a good woman. You should keep your choices open and find yourself a good woman to watch over you."

Lucas laughed and reflected on how he'd avoided relationships of any type. He knew he had left all those feelings of love behind him. He hadn't forgotten the lies, and he wasn't going to get hurt. Over the years, he'd built a wall around his heart shielding him from any emotional commitment, and he held no interest in having a steady relationship with any woman. He considered his past for a moment. "No, Charlie. I don't need anyone. I'm fine the way I am. I like my life, and I am in control of it."

"You're in control of it?" Charlie questioned.

"Sure! I come and go as I please, and I don't have to answer to no one about what I'm doing."

"If you say so, kid. But one day, some woman is going to walk through that door and knock you flat on your ass, and when it happens, you'll see what I mean. I can see it now; you be standing behind the bar and bam—there she'll be. You won't even know what hit you."

"I don't think that's gonna happen, Charlie. That's just not me."

Lucas wasn't going to give his heart to anyone. He didn't want the pain.

They moved over to one of the booths, and Charlie lit up a Lucky. Taking a long drag off his cigarette, he looked at Lucas through the smoke while pushing the brim of his floppy hat up with his finger. "Yeah, you done good kid, and you've come a long way. I appreciate your helping me with fixing up the joint."

Lucas smiled at his friend. "Thanks for the chance, Charlie, and thanks for helping me make something out of my life."

They sat and talked about the future, what they would do as the business grew, and how they would travel the world one day. Charlie leaned back and relaxed while blowing smoke rings. Lucas slid from the bench and said, "I'll get us another beer."

"You need to find yourself a good woman to watch over you," Charlie called after him. "You need to settle down and find someone to love. You can't go on like this forever."

Lucas smiled at his friend as he walked behind the new bar and grabbed two clean mugs. As he stuck the mugs under the tap, he said, "Did I tell you? I finish my college credits next week. With that, I will have my degree in journalism. Just like you said, Charlie—follow your dreams. Can you believe it? I'm not leaving, though. I am your man until you tell me to go away."

Lucas walked back to the booth and slid the mug across the table. Charlie sat with his eyes closed, and Lucas could see there was no expression on his face. His chin rested on his left palm with his elbow on the tabletop. In his right hand, his Lucky burned into his skin. Lucas knocked the cigarette out of Charlie's hand.

On a cold Sunday in 1934, Lucas sat in a church while a preacher spoke of an old friend. "Ashes to ashes, dust to dust..." the sound trailed off, bringing back memories of when he buried his father. He held Harriet's hand as she wept—as they all wept. Lucas and five burly men carried Charlie Leland to the hearse waiting to take him to the cemetery. As they left the church, gray skies floated endless overhead as the snow dusted the shoulders of their coats. The route of the procession took them past the bar. The hearse paused for a moment as if to salute the old building, to give Charlie one last look at the legacy he created. Lucas buried the only man he knew as a true friend that afternoon in a cemetery just outside the city.

Chapter 21

During the year since Charlie died, Harriet was a rare sight around the bar. She left Lucas to his own, running the bar, handling the business, and keeping the place moving. He knew she'd never been comfortable running the details of a bar business—the gambling, the girls, the late nights. For Lucas, this business was a natural, and he enjoyed the trust Harriet gave him. Lucas ran Charlie's as if it were his own—as if Charlie sat at the corner booth with the gang, smoking his Lucky and playing cards, watching the place as he always did.

Lucas believed he was to carry the legacy and keep Charlie alive in the hearts of the friends and customers coming to this place. The truth was, Lucas loved working at Charlie's. It was his life and the only thing he wanted to do.

After a busy night with a wild crowd, it was time to close. The last of the customers left, bidding an excellent night to Lucas, promising to return soon. A few moments later, Lucas heard the front door creak open, and without looking up, he said, "Sorry, folks. Closed for the night."

"Hey Lucas," he heard from a woman's voice. He looked up from the register and saw Harriet walking across the barroom floor toward him. He noticed she carried a folder containing papers in her right hand. She was smiling.

"Well. Good evening, Harriet."

When she arrived at the bar, she sat on one of the stools, placed the folder to her right, and watched as Lucas counted the night's receipts. "Looks like you had a good night, Lucas."

"It was a great night," Lucas said. "In fact, it has been a great week. Charlie would have been happy with a week like this."

"Charlie was happy, Lucas. In truth, after you came around, I think he was the happiest I had ever seen him. You made him a happy man, Lucas, and he was proud of you."

"Hmm," Lucas replied. He liked seeing Harriet at the bar. In truth, he wanted her around, but the sudden arrival aroused suspicion. It wasn't like Harriet to show up at the bar unannounced.

He walked around from behind the bar and sat next to her. "Speaking of Charlie, he taught me many things. Like reading people and understanding what they mean without their saying so. You know, like when someone is pulling the wool."

Harriet laughed. "No wool here, Lucas. I have a good reason to be here, and I think you are going to be a happy man by the time I leave here tonight."

Happy, Lucas thought. The unexpected visit made him feel more nervous than anything else, but he figured he'd been through worse situations, so he would be able to handle whatever Harriet threw at him.

"Let's sit at the table. It will be more comfortable," he suggested.

Harriet gathered her folder, and they walked across the room, sitting near the front window.

"Okay. Let me have it. I can't stand the suspense any longer," Lucas said.

Harriet cleared her throat and placed the folder between them. "I came here tonight because Charlie wanted it this way. Charlie always spoke well of you, Lucas. He always told me you were the son he never had. You meant a lot to him."

"Yeah, you know I thought a lot of Charlie, and if it hadn't been for him, I don't know what I would have done," Lucas confessed. "The truth is, Harriet, Charlie was the father I never had. He taught me so many things, and I will never be able to repay him."

"That's not true, Lucas. You've repaid Charlie a thousand times by just being here and helping him. Not a lot of people believed in Charlie Leland and his dreams. You not only believed in his dreams, but you also gave him hope. You didn't know it, but this bar was Charlie's last chance. He scraped together every cent he could find and bought the building. No one believed he could make it happen, especially during Prohibition, so there were no investors. Besides, after the crash in '29, nobody was taken a chance. He was doing it alone and figured that he could keep going if he had a little help. That's when you walked in that door over there. You didn't know, but that sign had been there for two weeks, and no one came in. Understand, jobs back then were scarce, and a lot of people needed work, yet no one came in here but you. Do you think that was an accident, Lucas? Or do you think maybe you were the one that was supposed to see the sign at that moment on that day?"

"That's grand, Harriet. I never knew the real story. Charlie never said anything about the day I showed up. I was happy I found work, and now I just hope you are happy with what I have been doing with the business over the last year. You know you make it look like something put me here. Don't get me wrong. I'm glad I saw the sign on the door. The truth is, I was down to my last nickel, and I needed a job badly. Charlie was my only hope, it seemed. I think I was just lucky to be in the right spot at the right time."

"I think it was more than that, Lucas, and maybe one day, we will see. Anyhow, to the business at hand."

"Business?"

"Charlie told me if anything ever happened to him, you could run this place and keep it going. You know, you could have walked away like the others, and this place would have died along with Charlie. I would have closed its doors if you had not stepped up and taken over the business after Charlie died. You know me, and there is no way I could have kept the place open without your help."

"Well, Harriet. Let me say this. I felt I owed it to Charlie and you to keep this place going. This is my home. It is who I am, and it has been my pleasure to keep Charlie alive through this place. If you don't mind, I would like to keep doing just that."

"I would like you to do just that, Lucas," Harriet said. "I think you're good at this."

Lucas smiled at this kind woman and reflected on his life, thinking, *Good at this! No one has ever said I was good at anything.*

"I am honored," Lucas responded.

"There is one more piece of business, Lucas."

Lucas paused for a moment in thought. He knew Harriet didn't like the bar business, and she was getting on in years. It was about time for her to spend her retirement in Florida or somewhere warm. His first thought was, she was selling the operation to a new boss, but then he figured it would be fine, and he would just continue doing his job. He wondered if he could swing the cash needed to buy the place.

"Now you have me nervous, Harriet. What do you mean one more piece of business?"

Harriet laughed. "Relax. I think you will like this." She opened the folder and removed a brown envelope, from which she pulled a document. Lucas noticed the name of Charlie's attorney printed in the corner. Her eyes scanned the paper, and she rubbed her finger across a paragraph and tapped the area with her fingernail. "Here it is," she said. "Charlie named you in his will."

Lucas, surprised at this news, asked, "Why would Charlie do something like that? I don't expect anything from him."

"Perhaps the point, Lucas, was Charlie knew you wouldn't expect anything from him and work this business as if it were your own."

"Why wouldn't I?" Lucas responded. "Charlie gave me a gift when he gave me a job. He saved my life. I had nothing to offer. I was just a kid from the street without direction. I don't pretend to understand how or why, but he saw through all of it. He taught me everything there was to know about this business and treated me like I was his son."

"Perhaps that's why he saw it right to leave you a gift."

"A gift?" Lucas asked. "What do you mean? Money? No Harriet. I don't want Charlie's money."

"I didn't say money, Lucas, and this is Charlie's Will and Testament that he left for you. This paper is a legal document, and you can't change it. Charlie and I talked about it many times, and he was set on doing what he wanted to do with his bar. You knew and understood Charlie like no one else, and this was his wish. He made only one stipulation."

"This is getting crazy," Lucas said.

"Not at all," Harriet countered. "He knew the business was tough, and he knew you were the one that could make it work. Somehow, he also knew you would remain here while the others walked away. He told me if you kept the place going for a year, I would sign over everything to you the year after his death. On the anniversary of his death, I had to meet with you and present the gift. Tonight is one year, and this is Charlie's gift to you."

"I don't understand. Did he ask you to give me the business? Charlie owes me nothing."

"Perhaps that's what you believe, Lucas, but Charlie didn't see it that way. Here, look for yourself."

Lucas reviewed the papers in front of him. He looked up at Harriet; her eyes damp reflecting her emotion. He tried to hold back his tears, but at that moment, all the years came back to him rushing hard like a river toward the ocean. In that flash of time, he remembered everything: his spent youth, his mother, her life, how she worked without complaint just to ensure his existence, his running for the train, and his chance arrival on a cold day in a strange city. It felt as if it were yesterday and Charlie Leland was sitting across from him with his Lucky hanging on the corner of his mouth—*you looking for a job kid*, he had said. Lucas stared across the darkened room at the table where they first met.

"I can't do this," he said to Harriet.

She placed her hand over his. "Yes, you can, Lucas. This place is yours now. That's how Charlie wanted it."

"But what about you, Harriet? What are you going to do?"

"I'll still be around. But there's no need to worry. Charlie made sure I would have everything I would ever need. He took care of me, and I do not need anything."

"You know, I will always be here for you."

"And I for you, love. And I for you."

"So, what's next," he asked.

Harriet smiled. "Have you found a nice young lady to settle with?"

Lucas laughed. "Harriet. You know better than that. Besides, I am too busy running this place to worry about my love life."

"Now that you are the big boss, maybe you can take some time off? You know. Find that special someone."

He folded the papers and placed them into the envelope. "I think I will take it one day at a time."

Chapter 22

Lucas knew it would be a quiet night at Charlie's and told the staff to leave early. Bonnie asked to stick around just in case some of the men stopped in. He considered it and reasoned he might be able to use the company. Bonnie was more intelligent than most of the chippies found hanging around Charlie's. Lucas had more than one thought of taking her home but knew you never mixed business with pleasure. He liked to flirt with her, and besides, she was a beautiful woman and knew how to stroke a man's ego. Then he figured if the business didn't pick up tonight, and Bonnie was free, who knows what trouble they could find.

He pulled a cigar from the humidor, struck a match, and lit the end. He walked across the dance floor and stood at the front window, staring and his mind wandering. The snow created a soft carpet along the sidewalk, hiding any evidence of recent footsteps left by the neighborhood's people. He thought about how he ended up in this place. Traffic was slow on this minor side road, and with a night like tonight, comfort would be found from a bottle of Macallan calling to him from behind the counter—just enough to warm the soul and ease his troubled mind.

He stared through the window occupying his mind with the thoughts of the past while watching snow flurries fall across the empty streets. Dancing through the air, carried by the hands of the wind, they gathered in the corner lines of the sash bars framing the large panes and covered the curb where he first sat after arriving in the city. He recalled his first sight of Charlie's, the sign beckoning him to his future. So much of his life changed in seven years. With Charlie gone, he could do as he wished, but the place just wasn't the same, as if life itself drained from the walls like the snow melting into the gutter. The days of the speakeasy ended as the crowd changed from the original locals to attracting a different crowd—more sophisticated and well-read. Charlie's speakeasy became a familiar place for the locals to gather. Lucas made many changes; some were Charlie's idea, but others were pure Lucas Colby. Either way, it was good, and even after giving up protection money, he made a tidy profit. Lucas built a new poker room upstairs, added more tables downstairs, and enjoyed his success celebrating with fine scotch, Cuban cigars, and beautiful women. He knew Charlie would have been proud of his dealings, although Charlie would have never given in to the mob. Lucas was more intelligent than that, however. He knew, in this business, it was give and take, and with the mob on his side, it worked out better in the end. This night, however, was going to be different. After a long and busy week, he was ready to settle in for a quiet, uneventful evening of solitude and peace. He thought, maybe after a couple of shots and quiet, he'd work on his journal like he always promised himself on slow nights. He pulled his notebook from his briefcase and laid it on the bar, then pulled the bottle of scotch from the top shelf and poured two shots in a glass.

He placed the tumbler under his nose and inhaled the aroma of sin. It was warm, understated, and just what he needed. The golden elixir fell down his throat, and it felt good, like sitting by a fireplace on a cold winter night. He was enjoying the rush of the warmth filling his gullet when he heard the creak of the front doors. The frigid curse of winter blew across the floor and slapped him in the face.

"Damn it," he said. "Perfect timing." He dropped the glass into the soapy water behind the bar and tried to focus his eyes in the darkness. *Who would be brave enough to come out in this weather?* he thought. He didn't have to wait long to find out.

She came through the door with purpose and with a pair of blue eyes that pierced the dim lights of the bar. His eyes transfixed on the face of a goddess. She was about to turn his life upside down.

Chapter 23

She was the kind of woman who, if you were lucky enough to be in the right place, would walk into your life only once. She was the kind of woman men held in their dreams. He imagined her untouchable by mortal men. She was the type of woman who gave a man cause to surrender his life just to follow her. Without speaking a word, she created the taste of desire on his lips and sweetness of innocence while exposing an air of the devil, and he could see she could betray your soul and destroy you.

She was bundled neck to knee in a heavy woolen coat, and he could tell there was something incredible hiding under all those clothes with how she moved.

Tall, her long auburn hair framed a perfect face, and through the dim light, he could see she was not happy. For the first time in his life, Lucas was without words and not blind to the fact that this was the most spectacular woman he'd ever seen.

She sat on one of the stools surrounding the bar. Her coat fell to the side, unveiling a perfect leg while she reached into her handbag, pulled out a dollar bill, and tossed it on the bar.

"Change for a buck. I need a phone," she said.

Lucas could hear a lilting melodic flow in her words, and struck by her presence, he smiled the way only Lucas could smile. "Sure, doll face, whatever you need, and maybe twice if you're nice!"

"Cut the doll face chatter and gimme the change, buddy. I'm in a hurry, and I gotta move it!"

Lucas, surprised by her retort, still found her attractive. In truth, like a butterfly hypnotized by the color and scent of a blossomed flower, she was a temptation beyond resistance. What he did know was he had to have her and would be willing to do just about anything to make it happen. He thought he had met every type of woman in the world, but this time, Lucas was lost, and he knew negotiating words with her wasn't an option. He figured he could live with her attitude, considering the package, for a little while.

He decided to change his tactics; acting as if he couldn't have cared less, he pulled the bar phone from under the counter and placed it in front of her.

"Listen, if you need a phone, you can use this one."

She looked down at the phone, then up at Lucas with eyes piercing his soul. "Thanks."

She picked up the receiver and dialed. Lucas watched. He noticed she wasn't wearing a wedding ring, a rule with Lucas. Single women were too much trouble, he would always tell Charlie.

He wiped down the bar and tried to ignore her actions, her voice, the way she moved—just another damsel in distress, he thought. He didn't need the complication. In his view, single women were clingy, needy, and always wanted you to hang around. It was simple—no ties, no commitments—none of this love business with a woman.

He walked over to Bonnie, sitting at the end of the bar keeping an eye on his new customer. Bonnie motioned toward the woman with a shake of her head.

Lucas shrugged and smiled.

"She's spectacular," Bonnie said as Lucas approached.

He couldn't help but listen to the conversation as she spoke to someone on the other end of the telephone. The rhythm of her voice, hypnotic as the inflection of each word would lift and fall from her lips.

"Hey. It's Savannah. I'll be a few minutes late," she said. "No, I'm calling a cab, and as soon as it arrives, I will be on my way. It shouldn't be but a few minutes."

Lucas wanted her, and he wanted her more than he had wanted any woman he had ever met before, but for the first time in his life, he thought he didn't have a chance. Lucas Colby, the man with a cold heart of steel, afraid of no one, found himself as nervous as a schoolboy on the first day of class.

He opened his mouth to speak, but his words jumbled as he said, "Need a drink or someone to talk to?"

Without a glance his way, Savannah said, "Coffee if you have it, and I am not in the mood to talk to anyone."

Lucas grabbed the pot of coffee behind the bar, "Bad day?" he asked as he poured.

She looked at Lucas and said, "No! Everything's been wonderful. My stinking jalopy stalled down the street, and I'm late for work. Nothing unusual, I guess. It seems all I have is bad luck lately. My boyfriend dumped me, telling me he needed to think about things, whatever that meant. Then the jerk had the nerve to leave me with this hunk of junk car and no money. The bastard emptied every penny from our bank account and split town with some stripper from Jersey. I hope he gets everything he deserves. As for me, at least I was lucky enough to get this job across town, but I have only been there a month, and now my car broke down. So, to answer your stupid question, yeah, it's an awful day."

"Maybe your luck will change," Lucas said as he placed the steaming coffee before her.

She picked up the mug with both hands as if to chase out the cold of winter and brought it near her nose. She inhaled the steam of the aroma. "This smells good," she said.

She didn't say another word and gazed absentminded into the darkness of the saloon. Lucas knew that gaze from his own life. It was the gaze from someone when their world was slowly falling apart, their mind a million miles away. They're not looking at anything yet everything at the same time. Nothing registers as your mind drifts of thoughts and things long ago—mistakes you have made, a choice, or perhaps what could have been, and you wonder how you ended up in this place and what would have happened, if only.

Lucas watched her from the other end of the bar while chatting with Bonnie, deciding to approach her. He had been with many women, but none like this. He knew she was different, but there was more—spectacular was the only word coming to his spinning head, and he was, without explanation or understanding, drawn to her like a butterfly to a wildflower. She sipped about half of the cup of coffee, and Lucas walked over for a reheat. Savannah looked at the journal he had left on the bar.

"That yours?"

Lucas looked over, "You mean the journal? Yeah, it's mine."

"Are you a musician practicing being a bartender?"

Lucas chuckled because that he knew he couldn't carry a tune if it were locked inside a barrel. "No. Just comments and notes."

"I see," Savannah said with a raise of an eyebrow. A writer, perhaps?"

A squeal of brakes outside interrupted the conversation. Lucas noticed, through the front window, the taxicab arriving.

"Is that for you?"

Her mood changed. She was quieter now. She turned and said, "Oh yeah. Good. I hope I still have a job when I get there."

"I think you will be fine," Lucas responded, trying to make conversation. His words defined more than the current situation; he could see she her mind was preoccupied.

She stood and pulled her pocketbook from the bar, removed a small change purse, and asked, "What do I owe you?"

"Not a thing. Don't worry about it. It's on the house."

She paused for a moment and looked at Lucas as if she were suspicious of his kindness. "Seriously buddy, what's this going to cost me?"

Lucas thought for a moment and wanted to see her again. Without thinking any further, he said, "You know. I'm quick about making up my mind when I see something I like, and I'm off tomorrow night, so maybe the timing is everything. How about a date?"

He thought there wasn't a chance when she smiled and rattled off instructions as if she were a Drill Sergeant. "That's a fair trade. How about eight o'clock at my place? You'll find me at 3rd and 52nd, near The Alvin. It's called Moe's."

Before Lucas could gather his senses and realize she

accepted, she continued, "I'll see you there, and don't be late. You never know what you might miss."

She left as quickly as she arrived, leaving Lucas wondering as to what had just happened. He was usually the one in charge of the conversation. He made the rules. This woman confused him.

Bonnie turned on her barstool and looked over at Lucas. "That was interesting," she said.

Lucas smiled. "We'll see just how interesting it will be.

Chapter 24

Savannah made up her mind quickly as well. The taxi pulled onto the quiet street, and her thoughts drifted back to the encounter with the confident man. Charming, she thought, her lips curved ever so slightly into a smile. The fact that his display of charm and wit appeared as finely tuned skills gave her reason alone to leave as quickly as possible. Yet she caught herself, more than once, wanting to stay and find out what made this man tick. She wondered what it would have felt like to be held in his strong arms, her lips pressed against his. He was, she thought, quite handsome. Something she was sure he knew very well. She was willing to bet he practiced those skills on the many women frequenting the bar, and she wasn't about to be one of them. He was tall; wavy brown hair, green eyes, emerald, she thought, intense and passionate. The way he looked at her as if he saw something. As if he were taking notes, remembering each detail. She felt he could see something she didn't see in herself; something hid deep within her soul. She couldn't put her finger on it, but she was impressed, intrigued. The way he stood with such authority, power, and yet she could see a softness, vulnerability, and a desire. She knew he wanted her, and it made her think about him. She knew when a woman thinks about a man, something always happens.

The night was quiet at Moe's. After wiping down the

bar and waiting for customers, Savannah decided she would play a little on the piano. She practiced whenever possible, and her voice was that of delicate beauty. She tried to focus but thought about the man at Charlie's. At that point, she realized he never mentioned his name.

"Just like a man, assuming I knew his name," she said aloud to no one. *Women*, she thought, *are nothing but conquests to him, or maybe a chapter in his book, and he can open his book to any chapter at any time.* The way he looked at the brunette at the end of the bar was enough to tell her that he wasn't a one-woman man. His broad, warm, and friendly smile, with just a hint of intimacy each time he spoke to her. A persuasive smile, Savannah mused, but it wasn't going to work on her. She was not interested in men who bounced from woman to woman. Yet there she was, with only one man on her mind.

Chapter 25

Lucas stopped by the bar the next day to finish the regular paperwork. Pete O'Reilly stood behind the bar, getting ready for the night ahead.

"What are you doing here today, Lucas? I didn't think I would see you tonight."

"Just a couple of things to tie up. Nothing big, and I will be out of here before you know it. Besides, I got a hot date tonight."

"That sounds great. Where you headed?"

"I'm meeting her at her place, which, so far, seems to be Moe's bar."

"Moe's? That's the piano bar over by the Alvin Hotel."

"That's the one."

The flurries fell across the slick pavement as Lucas drove to Moe's. He was weary of the cold and was waiting for a warm spring day, like a child waiting to blow out the candles on a birthday cake. Six blocks past his apartment and turning the corner, he saw a car on the side of the road. The hood was up, and hot steam rolled from under the vehicle covering the ground like a gray blanket. His eyes focused on a pair of high heels at the end of perfect legs. Lucas had a few extra minutes and thought he might be able to help. He rolled down the window of his coupe and offered his assistance.

"Good evening Miss. May I lend a hand?" He

recognized the long auburn hair as she turned around.

She looked toward him, exasperated, and raised her slender arms into the air. "I can't believe this." Without hesitation, she yanked the passenger door open and jumped into the front seat as if they were old friends.

Lucas, pleased with her excitement, asked, "Where you headed, doll face?"

"Cute," she said, never letting her guard down. "Can you step on it? I don't need to be late again."

Lucas pulled into the back alley of Moe's, dropping off his new friend. He watched as she went inside, then he drove his car to the front of the building and parked. He walked to the front door of Moe's, a nice little piano bar for the local crowd. He pulled open the mosaic glass doors and saw her standing behind the bar, getting ready for the night. She had tied her hair back with a black ribbon, making a ponytail, and placed a white apron around her front. She rubbed down the top of the bar, set up some glasses, and checked the cash register. Lucas pulled a stool from the bar and sat at the far end so he could continue to watch her every move. She looked over at Lucas and smiled. He could see what she had been hiding under her winter overcoat.

"Nice," Lucas said aloud, not thinking.

She turned toward him and asked, "What was that?"

"Nice place you have here," he answered, feeling stupid for his slip of the tongue.

"Thanks," she replied while walking toward him. She flipped the bar towel over her soft shoulder. "Would you like a scotch?"

"Scotch? How did you know I drank scotch?"

"I'm a bartender, and besides, you look the type."

"To tell you the truth, I would like three things."

"And what would those three things be?"

"The drink you mentioned would be very nice, and then a name—to start with."

She hit the bar hard with a tall glass and poured the golden liquid, never taking her eyes off his. Her poise was unnerving, and a shiver ran straight up his spine. She pushed the bottle down the bar and slid it right into his hand. She placed her hand on his cheek, rubbed his ear with her thumb, slid her long, graceful fingers around the back of his neck, and drew them across his face and chin. With confidence that would make any man tremble, her eyes unwavering, looking deep into his, she said, "Savannah Vaughn, and you?"

"And me what?"

"What do I call you other than my Knight in Shining Armor?"

"Oh, yeah, that would help, eh? Lucas Colby."

She smiled. "Lucas Colby. That's a strong name. Tell me, Lucas Colby, what was the third thing you wanted."

Lucas began to speak as a patron entered the bar, interrupting the casual conversation. He looked over toward the front door and said, "I guess it will have to wait."

Savannah curled her lips up and raised her brow. "Nice timing. I'll be right back, and don't move."

Lucas smiled and took a long drink from the glass, trying to regain his composure. After this latest introduction to Savannah, he needed a short break to catch his breath. He sat back and looked around the room. It was cozy and dark, with high ceilings. Large couches along the wall, high back chairs with end tables and lamps where you could enjoy a Brandy and a good cigar as if sitting in a rich man's study. A piano stood tucked away in a snug corner on a small, raised stage.

After she finished with the new customer, Savannah walked back and stood behind the bar near Lucas.

"How's your drink?" she said.

"Perfect," Lucas said, "and just what the doctor ordered. I see you hit the top shelf, the good stuff."

With a devilish smile, she said, "If you think this drink is good, wait until my shift is over."

Captivating, he thought as she turned and walked to the other end of the bar. He quickly tried to change the subject. "So, I'm gathering your family is Irish?" Immediately, he thought himself an idiot for stating the obvious.

"Gee, what gave it away?"

"Well, your hair, your eyes, and of course, my stupidity for even mentioning it."

"Does it appear that I meet with your approval, sir?" she asked as she slid another drink into his hand.

"More than you know."

Savannah leaned over and placed her elbow on the bar. She rested her chin on the palm of her hand. "So, what about you, handsome? What are you doing here?"

Lucas, caught off guard, said, "What do you mean? You asked me to come by. I thought we had a date?"

She laughed at him. "Well. We do. Sort of."

Savannah wasn't going to assume anything and taking it easy wasn't her style. She knew she wasn't about to rush into another affair and risk another broken heart.

"What's that mean, sort of?" Lucas asked.

"I mean, just because you rescue me doesn't mean I'm just going to fall into your arms."

"I didn't expect that," Lucas said, although he knew

this never seemed to be a problem for him in the past.

"Oh really? I guess your type usually has its way with most women."

"What in the hell does that mean?"

"It means I need to know you a little better before I start trusting you. I need to know your story."

"My story?"

"You heard me right, big guy. Your story. Where you are from. Where have you been? All the details."

"Details? That's a lot."

"I got all night, mister. Take your time," she said.

"It could take all night," Lucas replied.

Savannah smiled. "That is exactly what I am betting on."

Lucas liked the answer and decided to tuck the response away in his mind. "Anyhow," he said. "I arrived here a few years ago from Ohio. The short story is, after my mother died, there wasn't much left, and the town where I grew up—nothing to offer. I tried to enlist in Cleveland, but the doc said I have a heart condition, which they called a murmur. I told him it wasn't a problem, but he said there wasn't a chance I would be able to serve. To be honest, after everything I had been through, I didn't care. At that point in my screwed-up life, the setback didn't surprise me. I figured the best I could do was to get as far away from Ohio as I could. There was nothing but lies and heartache in that town. I hopped a train in Cleveland and jumped off here in New York."

"Sounds like you have had it rough over the years," she said.

"Rougher than you know. I found out my mother lied to me all my life about my father. She had always told me my father left us to fight in the war. She said he was a hero, and he died overseas. She took those secrets to her grave when she died of cancer in '29. After she died, I discovered a box she kept hidden under her bed. In the box, I found a journal, letters, and photographs. That is how I learned my family history, how we came to live in Ohio, and how this Finley guy destroyed my life. The letters from the hospital said my father was an alcoholic, and he had lost his mind. She had him committed to an asylum. The truth was, Finley, who my father worked for, had him committed to a hospital. Years later, when I was ten, he escaped. They found him dead the following day in the local supply store. Word had it, he went looking for Finley, the man responsible for locking him up and destroying his life. The shotgun was by his side, and his head blown off. I could have never proved it, but the sonovabitch that ran the town and owned the store shot him dead as sure as I'm sitting here talking.

"I don't know what to say," she said.

Lucas finished his drink and put the glass on the bar. "There's nothing to say. It was a long time ago," he said, then he paused for a moment as if reflecting. "Listen. It's all behind me, and there is nothing I can do about it now. Life in Ohio is something I would like to forget. We'll leave it at that." Lucas found himself sharing more than he wanted, and he knew doing so wasn't good.

"Okay. Let's leave it alone," Savannah responded. She could see the emptiness in his eyes, the loneliness she shared from her shattered love life. She changed the subject. "So. How did you end up in the bar business?"

"I fell into this little deal on 86th at Charlie's. It was a speakeasy back then, so there were some interesting times. I had been all over the city trying to find work, and I was on my last few cents. Somehow, I ended up standing in front of a doorway with a job sign on it. The owner, Charlie, gave me a job, took me under his wing. He thought I had potential and wanted me to make something of myself. He taught me everything he knew and one day asked me what I wanted to do with my life other than bartending. I said journalism rather than thinking I was going to be a bartender all my life. He thought it would be a great idea and sent me to college."

"He paid for your college?"

"Sure did."

"That's nice. It sounds like he is a great guy."

"Was a great guy."

"What do you mean? He's dead?"

"Yeah. Charlie died in 1934. That was tough."

"I'll bet. So, who owns the place now?"

"That's the crazy part. Harriet, his wife, comes in on the anniversary of Charlie's death and tells me the place is mine. Charlie willed the whole thing to me."

"The whole thing? You mean he left you the bar?"

"Sure did," Lucas replied. "I walked into this city with nothing but the clothes on my back and, by chance, ran into Charlie Leland. I guess he took a liken to me, taught me everything he knew, and set me up to run the bar. When I look back at all of this, I just wonder."

"What do you mean?"

"Well, for one thing, I didn't deserve what Charlie gave me. I had nothing to offer him but me. I worked hard and gave him everything I could, and in return, he paid me well and took care of me. I have been a lucky man. Oddly, my old man lost his mind and life because of alcohol, and here I am, a bar owner. Ironic, don't you think?"

She slid another drink into his hand and replied, "You know what I think?"

"No. What do you think?"

"I think everything happens for a reason."

"A reason."

"Yup. Like my car breaking down near your bar."

"Or again tonight?" he said.

"You know what I mean, Lucas. If my car had not died on the street, I would have never gone into your bar."

"And we would never have met. Is that what you're saying?"

"Yeah. Sort of."

"Really? So, if your car hadn't broken down, I wouldn't be sitting here, and by that, you are telling me we are supposed to be together."

"Yeah. I suppose you can think about it that way. I just think people meet each other for a reason. There are no accidents, and we are all here for something. Perhaps we only have each other to show us the way on our journey. You never know when you will touch someone just the right way or at that perfect time."

"Well. If that were the case, we would meet, one way or the other. Right? Look at it another way. You're saying that, regardless of what we do or have done, we would have met."

"You know what I believe, Lucas? Life is a journey toward a destination, and if we listen to the world around us, our providence will lead us."

"You mean fate?" Lucas asked.

"Sure. Fate or sometimes destiny; people call it different names."

"Fate?" Lucas responded. "I don't know if I believe in fate or if it had anything to do with why I am here, but I know everything has seemed to move along in the right direction after a bad start. You make your destiny."

Lucas, uncomfortable with the subject, quickly changed the direction of the conversation. "Of course, that's enough about me, Savannah Vaughn. Now it's your turn to tell everything about you?"

"My life's story?" Savannah replied. "There's not much to tell. I'm a pretty boring person."

Lucas chuckled. "Pretty? Yes. Boring? Not a chance would be my guess. So come on, let loose. Other than you blowing into my bar the other night, I know nothing about you."

"Me?" she responded mischievously.

Savannah Vaughn started life in a small town in Ireland, and soon after her mother died, she crossed the Atlantic with her father ending up in Pennsylvania. As a child, she dreamed of showbiz, performing as a singer at her school. Savannah showed a natural gift for music and studied voice as a child. Just after she graduated school, her father died, and she moved to New York.

"So, we are both orphaned," Lucas said.

"I guess we are," agreed Savannah.

Before leaving Philly, she married her high school sweetheart, and like many things, it looked good at first.

"It didn't work out?" Lucas asked.

"No, not by a long shot," she said. "I am happy to say the bastard is out of my life. He was abusive and a real jerk. He would get drunk and take pleasure in slapping me around. He got what was coming to him, though."

"How's that?"

"Believe it or not, he was slam drunk one night and coming out of his girlfriend's house. He crossed the street and stepped off the curb, directly in front of the oncoming bus, and that was the end of that." She lightly shook her head from side to side. "In the end, he got what he deserved. It's as simple as that, and I can't say it bothers me."

"So, the other night in my bar, you weren't talking about your husband but your boyfriend?"

"That's a whole other story," she said. "The boyfriend I was talking about, I met about two years ago at a party. At first, he was a nice guy, you know, roses, candy, gifts and all that. I should've known better. Women loved to throw themselves at him. I mean, he was good-looking, but I guess he had issues with keeping it in his pants. He also liked to slap me around." She reflected for a moment. "Clearly, I know how to pick them."

"Have you ever thought about moving back to Pennsylvania?" Lucas asked.

"No. Not really. I like it here. I mean, I wouldn't mind revisiting the area. My father built a small cabin in the northern woods, and we would sometimes stay there all summer and swim in the lake. Dad liked the peace being away from the busy city life he had. It's a nice place. We spent a lot of time fishing or hiking, or just time together. I haven't been back since my dad died, but maybe one day, I'll go again."

When Savannah spoke of her father, Lucas could see the pain his death caused. She had experienced a few tough years recently, and Lucas could see she needed a friend. The last thing her dad told her before he died was to follow her dreams and to use the money he saved for her college education.

"My father always said, between my singing and piano, I would be famous one day."

"Why not?" Lucas agreed.

"We will see," she said. "Maybe one day, someone will discover me.

"What's with the piano," Lucas said.

"Sometimes, local musicians come in and treat the customers with a few tunes. Other times, it's just me. Would you like to hear something?"

"Sure. How about a little Cole Porter?"

She smiled. "I love Cole Porter. How did you know?"

"Just lucky, I guess. Do you know Night and Day?"

She moved gracefully across the dark cherry wood floor toward the piano. She sat down, slid across the bench, and waved Lucas over.

"Come here so you can be closer to me," she said with a wink of her eye.

Lucas sat on a stool in front of the piano and watched her. Her hands floated over the ivory keys like clouds floating across a blue sky. He closed his eyes and heard the most incredible voice. The melody of her words flowed through the air as if carried by velvet hands, landing gently around him. He could feel a sadness ringing through her tone as if she had experienced her songs firsthand. Her voice was soulful. It gave comfort like a warm blanket across your shoulders while sitting in front of a fireplace. Hypnotized, Lucas watched her every move as each word dripped from her full lips. Never taking his eyes off her, he followed her every curve, from the top of her head, down her long, soft neck, and into her low-cut blouse. Her neck would tense and then soften with the melodious sounds of each note flowing like water through a brook.

The clock's hands moved closer to midnight, and they found more in common with each other and shared a few more laughs and stories. The time felt suspended, and before long, it was well into the twilight hours. The night was quiet, as if everyone had decided to stay home. They sat on a couch in a corner, and Savannah curled up under his arm.

"I can't believe I had only one customer come into the bar tonight."

"Maybe it's that thing you were talking about."

"What thing?"

"You know. The being in the right place thing, that journey deal you were talking about earlier."

"Lucas Colby. You are an impossible man."

"What do you mean, impossible? You're the one that said it."

"Well, maybe it's true. Maybe something kept everyone away tonight so that we could enjoy each other. Maybe it is supposed to be happening."

Lucas stood and straightened his clothes. "Yeah. Maybe we are meant for each other. You can be such a dreamer."

"You can be such a jerk," she said. "Let's get out of here."

They put on their coats, locked up the doors, and closed the joint down for another night. Outside on the streets, the weather had cleared. They bundled together to share body heat and walked; their heels clicked on the cold walkway echoing through the quiet streets. A diner sat as an oasis on the corner; the neon lights flickered and reflected on the iced sidewalk.

"I'm hungry. Feed me," Savannah said.

"I can manage that," Lucas said.

Lucas held the door as she walked past him. The room was warm and comfortable. With platinum blonde hair wrapped tight into a point on the top of her head, a heavy woman was standing at the cash register. She was chewing a large piece of gum, looked up, and pointed to a table. She pulled the pot of coffee off the burner and walked toward them.

"You lovebirds gonna eat?" she said as she poured.

"I would like to order breakfast. Whatever special is fine with me."

"Me too," Lucas said.

The waitress walked through a pair of silver doors and into the kitchen and yelled to the cook, "Two plates and make it snappy."

They talked and laughed. For the first time, life was good as two souls found comfort within each other. The sun was still resting below the horizon when Lucas paid the waitress. They walked back to his car, and Lucas opened the passenger door. Savannah sat inside, commenting on the cold interior. Lucas started the car to warm the heater. Ice had formed across the windshield, and Lucas scraped it off with a wide-bladed knife. When he sat down in the car, Savannah slid across the seat and snuggled close to him. It was still cold as he drove his car back to her apartment. Lucas wrapped his arm around her, holding her close, and she pressed against him. Lucas parked his car on the street below the window of her apartment. Savannah had dozed off after the long night, so he gave her a little nudge.

"Hey, we're here," he whispered. She roused up,

kissed his cheek, and snuggled closer.

"It's warm in here and feels good. Can we wait for a moment? I don't want to open the door."

He sat back in his seat and inhaled deep. He put his lips against the top of her head, and a subtle, delicate scent filled his senses. It made him feel comfortable. For the first time, Lucas felt at ease. He held a woman in his arms and felt as if he had known Savannah all his life.

"What is the perfume you are wearing?"

"I don't wear perfume. I never have."

They snuggled for a while longer, enjoying the quiet. Savannah raised her head and kissed Lucas on the neck.

"I guess we are going to have to brave the cold," she said.

Lucas jumped out of the car and hurried around to her side. Getting out of the car, she held him tight, trying to stay warm. He wrapped his arms and his coat around her. They walked ambled toward the steps. As they approached the doorway, Savannah paused and turned toward Lucas.

"I had a great time," Lucas said.

"Yeah, me too, and I am sure glad it was a slow night." Savannah ran her fingers along the lapel of his coat. "To be honest with you, Lucas, I didn't believe, with the rough start at Charlie's, we would hit it off so well. I guess I was wrong."

She released her keys as his hand covered hers. Feeling an emotion unfamiliar inside his heart, he hesitated.

"How about I call you tomorrow, and we spend the day doing something."

"Something?" she asked, confused at his mixed

signals.

"Sure," Lucas replied, sensing her puzzlement. "Maybe we can check out a movie, go to the park. Just be together and enjoy the day."

After a light kiss from Lucas, Savannah closed the door. She stopped for a moment and thought about the events of the evening. Savannah had seen men like this. She'd been with men like this, and she didn't want another hurt in her life. She had decided to be independent, to be her own woman. She didn't need a man in her life to complicate things, again.

She knew she had talent; everyone knew. She was a natural, like her father said. She believed with all her heart that she would make it to Broadway and beyond. She was going to be famous, and no one, not even a handsome, charming, irresistible man would stop her.

Chapter 26

Lucas arrived at Charlie's early the following evening. Pete was still cleaning up from the night before.

"What the hell happened here?" Lucas asked as he stepped over a chair.

"Vic came in last night and saw Bonnie flirting around, and all hell broke loose."

"Again? Jesus. That moron just doesn't understand what's going on, does he?"

"No. Not a clue. Anyhow, I called the cops and bounced his ass out. I don't think he'll be back for a while."

"How's that?" Lucas asked.

"Dumbass pulled a knife, and the cops shot him."

"They killed him?" Lucas asked.

"No. Just winged him and then beat the crap outta him. It was quite a sight."

"Normal night, then?"

"You could say," Pete answered.

"All right, then. I'll be in the back."

"Not so fast, kiddo. I want to hear about this new dame in your life."

"New dame? Oh. You've been talking to Bonnie?"

"Yeah. Bonnie said she's a beauty."

"You could say that."

"Gonna see her again?"

"Tonight."

Lucas stopped by his apartment and dressed in his best suit. Tonight would be special. He planned to meet Savannah at Moe's, charm her once again, and see where this would go. He'd met many women, but this time, it was different. She was unlike any woman he'd met. She was soft, intelligent, engaging, and it was as if she intuitively knew what he thought. He was captivated, and he didn't know it yet, but he was in love.

Lucas parked his car three doors down from Moe's, shutting off the lights and engine. He sat for a few moments and watched the activity around him. The weather had cleared, the snow melted, and the streets were quiet. Lucas noticed a few cars parked along the street and couples out for the evening enjoying the air, locals, mostly, strolling in the light of a full moon hanging low over the buildings. He'd grown to love the city, the noise, the traffic, and the flurry of people around at all hours.

As he climbed the stairs to Moe's, he heard Savannah's voice coming through the doors. He stopped and listened, without the distraction of watching her, and could hear the beauty, the clarity she possessed. Her voice was good; there was no doubt in his mind. He thought she was better than good.

She looked up as he approached the bar and smiled. He sat and listened as she finished her set and watched her as she slid from behind the piano and walked toward him.

"Starting with a scotch tonight?" she asked.

"Sounds like a good start," Lucas said as he stood, and she walked into his arms.

"You smell nice," she said.

"A new cologne, just for you," he said.

The night ended too soon as they explored each other's thoughts and dreams.

"I love your voice," he said.

"Is that all?" Savannah said.

"Is that all? What?"

"Is that all you love about me?"

Lucas knew a setup when he saw one. "There are a few other things, but I think we can save that conversation for later."

Savannah smiled and slid another scotch into his hand.

"You're tryin' to get me drunk? Perhaps take advantage?"

She laughed. "For some reason, I don't think I need to get you drunk to take advantage of anything."

She was right. Lucas Colby never lost his head and always kept his cool regardless of the situation. He remembered what Charlie had said. "You need to find yourself a good woman to watch over you. You need to settle down and find someone to love. You can't go on like this forever." They left Moe's after another quiet evening together and drove back to Savannah's apartment.

"Listen, Savannah, I think you're thinking what I'm thinking," he said as he unlocked the front door. "This was a great night, and I felt something."

She looked up and playfully said, "I'll bet you're right, and I'll bet you're feeling something right now." She pulled herself closer to Lucas. "I know precisely what you're thinking."

"Uh, yeah, but here's the thing, Savannah; I like you, and I want this to work, but I need to know this is not just another one-night stand. It seems my life has been nothing but one-night stands for so long. Truthfully, in the beginning, it was all I was looking for, but not after tonight. I gotta tell ya, Savannah, you make me dizzy." He paused for a moment. "Maybe we should call it a night, and I'll come back in a few hours. We could grab something to eat and maybe spend the day with each other at the park or drive out to the country. What do you think?"

Savannah smiled, leaned toward him, and began to kiss his neck. She slowly moved her soft lips up to his. He heard a slight moan of pleasure and a whisper in his ear, "You feel so good."

Lucas slid his hand around to the small of her back and pulled her closer. With bodies coming together as one, she turned herself into the doorway. They explored every curve. She reached behind him and gently pushed the door closed. Pausing for a second, she quickly glanced around her apartment.

"Don't mind the kitchen. I'm not much for cleaning up."

The room was dark, lit only by the light from outside the front window. Savannah pinned Lucas against the front door with her body. He felt her hand slide up behind him, and he heard the click of the cylinder lock on the door. She placed her hand around his belt buckle, and with a light tug, she said, "By the way, handsome, you're not going anywhere."

With passions rising, she pulled Lucas deeper into her apartment. His hands trembled as he slowly opened her blouse; each button surrendering to his grasp. He could feel her warm breath as it flowed across his chest. His eyes followed every curve of her entire body as each move revealed her desires. Her blouse fell gently down her arms to the floor. He playfully danced his fingers beneath the silk and lace, her soft skin excited by his touch. She reached behind her back, allowing the covering to fall. His hands moved lightly down her slender back as he unbuttoned her skirt. He gazed into the caressing eyes of this goddess standing before him and wondered how it was that he stood in her presence. Her hair flowed down around her soft shoulders, just barely covering her angelic skin. She tilted her head as she looked past his eyes and straight into his soul; her lips curved into a slight smile as her unspoken passion burned through him. For the first time in her life, she was happy and fulfilled.

Without words, slowly and deliberately, she unbuttoned his shirt. He wrapped his arms around her and pulled her closer. Her head fell back as his lips gently touched her neck. Lucas had never been with a woman like this, and heaven could not have been closer at that moment, he thought. Savannah gasped with sweet surrender as they became one, folding onto her bed. A touch, delicate and tender, she was warm and soft. Tomorrow would bring no regret. Tonight, there would be no moments of shame. They released their passionate desires, holding no secrets. They surrendered into each other's arms without regret as time passed two lost souls into the morning light.

Chapter 27

The ceiling came into view as Lucas opened his eyes. The bed was soft and warm. *This is not my bed,* he thought. He focused and could hear water—someone taking a shower. To his surprise, he had fallen asleep and stayed the night, and it took a moment for him to collect his thoughts. He had never felt so rested, so comfortable, so afraid of his feelings. He recalled the night and the unrelenting passion, knowing his presence after such a night was unusual. His thoughts were in turmoil; he wanted to stay, believing he should leave. True to his nature, Lucas rose from the bed, dressed quickly, and left quietly.

As the front door clicked shut, the shower stopped. Savannah pulled the curtain away from the bathtub and stepped out onto a small rug. Wrapped in a towel, she walked from the bathroom. Her towel did not cover her sleek physique. She looked over at her bed with fond remembrance, the sheets twisted in disarray, a testament to last night's performance. She looked at her clothes tossed across the floor and allowed the towel to loosen and fall as she approached a full-length mirror that stood sentinel in the corner of her bedroom. She paused to admire her shapely figure while recalling Lucas' warm, muscular hands. She pulled a night coat off the post on the mirror stand and slipped her long arms into the supple cloth. She tied the coat around her waist and walked into the front of her apartment, expecting to see Lucas waiting for her, but there was only silence. She rushed to the window and watched as his car pulled away from the curb. Her heart sank as she watched his car turn at the corner. She sat in the chair by the window, disappointed, and wondered if she would hear from him again.

Lucas drove, without thought, to the edge of the borough and continued beyond the city limit. He came upon a small diner in a little town outside of White Plains, pulled into a parking space, and stepped out of his car. The weather was clear and cold, and he could see his breath in the morning light. He pulled open the door to the café, and a hook caught a small bell hanging from the frame. It jingled, and a man looked at him through a small, rectangle hole behind the counter. Lucas acknowledged the cook's presence and walked past—the cook's eyes following Lucas to a booth near the front window. Scattered across the bench seat, Lucas pushed the morning paper left by a previous patron onto the floor. He slid across the center, placed his elbows onto the table, and rested his head on his hands, staring out the window through white laced curtains as the sunlight spread across the parking lot.

"Coffee?" she said.

Turning his head from the dawning day, he viewed a young girl, belly extended. She held a pot of steaming coffee in her slender hand.

"You want coffee, mister?" Lucas found her soft southern accent intriguing but could see she was agitated from carrying the weight of an unborn child.

"Yeah, coffee, that's fine, thanks," he rattled off absentmindedly. His thoughts focused on Savannah. The young girl's belly protruding beneath her stretched uniform caught his attention as she turned toward him.

"Three days," the girl said.

"Three days?" Lucas responded as he looked up and into her almond-shaped, brown eyes holding her secrets and the suffering she experienced.

"You were looking at my belly, Mister. I got three more days 'fore I squirt this boy out."

"And you're working?

"No choice," she said as her eyes wandered to the distance, the corners of her thin lips curling downward.

"How do you know it's a boy?" Lucas asked.

"Don't know, but my neighbor, she said the way I'm carrying, it's a boy. She got eight of her own, so I guess she might know something about babies and things like that. But you can never really tell until they get here."

"Oh. I see," Lucas responded. "Well then, best of luck to you and your husband."

"Husband?" the girl said. "There ain't no husband, at least not the lazy bum that knocked me up. He's worthless as far as I'm concerned. Besides, if I had a husband, do you think I'd be working in this place serving greasy food?"

Lucas was indifferent to the young girl's plight and ordered breakfast: fried eggs, ham, and toast well done.

Moments passed, and Lucas tried to focus on the events of last night, trying to understand the torment he felt in his heart. The waitress returned and slid the hot breakfast onto the table. Lucas stared at the plate until the food was cold. His languid mindset interrupted as the young waitress waddled past the empty tables. She would pause and release a quiet moan, placing her frail hands on her arched back, stretching to ease the discomfort of a third trimester and the inevitable delivery of a fatherless child into a world of unknown. He wondered if she would make it through the day.

Lucas pushed the cold plate aside and stood to leave the small diner. He turned and saw the young mother, alone at the end of the counter as she thumbed through a variety magazine. She was, at best, nineteen years old, he figured. Her tawny hair held back behind her small ears fell straight down the side of her thin face as she bit the side of her lip, concentrating on the story she was reading. She reminded Lucas of his mother, his childhood. He approached her. Lucas could see his past reflected in the young girl, and he understood what she held within her heart. She was afraid, alone, without someone to love, without someone to love her. He remembered what Savannah said. *I just think people meet each other for a reason.*

Lucas walked past the empty tables and toward the young girl. She looked up as he approached and smiled.

"Listen," he said. "I hope everything works out for you. I know how tough it can be for a kid without a father. If I can give you any advice at all, it's this; give him all the love you can and be there for him. Forget the father but love your son enough to tell him the truth." He took her small slender hand into his and quietly folded a one-hundred-dollar bill into her palm. "This may help," he said. She watched in silence, struck by a stranger's generosity, as Lucas maneuvered past the tables and into the cold morning air.

Lucas slowly backed his car out of the parking space and drove back into the city. He parked under the window of Savannah's apartment and walked up to her door. He knocked, but there was no answer, and he turned to leave. Approaching his car, he looked down the street and saw Savannah walking toward him. She paused for a moment and looked away as if embarrassed to see Lucas. He walked to the front of his car and leaned against the fender. She walked toward him with ever-increasing speed until she was running. He, in turn, stood and approached her with a final understanding. A thousand thoughts unsaid, feelings never felt before, and warmth they understood without words. He held her tight and lifted her off the ground, and she said, "I thought you were gone."

"No," Lucas responded. "As I told you, Savannah, you make me dizzy."

Savannah buried her head on his chest and held him tight as if she were falling and only he could save her. She held Lucas so close, that he thought he could not take another breath, and he felt as if he never wanted to breathe again without her by his side. As words passed between them without sound, Lucas felt the lies he had held so close to his heart dissolve. In his arms, he knew he held everything a man could want and everything he could be.

Chapter 28

The turn is just ahead," she said. "You will see a large tree and a fence. Turn left when you get there."

Lucas looked ahead and could see a dirt road meeting the highway. They traveled up the winding road. Nearly five years had passed since Savannah had last seen the place.

"Where's this property of yours?" Lucas asked.

Savannah smiled in response. "We've been on my property since you left the highway, silly boy!"

Lucas was surprised. "Since we left the highway? How much land do you have?"

"Oh, I don't know exactly, but Dad would tell me it was around two hundred acres." Savannah looked around. "He loved this place, and we enjoyed a lot of summers here."

Rounding a turn, Lucas noticed a log home with a surrounding porch. To the left of the cabin was a small barn.

"We're here," Savannah said as the car rolled to a stop. She had the door open before Lucas could get out. "Come on, slowpoke," she called to Lucas as she ran to the front door.

Lucas stretched as he stood by his car and looked around the property. "It's beautiful," he said.

From the cabin's front, you could see the lake where Savannah would swim and fish in the summer. The trees—oak, poplar, and maple—filled the grounds providing shade and comfort.

The land was nothing like the flat land of Ohio and unlike the grime and dirt of the city. He noticed a small stone trail leading to the lake's clear waters where he could see a small dock and a boathouse on the water's edge. He heard the sound of birds and wind rustling the leaves of the tall trees. He carried the luggage into the house and returned to the car for the groceries they picked up in town. Savannah walked into the kitchen, filled the cabinets with canned goods, and pulled out plates and glasses to prepare dinner. The house was as she left it the last time she was there with her father.

Lucas came into the room and approached her from behind. Wrapping his arms around her, he buried his face into her neck.

"Let's go for a walk," he suggested.

Savannah turned and, after a long kiss, said, "Walk now, play later?"

Lucas smiled, and they held each other's hand as they followed the path to the lake.

After dinner, they sat on the porch and enjoyed a glass of wine while watching the orange ball of sunset fall beneath the trees across the lake. In the dark of evening, only the glow of the candle lit their faces.

Savannah pointed out the constellations. "Look, a falling star. Make a wish."

Lucas smiled at her uncomplicated purity and leaned toward her. "What was your wish," he asked.

She gazed deep into his eyes and said, "I have never been this happy, and I never want this to end."

Lucas took her into his arms. "I love you, Savannah."

She pulled him close. "I will love you, Lucas Colby, forever."

Lucas slept without his usual waking in the middle of the night. Savannah held him close. He awoke in the early morning to the sounds of the songbirds in the woods. As days passed, each night, they listened to the gentle questions of the owl. Each morning, they would enjoy coffee on the porch while watching the wildlife by the lake. Later, they would canoe and explore the shoreline. They would skinny-dip far from shore in the middle of the lake or make love under the heavens.

Nearing the end of the week, Lucas woke early. He lay in bed while Savannah continued to sleep, and he watched her and studied the rhythm of her breathing, the curve of her nose, how her hair framed her beautiful face, lips, and chin. *A face of a goddess*, he thought. *This is not something I should have.*

He stood and left the room once again, finding himself at a crossroad. Quietly, he slipped out of the house and walked along the shoreline of the lake. His mind couldn't make sense of this thing called love, thinking to himself in the morning sun, *I am not one to fall in love. I don't want love, and I don't need it.*

He was afraid of love, fearful of the loss that always followed him. His mother's words echoed in his mind. *Life ain't worth living without somebody to love.*

To Lucas, love was a peculiar emotion always trumped by the lies within your heart, words wasted as promises of better things to come rather than an expressing truth. Love was not to be trusted, and at best, love was a poignant reminder of something that would never last and always end in pain. It was easier to turn his back on love. It was easier to run.

He thought about Savannah, but he'd never met anyone that could define love to a point where it made any sense to him, and yet, with all the confusion and misguided understanding, he found himself in love— hopelessly and entirely in love.

"Hey! What are you doing down there?" Her voice calling to him from a distance interrupted his thoughts. Lucas looked toward the cabin to see Savannah bounding down the stone path toward him. He knew in his heart; Savannah was everything he could ever hope for in a woman. She was nothing like the person he met a year ago on that cold night in December when she busted into his bar. Time had passed unnoticed, and Lucas had never experienced a woman like this. They walked, hand in hand, on the soft earth surrounding the waters of the lake.

"Did you sleep well last night?" she asked.

"Like a baby in your arms."

"Oh really? Speaking of babies."

Lucas stopped and turned. With a look on his face, Savannah considered the surprise. "You're pregnant?"

"No. But I could be if you-"

"No. That's fine. I'm good."

Savannah laughed at Lucas. "I got ya on that one, didn't I?"

"You could say, but that would have been okay."

"You mean having a baby?"

"Well, yeah. I mean. Not right now, but it is something to think about."

"Think about this, Lucas Colby." She took him into her arms, and she pressed her lips to his.

Afterward, Lucas asked, "How long do you think we can keep this up?"

She reminded him she had said forever.

Chapter 29

Returning to the city, Lucas stopped by Charlie's.

"A couple of Bettys were in last night asking for you," Pete said as Lucas walked into the bar.

"Is that right," Lucas responded.

"You don't sound very excited, Lucas. You okay?" said Pete.

"Sure. I'm fine," Lucas said. "Why would you ask such a question?"

"Why?" Pete asked. "I've known you for a few years now, and I have never seen you not excited about a dame."

Lucas laughed at Pete. "Now you know why I hired you to bartend, Pete. You have always had a way of pulling the talk out of someone."

"Aye," Pete said as he wiped down the bar top. "I think I can get anyone to talk about anything, it seems."

Before the conversation could continue, Harriet walked around the corner from the back office. "I thought I heard a familiar voice," she said. "How was the weekend, Boss?"

Lucas glanced over at Harriet as she approached the bar. "Don't call me Boss, and the weekend was fine."

"You sound cranky, Lucas," Pete said.

"Yeah, Lucas. Are you okay? " Harriet chimed in.

Lucas sat down at the bar. "Pete, toss me a beer."

"Aye. Be happy to." Pete filled an iced mug from the

draft and slid it to Lucas. "So? Spill it. What's a cracka lackin sport?"

He took a long drink and said, "Well, to tell you the truth, I think I've met the woman of my dreams."

Harriet pulled up a barstool and sat next to Lucas, "I certainly hope you mean Savannah."

"Aye," agreed Pete. "You'd better be talking about the doll face you've been seeing lately."

"Yes, both of you. I am talking about Savannah. We spent the weekend at her father's place in Pennsylvania, and it was quite a weekend."

"What was it like?" Harriet asked.

"It was nice, Harriet. Her father left her a beautiful cabin in the woods, and we had a great time. I can't recall ever having such a good time with someone. She's unlike anyone I've ever met."

"Aye. It sounds like someone's talking about settling down," Pete said.

"Settling down?" Lucas responded. "I don't know, Pete. I mean, I like her. But for me? A one-woman man? Do you think that's possible?

"Don't worry, Lucas. You will know when it's right," Harriet said.

"You're right, Harriet," Lucas agreed. "I think I'll just take it as it comes."

"Aye. No rush is what I always say," Pete said. "You have to be careful with women. They'll break your heart."

Lucas nodded. "Fill me another beer, Pete, and you're right. Women will break your heart."

On the way back to his apartment, Lucas' mind drifted back to thoughts of Independence, the farm, and childhood—the lies he survived. So many things changed in his life. In less than ten years, his world was nothing like the world he left behind. Everything was good, and his future looked solid.

He worked hard, and Charlie had treated him well. Lucas had built the business into a successful operation with a great staff. Still, in the dark corners, his past haunted his thoughts. Surrounded by so many lies for so long, he harbored nights of solitude while endless dreams of the past disturbed his sleep, waking him throughout the night. He remembered muffled voices from thin walls, the deceit, and improbable childhood. In his mind, he never felt he could trust anyone. *Get too close, and they will break your heart. Fall in love, and they will leave you,* he thought. Lucas decided to play it cool with Savannah. He did not plan to fall in love and believed he was in a relationship he didn't need.

Chapter 30

A few days passed when Savannah walked into Charlie's. Even in the daylight, Charlie's was a dark room, and the outside light created a long shadow as she opened the door and arrived quietly. Without words, she sat at the end of the bar. His heart jumped when he saw her, and her sight pleased him, but he approached her with caution in his heart.

"Hey," he said.

She looked up and responded, "Hey."

There was an uncomfortable silence between them. Both were at a loss for words that would bring them to the conversation.

"Savannah, I think we need to talk," Lucas said.

She smiled back at Lucas. It was a sad smile, but she needed him to talk. "That would be good," she said. "I have a lot on my mind."

Lucas looked across the bar to find Pete.

"Hey, Pete."

"Aye, Lucas."

"Watch over the place for me. I need to go and take care of some things."

"Gotcha. Don't worry. Things here will be fine."

Lucas wiped his hands on the towel stuck in his belt and threw the towel on the table. He walked to the front door, grabbed his coat, and he left with Savannah.

Harriet walked in from the back office and asked,

"What's going on? Where's Lucas?"

"Savannah came in," Pete said.

"Everything okay?" she asked.

"Dunno, but there wasn't much smiling happening, if you know what I mean," said Pete.

As the front door closed, it shut off the sunlight, leaving Charlie's a dark place again.

Where would you like to go?" Lucas asked Savannah as they walked down the street.

"I don't know," said Savannah. "Can we just find someplace quiet so we can talk?"

"There's a spot in the park I know of."

"Sure," Savannah agreed.

They walked to a gazebo overlooking a large, grassy field surrounded by trees. Sitting down on the bench, Lucas said, "Listen, Savannah. I think I've not been fair with you."

"You think?" Savannah said. Lucas could feel the tone and the hurt in her voice.

He stood and walked to the railing. "I tried to tell you on our first night. My life has been nothing but a series of one-night stands, bar fights, wrong women, gambling, and drinking. And then you walked into my life. Everything I don't deserve and nothing I have worked for. I'm no good for you, Savannah."

"Oh, you poor baby," Savannah responded. "You're acting the gom."

"What?" Lucas turned and walked toward her.

"You, Lucas Colby, are a fool."

"How can you say that? I am trying to talk to you."

"Yes, you are, but after I came to you. If you were any sort of a man, you would have come to me and not just left me hanging without as much as a word. I thought we had a perfect weekend. I thought we had a good start. What did I do to you, Lucas?"

He sat beside her once again and said, "You did nothing wrong, Savannah. Truth be known, you did everything right."

Lucas hung his head and leaned his arms on his legs while staring at the wood decking below his feet. Words escaped the expression of feelings held hostage deep within his heart and mind. He could hear Savannah's gentle breathing, her scent filling the air and surrounding him. Thoughts circled in his mind like a carousel on the fairground. Why did he feel so comfortable in her presence? What was this hold she had on him? He wanted to reach for the prize—the golden ring, just out of his reach. He thought he'd found love in the past, only to end with an empty heart, torn and damaged as each relationship ended without reason. How does one recognize his life's destiny? How does one know when the right person comes along? Lucas had been with many women, and many women said they were in love with him. With each passing affair, his heart fell deeper, and the walls became thicker. His emotions tucked away in a hidden place. Savannah could see past his front. She knew the shell of Lucas Colby was not the soul of the man. She knew deep inside, a boy screamed out for love. He knew deep within. It was time.

Summoning the courage he needed, he turned to Savannah. "For so long, my life has been screwed up. Any relationship I have ever had, it always ended in a lie. I don't want to lie to you."

Savannah sat beside Lucas, placing her arm across his shoulders. Lucas sat with his face hidden within his hands.

"You just need to be you, Lucas. There is a wonderful man inside this persona you carry. I saw him. I know him," Savannah said from deep within her heart.

"You think so, eh?" Lucas said.

"No, Lucas Colby. I know so. You are the one in my dreams. You are the only man I need." Savannah brushed her soft fingers through his hair. "I know your life started rough, and that's why we need each other. We can start new. Forget yesterday, leave the past in the past, and let tomorrow come with us."

Lucas stretched out on the bench and rested his head on Savannah's lap. Unexplained, he felt entirely at ease in her arms as if the world could stop and no one would notice. Savannah hummed a quiet song.

"I've heard that song before," he said.

She smiled. "I sang this song to you, our first night together when it was just you and me."

"Just you and me," Lucas repeated.

Chapter 31

"What do you think about spending the weekend at the cabin?" Lucas suggested.

"Why? We have so much to do here in the city. You know, Christmas is not far off, and you said you wanted to do some shopping. Perhaps we should wait," Savannah said in turn.

Savannah, always the planner, knew there were things in town needing attending. Lucas loved her for her tenacity and organization, but he needed her to listen this time.

Pushing the issue, he said, "Savannah, amuse me. I think we need the break, and besides, I'm your favorite guy, right?"

Savannah wasn't one to allow anything to stand still for very long. Her drive and intensity sometimes moved in between her and Lucas. He would have to remind her about life. She laughed at his childish antics and said, "Fine, silly boy. Let's make it a weekend."

Lucas contacted a local florist asking to have flowers placed throughout the cabin. Arriving the next day, Lucas hurried to the front door and stepped inside. Savannah walked in after him.

"Lucas?" Savannah called out.

"Yes, my love," Lucas answered from the kitchen.

"There are flowers on the table," she said after enjoying their scent.

"Yes, my love," Lucas agreed. "I believe those are for you."

Savannah walked into the kitchen. "And my favorite wine?" she asked. "What's going on?"

Lucas walked up from behind and wrapped his arms across her. "Nothing at all, my love. I know you have been working very hard, and you needed a break, so I made a few last-minute arrangements to give you a special weekend."

Savannah, always thinking ahead, was suspected something, but Lucas held his ground. He dismissed himself to gather a few logs to build a fire in the hearth.

The embers slowly grew into warm comfort. Lucas poured Savannah a glass of wine as she warmed by the fireplace.

Tapping his glass to hers, he said, "A toast to our future."

"A toast for tomorrow, for we live today," she replied.

"A toast for two hearts in one, and to our love forever."

"Forever," she said.

After dinner, they sat on the porch swing and enjoyed the sun setting beyond the lake. In the twilight, they moved back into the house while holding each other. They warmed together near the fireplace. Lying on the floor, Lucas pulled an elaborate quilt from the couch. They watched the embers dancing up the chimney. Savannah pressed against him, her slender hands rubbing his chest as she reminded him of their first night. Lucas looked at Savannah and knew he had to spend the rest of his life with her. She lifted her head; the calmness and serenity of the night filled her heart. She had found the man she dreamed of, and her life was perfect.

"I love you, Lucas." Without words, she moved up and kissed his lips. "Hmm."

"What is it?" he asked.

"This must be a special night."

"What makes you think it's special?"

"Well. For one, it is the weekend."

"And?"

"You shaved."

Lucas laughed, and he knew how lucky he was to be in her arms. She rested her head on his chest. "I have a surprise for you," he said.

"And what more could you have?"

"I'll be right back." He stood and walked to the kitchen, opened a bottle of champagne, and carried two glasses back to the hearth. Holding the stem, he handed her a long, slender glass as bubbles rose.

"Do you remember the first night we met at Charlie's?"

"How could I forget?"

"You know I had all the wrong ideas about you then," Lucas reminded her.

"Yeah, no kidding," she said. "You were quite the piece of work, I might add."

"Me? I wasn't near drunk," Lucas responded, "and I believe it was you who set the place on fire."

They laughed, and Lucas asked, "Do you know what day this is?"

"Sure. October 14th. Why?"

"Silly girl," Lucas said. "It was October 14th—one year ago tonight—when a beautiful woman stormed into my life and turned everything upside down."

"And?" Savannah responded, her suspicions rising.

"And I just wanted to say I love you."

Savannah smiled and toasted. When she brought the glass down, she noticed a small box in Lucas' hand.

"What is that?" she asked.

"What's what?"

"In your hand, what do you think?"

"Oh. This?" Lucas held the small box up to examine and smiled at the woman he wanted to spend the rest of his life with. "A little something I picked up in town. More champagne?"

"It tickles my nose," Savannah said.

Lucas smiled and asked, "What does this tickle?" as he opened the box.

"Lucas!" her voice was rising to meet the occasion. "It's so big. Are you crazy? Can you afford this?" She paused only long enough to slip the diamond ring onto her finger, admiring the sparkle given from the fire. "Oh, my Lucas. Oh, my love. A thousand times, yes."

Chapter 32

Harriet knew what to do. Savannah was familiar with a small church upstate. Lucas scheduled an appointment with the Pastor. Charlie's was the perfect place to hold the party. They gathered their friends and toasted the future and starting their new lives. At the reception, George Robbins approached Lucas.

"Congratulations on finding the most beautiful woman in New York."

Lucas smiled at his college friend. "Not to worry, George. My guess is there is someone out there for you."

"Not like yours, Lucas. You have yourself a one in a million, my friend."

Savannah walked over and hugged George. "Am I going to get a dance with you?" she asked.

"Do I get to dance with the bride, Lucas?"

"I tell ya what. You two go tear up the dance floor, and I'll find the bartender. I'll bet there's one around here somewhere."

George and Savannah walked through the crowd toward the dance floor. Her reach barely touched George's shoulders.

"This place was once a speakeasy. Did you know that?"

Savannah laughed. "Yes. And right over there," she pointed to a stool against the bar, "is where I first met Lucas."

"You know, he is a fortunate man."

"No, George. I am the lucky one, but sometimes, I wonder, however."

"How's that?"

"How we met. How we ended up together. It was all so coincidental like it was supposed to happen."

"Life turns out like that sometimes," George said. "Just enjoy it when it does."

The music stopped, and they walked back to the table. "Where's the honeymoon?" George asked.

"Lucas found a small village in France. Brantôme. He tells me it is beautiful."

"Not as beautiful as the bride, however," answered George.

Savannah smiled. "I can always count on you to make me smile, George Robbins."

****

Lucas and Savannah left for France the following week. They taxied to the ports and arrived at "*Isle de France,*" a luxury liner of the *Concord Line* and the pride of France. Crossing the gangway and finding dry land once again, Lucas met with Louis Rousseau, a Parisian citizen. Lucas provided the porter with his first-class reservation documents. The porter escorted them to their suite. After almost a week at sea, they arrived outside of Le Harve in the north of France. Lucas arranged for the guide to escort them for the remainder of their trip.

"Lucas, a man is waving at us," Savannah said as they walked toward the baggage area.

Lucas looked over to the street. "That must be Rousseau. He said he would meet us here."

"Who is Rousseau, and why would he meet us?" Savannah asked.

"He will be our guide for the next few weeks while we are here. Since we have never been to France, I thought it best to hire someone to take us around," Lucas said.

Rousseau approached Lucas and Savannah and graciously introduced himself. "Good morning, or as we say here, Bonjour. I am Rousseau, and I am at your service." Louis Rousseau took a deep bow and kissed Savannah's hand.

"Le plaisir est à nous," Savannah responded.

"Yes," Lucas echoed. "The pleasure is ours."

"I have made arrangements to have your bags delivered to your hotel in Le Harve, Mr. Colby," Rousseau explained.

Over the next fourteen days, Lucas and Savannah toured the areas of France while falling in love with each other and the beautiful countryside.

Sitting in a small café outside of Le Harve, Lucas said, "How about tomorrow we visit Brantôme? I think you will like it there."

"That sounds like a beautiful trip to take, Lucas," Savannah said. "How far is Brantôme?"

"Not far, and Rousseau will drive us so that it won't be tiring. He tells me of a villa located near town. His description was intriguing. Would you like to look at it?"

"Are you planning on moving to France, Lucas?" Savannah asked.

"Perhaps later in life. I love this countryside, and it is all so beautiful," Lucas explained to Savannah.

The following day, they left for Brantôme, a small village on the river Dronne. After lunch, they arrived at the villa. Fragrant vines grew atop the shutters and hung across the wooden window frames. The area would afford them the privacy they desired, yet it was close enough to town, so they were not isolated. The land carried a small creek past the property, flowing southward toward the river.

"What do you think?" Lucas asked.

"I think it is beautiful," Savannah replied. "But what are you thinking?"

"I think this could be our retirement one day," Lucas told her.

"One day, I hope," said Savannah. "This is the most beautiful place I have seen. But it is only a dream, I am afraid."

"What are we if we don't have dreams, Savannah?" Lucas said as he put his arm around her.

Rousseau approached from the rear of the villa. "Mr. Colby, we must leave now to make your dinner reservations for this evening."

Lucas kissed Savannah. "Dinner tonight, dreams tomorrow."

A few days more in Paris, and they planned a return trip back home. Rousseau left them at the port and said goodbye for the last time.

"What do you think the Germans will do?" Lucas asked of Rousseau.

Rousseau shrugged and laughed. "I am French, and I take each day as it comes. Today is my only worry, for tomorrow may come, or perhaps it may not."

Chapter 33

The first year of married life passed quickly. Savannah's career increased in popularity, and Lucas continued with success at Charlie's. Savannah's voice grew more robust and more resilient with each performance. Lucas could see her gift and love for songs and watched the crowds at Moe's grow larger each night. She was a natural entertainer with a voice that touched the center of your soul.

Most everyone had left the bar, and she gathered her things together to go for the night. One evening, after her last performance, a well-dressed man in a black pinstriped suit approached Savannah. With his business card extended in his hand, he said, "I'm Tony Costa. I represent Swan Music, and I would like to talk to you."

"Sure," said Savannah. "What would you like to discuss?"

"I've been coming to Moe's for about a month now," said Costa. "One thing I see, besides a beautiful woman and an incredible voice, is your ability to draw the crowd. You're quite good, Miss Vaughn."

Savannah, more visionary than Tony could understand, responded, "Your point, Mr. Costa."

"My point, my dear lady, is I can give you what you don't have."

"And what would that be?"

"I would like to be your agent, Miss Vaughn. I've

been in this business for a long time, and I know I can get you a contract with a real music company. I can represent you in this business as no one else can, and I will make you famous."

Anxious to have her career begin, famous was all she needed to hear. Savannah jumped at the offer. The music business was a tough one, and somehow, Tony made a meager living finding solid music talent. Savannah, in her desires, believed this was her chance at the big time.

"A contract would be nice, and you are correct, Mr. Costa; I will need an agent," Savannah said.

"Of course, you will, but please, call me Tony. If we are going to work together, we need to be comfortable," Costa said.

Within just five days of their meeting, Costa arranged a session in a small recording studio at the city's north end. Everyone in the music business considered this studio a cut-rate shop that took advantage of young talent.

The equipment was old but seemed to work well enough to record her singing some of the latest songs. The time moved so quickly, Savannah hadn't time to think, and before she knew it, she had a recording, and Tony Costa pushed himself and her music into every music house he could find. He had stumbled onto a gold mine, and he knew it.

Early one morning, about three weeks after they had completed her first demo, Costa called Savannah.

"I just got off the phone with Jimmy Cintrone. He plays at a supper club in town. He listened to your recording, and he wants to see you," Costa said.

"When?" Savannah asked.

"This afternoon, about five o'clock. Is that good?" he asked.

"That's perfect! Let me tell Lucas," she said and hung up the phone.

Chapter 34

Over the next several months, Lucas passed his time at the bar. When he wasn't working behind the counter, which became less and less, he played cards and gambled upstairs in the game rooms while drinking the night away. Savannah stayed busy and began to work with some of the top names in the music business.

As luck would have it, and clearly, Tony Costa had plenty, he sold her contract to Entertainment America, a small outfit highlighting talent from around the area. The organization wasn't the most incredible break, but she knew what she wanted, and she believed this would lead to bigger and better. Entertainment America sent talent on tour for movie houses, special events, and USO. Their reputation was a little better than Tony Costa's, but not by much. They would push the talent to their limits, and the pay was low. If you had talent, natural talent, you might get lucky, and someone would discover you.

The work took Savannah on a whirlwind tour with a small vaudeville act with some other entertainment. The manager pushed Savannah to the front as the star of the show. Although this was a small outfit, she received much exposure. After finishing a set one night in Iowa, the show manager motioned to her as she exited the stage. A tall, handsome man was standing next to him.

"Savannah! I would like you to meet Ray Carter. Ray is the bandleader for a small horn group and would like to speak with you."

She called Lucas that night from her hotel room to tell him of the news. He was at Charlie's.

"Hello, Charlie's," Lucas answered.

"Hey there! It's me!" He could hear the excitement in her voice.

"Hey superstar, how's the best voice in the business?" he asked.

"Lucas, you are not going to believe this! Tonight, I met Ray Carter. He is the Ray Carter from the Ray Carter Band in New York, and he wants me to tour with them!"

"Tour with Ray Carter?" Lucas replied. "That sounds great."

"I will be home in two days," she said.

Lucas took a deep breath as he hung up the phone. He was happy for her, but something didn't feel right. The nights were becoming lonely. Knowing Savannah was doing the right thing, he tried to keep his focus, but the demons came back and haunted his nights, telling him something was wrong.

The train arrived at the station early on Saturday morning. As the train pulled to a stop, he could see Savannah standing by the door, excited like a schoolgirl on the last day of class, jumping up and down, waving frantically. She leaped from the platform and ran toward Lucas with arms open wide. Lucas almost lost his balance as she slammed into him, smothering his face with kisses.

"I am so happy to be home. I have missed you so much," Savannah said, wrapping her arms around him.

That evening, Lucas and Savannah went out for dinner. There were so many things to talk about with her new career. They sat at a corner table near the window with a view of the park. In the early evening twilight, they watched young lovers stroll along the pathway around the pond. Lucas ordered a bottle of their finest wine to celebrate their reunion.

He raised his glass to the woman of his dreams. "A toast to the next superstar of stage and radio."

Savannah smiled and sipped from her glass of wine.

"What's next, my little canary?" Lucas asked.

"Lucas, you are too funny," Savannah replied.

"I'm serious! Tell me about the tour, Ray Carter, everything."

She looked at Lucas pensively, her blue eyes cutting into his soul. He could tell he wasn't going to like what she had to say.

"We begin touring next week."

"Okay, fine. What does it mean? Two weeks? Maybe three?"

"Well, that's the problem," she said. "The schedule is eight weeks." Then she quickly added, "But you can meet me when we are on tour! It's not like we have to be apart for the entire time."

Lucas sat back in the chair and pondered for a moment. "The last time we talked, I thought you said you'd be working with Ray Carter. That means you would be here in New York. Right?"

She shrugged. "That's what I thought as well. It's my understanding this is temporary, and most of the time, we will be here."

"What the hell's going on, Savannah?"

"What do you mean? That's how it works in this business, and I told you. It's only temporary."

"And when it's not temporary, you're what? Running all over the country with Ray Carter?"

"It's not like that, Lucas. Grow up."

Lucas threw his napkin on the table along with a hundred-dollar bill. He motioned to the waiter and stood up. "Let's go. We can talk about this later."

The ride home was silent; Savannah stared out the window. It was late, and there were many things left unsaid. Lucas knew better than to let his thoughts run. He knew Savannah was faithful, and if there were another, it would be her career and not another man.

Savannah sat in front of the mirror and combed her hair. After a few moments, she climbed into bed, and Lucas reached over. He moved her hair back and gently kissed her shoulder.

"Not tonight Lucas. Okay? I'm pretty tired," she said.

Chapter 35

The following morning, as Savannah slept, Lucas was up early and decided to take a walk. He left quietly. He had been walking for about an hour when he passed by Charlie's. He noticed Harriet's car was around back, so he went inside.

"Hey. Anybody home?" he yelled as he came in the back door.

"Over here in the office," he heard Harriet say.

He walked into the office to see her behind a desk piled high with papers and invoices.

"Hey there, Harriet. What's up?"

She looked up at Lucas. "Just trying to make heads or tails of this mess. We have to get some bills paid, or we are going to get cut off."

Lucas said, "Move, and I will sort it out. It won't take long."

She looked back up at Lucas. "Why do you have time for this? Isn't Savannah in town?"

"Yeah, she's here, but she was sleeping when I left, so I have some time."

Harriet was a wise woman, and she knew something was up. "Bullshit," she said.

"What?" Lucas answered.

"Lucas Colby, I know when you're feeding me a line. Something's up. Now talk. This can wait."

Lucas pulled up a chair and sat down. "It's the tour,"

he said.

"What about the tour? Isn't touring what she does?" Harriet asked.

He looked up at Harriet. "Yeah, but this is different. She tells me she will be gone for maybe eight weeks! I didn't expect that."

"Listen, you're a big boy now, and you can take care of yourself." Harriet said. "You don't need to have Savannah around every day. Besides, a little separation could do you good."

"True. I can spend more time with the boys."

"The boys," Harriet said. "You need to spend less time with those boys."

"For what? We have our fun."

"Yeah. Drinkin' and gamblin' to the wee hours every night."

"That's fine, Harriet. I can handle it, and besides, what else am I going to be doing since Savannah is running all over becoming famous?"

"I'm just saying, Lucas. Watch yourself. This life will sneak up on you, and you could be sorry."

"I'll be fine."

Harriet grinned. "I bet you will. Anyhow, how was it the other night when she first arrived back from the tour?"

Lucas thought back and said, "That was nice."

"See what I mean?"

"Well. Nice until I insinuated she was screwing Carter."

"Awe. For chrissake, Lucas."

"Yeah. I know. I came short of telling her, but the thought was there." Lucas stood. "I guess I better be getting back. Thanks for coming in to take care of the books."

"Not a problem, Lucas. You know I am always here if you need me."

Harriet called out to Lucas as he approached the door.

"Lucas."

"Yes. Harriet."

"Take a few days off and enjoy them with Savannah before she leaves."

Lucas walked back to the apartment and opened the door.

"I saw you were coming up the street," Savannah said. She was up and having her coffee while sitting at the window.

She looked like a teenager sitting in the chair with her hair pulled into a ponytail, wearing a long T-shirt, and not the star of the stage she had become.

"You looked like you were in a hurry," Savannah said.

"I am. I wanted to get back here to be with you." Lucas could sense something about her. "What's wrong?"

Savannah shrugged. "Ray just called and said we need to go over the act, so I don't have much time. I was just about to shower and leave."

"I see. Okay, fine. I guess I will find something to do today."

Standing close to Lucas, she stroked his chest. "Why don't you start that book you keep telling me about?"

Savannah went to the bedroom to dress. Lucas spoke from the other room. "Harriet will handle the bar until Monday, so don't take long, and we can do something this weekend," he said, hoping for an answer. He heard the shower start. He walked into the bedroom, and the bath door was open. The steam poured from the hot water; Lucas could see her contour in the mist of the shower through the glass door. His view reminded him of what he missed most.

He said to Savannah, over the sound of the rushing water, "I'm going to run to the store and pick up some things."

"Okay. I'll see you tonight at about six," she replied.

Lucas thought she was just tired and preoccupied with everything going on. He picked up her favorite food from the grocery store and the best wine he could find. He bought a couple of candles and a bouquet.

After arriving home, he cleaned up the apartment. While dinner was cooking, he dressed the table with the candles and place settings. At six o'clock, he lit the candles and poured the wine, knowing she would be home at any moment. Savannah was still working at eight o'clock, and before Lucas realized it, the bottle was empty.

"I gotta go," she whispered in his ear.

"Gotta go?" Lucas responded, half-awakened, the sun shining bright in his eyes, "Gotta go where?"

"The tour. Ray told me last night we had to leave this morning because we need to be in California in three days," she said.

There wasn't much left to say. Lucas heard the bus in front of the apartment blowing its horn.

Lucas spent the day quietly at the apartment. He didn't know if his head hurt from the wine or Savannah. He decided, rather than sit and wait, he would go to Charlie's for some entertainment.

Harriet was in the back, and Pete O'Reilly tended the

bar. Lucas came in the front door.

"Hey, Pete!"

"Lucas. What the hell are you doing here?"

"Long story, Pete. Where's Harriet?"

He pointed over his shoulder with his thumb. "She's in the back office."

Lucas sat with Harriet for a while and brought her up to date. She said, "Don't worry. Everything will be fine. Show business is a tough road, but you know she loves you and will be back sooner than you realize."

Lucas pulled up a stool at the bar, resting his forehead on his palms. "I'll take a scotch, Pete."

Chapter 36

Lucas stared through hazy eyes at the ceiling above him. The last thing he remembered was something Pete had said, although the words were about as clear as his head felt on this day. He knew one thing for sure; this was not his bed and not his apartment.

He looked across the room and could see his clothes neatly stacked in a chair. He lifted the covering and saw he wore only his boxers. His mouth was pasty, a feeling he was familiar with after a long night of cigars and scotch.

He rose from the soft mattress covered with a dainty blanket and tried to get his bearings, still intoxicated from the night's activities, not sure of exactly what happened. Balancing himself on the door frame, he stepped into the bathroom, splashed water on his face, and dried off with a laced towel. *Not mine*, he thought.

He looked around the bathroom for clues as to his location. It was plain to him; a woman lived here. Brushes, makeup, and all the other things a woman uses to preen herself. Without further thought, he dressed and walked into the front room.

She sat at the table facing the window wearing a powder blue housecoat. Long legs slid from beneath, revealing a slender foot with red nail polish on her toes. She sipped from a mug of coffee while looking out the window to the street below. Approaching from behind,

Lucas could see her long, black hair falling across her delicate shoulders. She turned around as he came.

"Hey! Good morning Lucas! I thought I heard you moving around back there. How's your head feeling?" she said.

"Bonnie?" Lucas replied.

"Yeah! Who did you think I was?" she said.

"I didn't know. What am I doing here?"

"Someone had to rescue your sorry butt last night."

Lucas sat down on the couch and buried his face in his hands. "What the hell have I done?"

"What do you mean? Done what?" Bonnie asked.

"Here, Bonnie. What am I doing here? Why was I in your bed? What the hell did we do?"

She stood up, walked over to the couch, and sat down next to Lucas. Putting her arm on his shoulder, she said, "You know Lucas, that's not saying much about me."

"What do you mean by that?"

"Well. If we had done something, I think, or at least I hope, you'da known about it. You know, a girl has a reputation to keep up."

Lucas smiled at Bonnie and lay back on the couch.

"You are something else, Bonnie. So, you didn't take advantage of me, eh."

"No. But that's not sayin' I didn't want to."

"So then why am I here?" Lucas asked.

She looked at Lucas and shook her head softly. "Pete told me Savannah was out of town. You tied one on last night and passed out drunk in the corner of Charlie's. Since I live right around the corner, and being the nice girl that I am, Pete helped me get you here and into bed so you would be safe."

Lucas wouldn't have thought twice before climbing into bed with Bonnie or any other woman, but times had changed from the old days. "Oh. Thanks. I'm sorry to put you through this."

"It's not a problem, Lucas. We have known each other for a long time. You're just like a brother to me," she said.

"Sure, that's what every guy wants to hear from a beautiful dame."

"Lucas. You are too funny. You know nothing could happen between us. Besides, I wouldn't be able to face Savannah."

Bonnie, beautiful as she was, was the sister Lucas never had.

"Tell ya what. Let me buy you breakfast," Lucas said.

Chapter 37

Lucas spent the rest of the day thinking about Savannah and wondering if she would call. He slept on the couch and awoke about six that night. He decided to go to Charlie's and play some cards with the guys. Charlie's was busy for a Wednesday when he arrived, and Lucas was happy to see the business going strong.

"Hey, Pete. Is there anything going on upstairs?"

"Aye. We got a few playing cards."

"Good. I'm going to help them lose some money. Send up a bottle."

He climbed the stairs to the gambling rooms and opened the door. The air was thick with smoke, and four men sat at the table. The big, ugly one looked up at Lucas.

"Hey, Lucky Luke. You going to give us some of your money?"

"I think quite the opposite, Joe. Deal me in."

Lucas pulled a chair from the table and sat down. He lit one of his cigars and poured a shot of whiskey from the bottle on the table.

"Good thing I told Pete to bring another bottle. You guys have already polished this one off."

Jimmy the Nose sat across from Lucas. Jimmy, a two-bit hustler from Chicago, liked to play billiards for money but didn't have a clue when it came to poker.

Johnny Two-Step sat at the right of Lucas. He was

happier dancing with a woman and drinking, but tonight, his heart was in the cards, and considering the pile of chips next to him, he was doing fine.

Billy Wannabe, the youngest of the group, sat on the left of Lucas nearest Joe. He was just a kid and barely eighteen but would do anything to get into the club with the boys.

"You gonna deal those cards or are going to sit here all night watching you flip 'em around?" Lucas asked Joe.

"Yeah. I'm gettin' there, Colby. Hold on to your skirt." Joe slid the deck toward Lucas. "Here. Cut the deck, quit your bitchin, and prepare to lose all your money."

Lucas reached across Billy and split the deck in two. Joe picked up the cards, shuffled, and tossed them across the table while giving Lucas a sly grin.

Two cards dealt, Lucas heard shouting downstairs. "Start without me, boys," he said as he bolted toward the door.

"Are you going to leave your cards on the table?" Billy asked.

"If you like them better than yours, you keep them," Lucas said as he shut the door.

Joe motioned to all the players to return their cards. Billy flipped Lucas' card and found a Jack and an Ace of Spades. He flipped them over to show the guys, and Jimmy said, "You expected less?"

Lucas hopped down the stairs taking two steps, and approached Pete, who was busy talking to a patron who believed one of the girls cheated him.

"What's going on?" Lucas asked.

"This guy says one of the ladies took his wallet

while dancing."

"Yeah. That's right," the man said. "It was the blonde in the blue dress." He pointed to one of the women sitting at a table across the room."

Lucas walked over to Sawmill Sally. "Did you?" he asked.

"Did I what?" Sally said as if it was just another night.

"Give me the guy's wallet," Lucas said.

"Jumping Jesus, Lucas. He's loaded. He ain't gonna miss his money."

"Not the point, Sally. Let me have the wallet and get the hell out of here. We don't need to rob our customers to make a living."

Sally grimaced at Lucas. "You know, I make a lot of money for you in this dump."

"Maybe so," Lucas said. "But if I can't trust you, you're not going to work here anymore. Now, get out and don't think about coming back in."

Lucas walked back to the bar and gave the man his wallet. "Listen, pal. Sorry about that. She won't be back."

"Yeah. Well, that's a good thing. I don't need anything like that.

"Tell ya what. How about I set you up with one of my finest girls and a bottle of our best champagne.

"Now we're talking," the man said, quite pleased with the offer.

Lucas glanced to Pete with a nod.

"I got it, boss. Get back to your game."

"Nah. I'm not in the mood anymore. Give me a shot, and I will be on my way."

Lucas walked back to the apartment. The following day, he woke up on the couch. He decided to take the day off and catch up on his writing. He had a few ideas he wanted to work out, and perhaps with Savannah out of town, things would be quiet.

Three days passed before she called.

Chapter 38

"Where the hell have you been?" Lucas asked.

Even over the telephone, she could hear the aggravation in his voice. She knew he wasn't going to be happy.

"I know. I'm sorry," Savannah said. "It has been so hectic, and I have just not been able to call."

"Savannah," Lucas answered while trying to control his temper. "It takes only a minute to let me know where you are."

"I know, honey, but please try and understand."

Lucas could hear the background as someone yelled, "Let's go!"

Savannah tried to continue. "Please try to understand. I am doing the best I can."

Again, someone yelled, "Let's go, Savannah."

She said, "I'll try to call you in the morning."

The same pattern continued night after night, day after day. At best, a few short words here, a quick hello and good-bye there. It was getting old fast, and it didn't take long until their first serious argument. After the eight weeks of touring, Savannah arrived home exhausted, and her timing could not have been worse. Lucas had just come home from an all-nighter with the boys. When he walked into the apartment, she was sitting at the kitchen table. Savannah turned toward the door as he entered.

"Nice to see you could make it home," she said.

"Well. If it ain't the famous Miss Savannah Vaughn!" Lucas replied as he staggered through the front door.

"Good lord, Lucas. You're drunk. Is this how you've been spending your time?" she asked.

"What do you care?" Lucas said. "This is the first conversation we have had in eight weeks."

"What do I care? Do you even have the slightest idea about what I go through on the road? Do you understand how demanding the schedule has become?"

"I know this," Lucas said. "I am alone and without you. I know my wife is running around the country with a bus full of men and no time to call her husband!"

"Lucas, it's not like that, and you know it. You need to slow down, and you're drinking too much."

"I don't drink any more than anyone else. Besides, I own the bar, so it's only natural. And what the hell do you care; you and your touring, Miss Famous."

"At least I have dreams, Lucas. At least I want to do something with my life other than getting slap drunk and gambling my life away every night. Maybe you enjoy drowning your sorrows. Maybe you would rather drink than do anything else?"

Lucas was silent. More, he was tired of waiting and beginning to believe marriage was a mistake.

He thought, *Women. What the hell do they know*?

Lucas walked out onto the balcony, and he heard Savannah call a cab. He watched as the taxi pulled up, and she left. When he went inside, he found she had left a note that she'd be at the cabin.

Chapter 39

The cab driver drove his car through the city as if he had all day. Savannah watched the storefronts as they passed through the streets. She saw Moe's on the corner.

"Driver. Could you stop here, please?" She needed a distraction after the long road trip.

Walking in, she saw George Robbins sitting at one of the tables near the front window. He looked up as she entered the room.

He called out, "Savannah! Over here."

She walked over and gave him a friendly hug.

"I heard you have made it to the big time!" he said. "Sit down, please. Let me buy you lunch."

"How about a coffee," she said.

"Coffee it is." George motioned to the waiter.

"Hey, Savannah!" She looked up, "Hey, Jimmy. How have you been?"

"Where you been? " George interrupted. "What's been happening? I haven't heard from you and Lucas since the wedding?"

She looked over at George, and her eyes welled up, and she started to cry. George was a bit surprised and moved closer.

"Savannah. What's wrong? What happened?"

"Oh, George. I am so sorry. I didn't mean for this to happen."

"Happen? What happened? Is it Lucas?"

"Sort of. It's both of us, I guess. I've been traveling, and he doesn't like it. Jealousy is part of it, and I guess loneliness is the other, or perhaps he is just selfish. All I know is he is wasting away, I am trying to make a career, and we are traveling on separate paths."

"You could stop."

She looked at George. "Stop what? Singing? Touring? I don't think so. My career is just starting to take off, and this is my dream, George."

"Yes, I understand. But you have to weigh the consequences, Savannah."

"George, I understand, but I don't see another choice other than being the bar owner's wife. Lucas needs to understand. I must do this. I love him, George. More than anyone or anything. He is the only man I have ever loved or will ever love. I don't know what to do." She quietly sipped her coffee while her looking across the room at the piano. "George. I can be a star—a big star. Ray Carter said he has never seen a talent like mine. But I don't want to do this alone. I want Lucas, but he thinks I don't want him."

"Do you?"

"Yes, more than anything, and when I make it, we won't need the bar and the trouble it brings. He must understand. I told him he could sell Charlie's, and he could manage my career. You know he would be a good manager, and we would be fine, but he just doesn't believe it. He has this thing with the bar as if it's a part of his life and he can't exist without it. The problem is, his drinking is going to kill him, just like it killed his father. He doesn't see it coming."

"I can understand the drinking."

"What do you mean, George?"

"Drinking almost killed me."

"I never realized."

"Sure did. There wasn't a day going by I didn't end up passed out somewhere—most the time not at home."

"What did you do?"

"I didn't do anything but hit rock bottom. I mean, everyone tried to tell me, but I wouldn't listen. I'll bet it's the same with Lucas."

"You're right. He won't listen."

"Let me guess. He thinks he is fine, and it is something everybody does. Right?"

"Yes. Exactly. I just don't understand."

"I do."

"What can I do, George? How can I get him to stop?"

"You can't, and that's the biggest challenge. A friend pulled me out and introduced me to Alcoholics Anonymous. The outfit was smaller back then, just getting started, and the folks who found me had just moved here from Ohio to start a new branch. The point is, I have been dry ever since. But there's nothing that is going to happen until Lucas makes up his mind to stop."

"I never realized it could be so difficult."

"Wasn't his father an alcoholic?"

"Yes. And it looks like he will follow in his footsteps. Can you help him, George?"

"I can tell you this. People like Lucas, like me, won't listen and need to learn for themselves."

"But I worry about him."

"I'm sure you do, but Lucas needs to decide on his own. Only he knows when the time is right, and there is nothing you can do right now except wait."

"But it's because of me, George."

"No. You're looking at it wrong. His drinking is not because of you. It's despite you. Listen. You know Lucas hides his emotions. However, you need to be strong and stand back until he learns he can't have a crutch. If you continue to rescue him, he will only fall farther. He may pull himself out, but that's not normally how it goes. Let's watch this for a while."

They talked as old friends, and after the long evening, she told George she would spend a couple of weeks at the cabin.

"Let me do this for you guys. You head for the cabin and try to focus your mind on other things. I will keep a watch on Lucas the best I can. I can't make any promises, but I can at least try and keep him moving forward and out of trouble."

Chapter 40

Waking slowly in the morning, Savannah thought, was the best thing about staying at the cabin. That and clinging to a dreamy state of mind halfway between awake and asleep while listening to the sounds of chirping birds and the sunlight and soft breezes shivering through open windows, dancing on half-closed eyes. Savannah knew there was nothing to do but enjoy the quiet of the country. There were countless things for her to accomplish, but she thought they could wait. A life filled with have to and need to, schedules, studio time, and people clamoring for this or that. Here, no one told her what she needed to do.

Her stomach forced her to the kitchen, and she made coffee and toast. She decided she would have breakfast on the porch and overlook the lake below her property. Then, maybe later, she would place a record on the player and putter around the garden planting flowers and cleaning out the weeds. There was no show to do, no luncheon to attend, no phone calls or agents to deal with—nothing to clutter her quiet. More important, no spats between her and Lucas and no hurt feelings and sorrowful looks because she felt she had to indulge his anger. The only thing she needed to worry about today was where she should plant the flowers and their arrangement to show off their color. She thought about the lazy enjoyment of the day where she could just sit back, enjoy the quiet, and perhaps read a book or just nap.

In all the years of driving toward success, she had never once taken life for granted. Every day had a point, a goal, and by the end of that day, she had accomplished what she'd set out to do. But this morning, she stood upon her porch looking over her front yard and the path leading down to the lake, realizing she had never lost a drop of pleasure while here, engulfed within the beauty of this place. She could admire her private curve of the rocky path leading toward the peaceful waterline. There were no city streets, taxis, horns, yelling, or brownstones to get in the way and make her think of people when she only wanted to be alone. The leaves began their change into winter clothing, leaving the trees looking as if there was an explosion of beauty and color. A walk to the lake showed the marsh grass as it brushed against the old boathouse. Savannah could hear the birds, the breeze, and she watched as the fish jumped, leaving a rippled circle of water.

Forgetting the coffee she'd made, she wandered back to the house and through to the front door, still dressed in the long shirt she'd slept in. She decided her clothes were perfect for the event with no photographers, no, reporters, and no Lucas to worry over. There was only a lovely quiet peace.

Later, she poured a cup of coffee, noticing the aroma, and sipped from the mug and then picked up her watering can she had carried inside to fill. She thought about what George had said. He was right about one thing. Lucas needed to come around on his own, and she couldn't do anything but wait. She was a woman who knew what she wanted, and she went out and got it when she had to. However, she needed to be patient; let time run its course, not a trait Savannah preferred. It had taken her some time to realize what she needed to do, and with George's help, everything should work out perfectly.

She just wanted two things in her life: a good man and to sing. She didn't think that was too much to ask. She considered just continuing to sing at Moe's or perhaps at Charlie's, but with a contract and an agent, it was apparent she had talent. If her voice could bring her fame and fortune, she believed she should take every advantage. Her dreams, after the fame, included a small town where the pace was leisurely and the demands few. She wanted a simple garden to grow roses, she thought, and perhaps near water. Most of all, she wanted Lucas.

The metropolis had become routine; the dissonant relationships of the city seemed just part of the landscape. She longed for a piece of life where she could just be herself. Where she could enjoy life, love, and quietly walk with Lucas. But at this point in her life, she knew that distance was the answer, geographically and emotionally.

She carried the watering can outside to tend to her flowers. She thought how nice everything would look in full bloom and how it would balance the cabin. A sound behind her drew attention. She looked over and watched as the geese landed in the crystal blue waters of the lake below.

She decided to skip breakfast, and for more than an hour, she enjoyed the warmth of the sun on her back while she worked on a new patch of dirt where she was determined to establish a rose garden with smaller wildflowers as a border.

Chapter 41

Lucas sat alone on the balcony of their apartment, unshaven and bewildered. He watched the traffic and the street below and thought of Savannah and her new life. *What would I do now with Savannah gone?* he thought. He didn't know his life was so bad. Life was simple according to the rules of Lucas Colby; she needed to be where he said she should be, and he needed to have a wife at home where she belonged. Lucas had dreams of infamy. Savannah just wanted to be famous. But as rain dampens the leaves of autumn, muting their bright colors as they surrender to the harsh realities of a dismal winter, love abandons all hope, and everything we have trusted becomes the lie within our hearts.

Savannah moved forward with her singing career, and her words echoed inside his head, "At least I have dreams!" she'd said. "At least I want to do something other than drink my life away." Savannah's passion and her resolve to be famous made a deadly combination. Lucas didn't think he changed much from the time they first met. He was still the same fun-loving guy. He believed Savannah had changed. There were no silly make-believe ideas of where he was going. Savannah will come around, he thought. Lucas was confident she would see his way eventually. Two weeks passed when she walked into Charlie's.

"Are you planning on coming home anytime soon,

or do I need to change your mailing address?" she asked. Her arms folded across her body, foot tapping the worn wooden floors as she waited impatiently for a response.

Lucas looked up from the booth. "What's your problem? I just had a few drinks with the boys, taking the edge off. Besides, you've been hiding at the cabin. I don't have a reason to be at home right now!"

Her temper flared. "Taking off the edge? You stupid, lazy bastard! You haven't been home in two weeks! I thought some time away would help us." Savannah turned and walked toward the door, then stopped.

"You know, Lucas. This isn't right. It just isn't right."

Lucas ignored the tears in her eyes, and her trembled words fell on deaf ears. Savannah gave up and left.

Harriet walked over to the table. "Lucas. What the hell are you doing?"

"What do you mean, Harriet?"

She looked at Lucas with scowled face and demanded, "Answer the goddamn question!"

"Drinking my scotch?"

"Quit the smartass routine, Lucas. You're drowning in your self-pity, and you need to straighten your ass out before you get into something you can't get out of."

"Yeah, thanks Harriet, I'll think about it. Thanks for the advice."

"Perhaps you should think about it and think hard, Lucas Colby," Harriet's voice raised in anger. "Quit thinking you're the only one in this world. Charlie and Savannah believed in you. Why in the hell do you think she works so hard? She's building something for both of you, and as I see it, you must be too blind, too drunk, or too stupid to see that. Besides, this is your bar, and you need to run it or lose it."

Lucas stood, grabbed the bottle of scotch off the table, walked across the dance floor and out of the bar. Harriet continued her castigation as Lucas waved her off with his hand and walked through the same door where he found his beginning, where he first met Savannah, and where he found his end.

Chapter 42

He wandered around the city until his bottle was dry. He picked up another bottle from a bar down the street and went to the park to sit down on a bench. Slowly, the liquor took over, and he fell asleep.

He awoke to three young men screaming at him. "Gimme ya money, ya dumb bastard!"

They pulled Lucas to the ground and started kicking him in the ribs and back. One of them climbed on his chest and started beating his face. He fought them off as best he could, but they yanked his wallet out of his back pocket and disappeared into the night.

A police officer ran up to Lucas, seeing him sprawled out on the ground, torn up and bloody. He vaguely remembered hearing something about needing medical attention, a siren in the distance, men yelling.

He awoke in a hospital bed as a nurse straightened his bedsheets. She heard Lucas stirring and said in a cold tone, "Well, looks like someone is finally waking up."

"Where am I? What the hell happened?" Lucas said as he felt the bandages around his chest and face. He felt like a train hit him. He couldn't move a muscle without hurting.

"You're at County General, and you've been here for about five days. Here, I have some medication to help you sleep." The nurse handed Lucas a hand full of colored pills and poured a glass of water. He tried to move as every inch of his body screamed in pain.

"Five days? I was in the park, and there were some kids. Three of them, I think."

The nurse interrupted. "Fortunately for you, Mr. Colby, a couple of park police were nearby as well. You were lucky. Those thugs got your wallet, and it didn't look like they cared if you lived or died. What were you trying to do? Kill yourself?"

Lucas laid in bed, quiet for a moment, rethinking the events as the nurse adjusted the bandages.

"Looks like you might make it out of here, Mr. Colby."

"Wait a minute," Lucas said. "How do you know my name? You said those guys took my wallet?"

"This woman was in a few days ago to see you and told us your name."

"Woman? What woman? Who was she? What did she look like? Was it Savannah?" he asked.

The nurse paused as if she was trying to remember, "I didn't catch her name, Mr. Colby, but I can tell you she looked like she cared about what had happened to you."

"What did she look like?"

"She was a beautiful woman," the nurse said. "One might say, spectacular. She was tall and slender, with piercing blue eyes."

Lucas knew it was Savannah, which meant she still cared, and maybe she even still loved him. His medication was beginning to make him tired, and he tried to stay awake, hoping she would return. The room was quiet, giving Lucas plenty of solitude to reflect on, and he thought to close his eyes for a moment. He drifted off into a deep sleep.

Somewhere between that sleep and consciousness,

he heard a knock at the door. His eyelids felt heavy, and he couldn't move. He thought he could see a man standing in the doorway wearing a floppy hat, an open shirt, and a loose tie around his skinny neck. He was tall and had a rough face with a ruddy complexion.

"You okay, kid?"

"Charlie?"

"Yeah, kid, it's me. Screwed up, eh?"

"I think so. Charlie?"

Charlie pulled up a chair and sat next to the bed. Pushing the brim of his hat up over his forehead, he said, "Listen, kid. It looks like you got a little more jam on your toast than you need."

"Yeah, Charlie, I've really screwed it up."

"Let me see if I can help you out. I've been through three wives and a boatload of girlfriends. I know about two things. One is managing a bar, and the second is women. I can manage a bar better than managing any woman, but that's another story. Anyhow, I think I can help you out here.

Listen up, kid. This is how I see it. My first wife was a tough bird. Of course, she died young, so I didn't have to put up with much. My second wife was fiery like Savannah, but there was a big difference. She wasn't a babe like Savannah. The worst part was, she wasn't too bright. She was a crazy platinum blonde with a body that wouldn't quit, but I had to tell her how to do everything. The problem was, hot temper and dumb don't mix too well. You see, with Savannah, you got babe and brains. That can be a good combination for a guy. She also has talent, and I think she is going to go far.

Now for the fatherly advice, not that I am much of a father, but even I can see you need to straighten your ass out and grow up. It's that simple. I remember the day you walked into my bar. You were a tall, skinny, wet behind-the-ear punk who thought he owned the world. You found out different, didn't you? Getting your ass kicked in a couple of bar fights will teach you a thing or two. But you survived, and now look at you. You were on the right track, but you've screwed up badly. As I see it, you got a couple of choices. You can keep your sorry ass like it is or beg for forgiveness with Savannah. Just remember one thing. I can see something in Savannah that's good for you. You ain't figured it out yet, kid, but you two are supposed to be together.

There is a damn good reason why she walked into the bar that night. My best advice to you is that you need to quit looking for the perfect woman. You ain't perfect and, as a matter of fact, a long way from it. Maybe Savannah ain't perfect either, but I'm telling you, she is the one. "

Charlie continued to talk for a while, and Lucas listened. He had good things to say. He was a kind man.

When he finally stood to leave, he said, "I've taken enough time, and you need to rest. I'll be back to check on you.

Chapter 43

"Whatever you do, don't tell Lucas. It would make things worse," Savannah told Harriet.

Savannah was lost and didn't know where to turn. She stopped at Charlie's to ask the advice of Harriet. Harriet was a wise woman and asked, "Do you love him, Savannah?"

Savannah thought, *What an odd question.* She responded, "What do you think, Harriet? Why wouldn't I love him? Of course, I love him. I married him, didn't I?"

Harriet, in her wisdom, looked at Savannah. "That's not what I asked. Do you love him?"

Savannah's eyes welled, and she looked down. "I love Lucas more than anything in the world. But I don't know if I am the right woman for him. You know, sometimes people just don't mix."

Harriet hugged her, and Savannah leaned her head into Harriet's shoulder. Crying, she said, "I'm no good for Lucas. It's my fault things are screwed up."

Harriet comforted Savannah. "No. It's not your fault, and you can't blame yourself for his ways. I think that maybe you two just need some time away from each other. Between his running the bar and your traveling, that's a lot of stress without a lot of time. Take some time away, search your heart, and find solitude. It will work itself out, Savannah."

"It's so hard, Harriet. I feel so helpless."

"It's not your fault," Harriet told her.

"You know I love him," Savannah said.

"Of course, you do, honey. You wouldn't be here talking to me if you didn't love Lucas."

****

For many couples, love gives way to comfort and the warmth of familiarity. What can seem so perfect—so inseparable—can sometimes resolve a false face. A love not settled within the heart; a love not yet ready. The flames of their passion changed to embers and then to ashes. It melted away like the snow of winter, but instead of bringing forth the birth of spring, the absence bared their naked souls, exposing them for what they had become. It all left them empty and without hope.

Alone in his hospital room, Lucas reflected on what he could have done, should have done. He thought about his dream of Charlie. It felt real. He settled he had destroyed both lives and every opportunity. It was time to start over. The difference was, he didn't care anymore. He was beginning to see the booze had affected him more than he wanted to admit. He had become his worst nightmare. He had become his father. More important, more tragic—he didn't care.

Drinkin' is the work of the devil. His mother's voice echoed. He remembered: *Life ain't worth living without somebody to love. If nobody loved you, or you didn't love somebody, you might as well be dead.* In his heart, Lucas believed those words true; he may as well be dead. He'd allowed love to enter his heart only to find love was not the perfect answer, and the love of a woman could not save him. The lies held within his heart faced him and told him no one could love him. There was nothing to live for, and no one cared. As the week passed, he believed his time passed as well, but to his disappointment, he survived. Harriet picked him up at the hospital.

He limped to her car, still sore from the beating. The doctor said he would be fine in a few weeks.

The doctor didn't know the whole story.

Chapter 44

Arriving at his apartment, he got out of the car and thanked Harriet.

She looked up and said, "No thanks needed, Lucas. Take this week off and get your health back. I will handle the business until you return." Lucas turned and started up the stairs. He wanted to know about Savannah, and he paused.

"You okay, honey? Is there something you need?" Harriet asked.

He stared at the ground for a moment. "No. All is good."

He limped to the manager's office. The manager pulled the spare from the pegboard behind him. "Here you go, pal."

Lucas didn't say much. He mumbled thanks and headed to his apartment. He put the key in the lock and opened the door, not knowing what to expect. The apartment was quiet. Savannah wasn't home, and it looked like she hadn't been home in a while. He walked to the cabinet and pulled out his bottle of scotch. He poured the liquor into a glass and took a drink. The feeling of warmth down his throat and into his chest felt good. The drink settled in his stomach like an old friend, warm and comfortable. He had another drink, and then another, then a few more.

Savannah returned to the apartment, hearing Lucas

was home. Perhaps she was hoping for one more chance, or maybe she thought his encounter with near-death would have changed him.

She found Lucas on the couch, bottle in hand and out cold. The front door sounded like a clap of thunder as she slammed it shut, then silence. The ending was a stark contrast to the first night they were together. It was Sunday. Lucas could remember her going on about being a worthless no-good son of a bitch that would never amount to anything but a drunken, useless bastard. She walked out of his life.

****

As the drugs and liquor wore off, he began gaining consciousness. It was sometime later when he tried to focus on the ceiling above him. The inside of his head screamed with pain; like hot coals, his eyes felt as if being crushed. He stumbled into the bedroom, shielding his eyes from the daylight streaming through the window. He could see her closet was bare. He stumbled into the bathroom. Trying to stop the fire in his skull, he climbed into the shower and turned the water on. Leaning against the wall while the water cascaded down the back of his head, his mouth was dry, his tongue like sand. Thoughts of his life, reflections of Savannah filled him. *Who would want a worthless soul like me?* he thought. His legs felt weak, and no longer able to hold his weight. He could feel himself slipping as the room turned to shades of gray. He collapsed to his knees, no longer able to stand.

The water felt like hot rain on his back, and he wept as if the gates of hell had opened. Tears shed down his hardened cheeks and fell like raindrops on a tin roof.

Disgraced, as God's hand had stretched through the

heavens and singled him out, knowing the lies, the deceptions, and it felt as if God's fist ripped through the emptiness left in his heart where Savannah once lived. Lucas hunched over on his knees as the water fell across his back, and he sobbed from deep within his soul, then cried out, "God. Oh, God. What have I done?"

Chapter 45

Savannah stopped at Charlie's on her way out of town. Pete was there, holding everything together.

"Hey Savannah," Pete said as she walked up to the bar.

"Hey, Pete. Good to see you. Is Harriet around?" she asked.

"Sure is. She's in the back. I'll get her for you," Pete said.

Savannah walked over to a booth to sit down. Charlie's held many memories for her. As she sat, she thought of Lucas and prayed that he would come through. Harriet sat down across from her.

"Hi, Savannah. How are you holding out?" Harriet asked.

"Oh, I'm fine, Harriet. You know me. I adjust the best I can. Have you heard from Lucas?"

"I dropped him off a couple of days ago at the apartment. I told him to lay low for a while." Harriet said.

"That was kind of you. Thanks for watching out for him. I heard he was back home, so I stopped in yesterday," Savannah said.

"Is he doing okay? I've asked Pete to stop by this afternoon after work to check on him," Harriet said.

"Yeah. He might want to do that. As I said, I went to the apartment yesterday, and damn if he was completely out of it. I guess he decided to wash down his pain pills with his goddamn scotch."

"Oh, Savannah. I'm so sorry to hear that."

"I've had enough, Harriet. I grabbed my things and left him there lying on the couch. I don't even think he knew I came by." Tears fell from Savannah's eyes. "I don't know what to do anymore. I can't go back."

Harriet motioned to Pete and asked him to go by the apartment to check on Lucas.

When Pete arrived, he found the front door unlocked and unanswered.

"Lucas?" he called out. "Are you here?" Pete heard the water running in the shower and entered the bathroom seeing his friend crumpled on the floor.

"Hey, man! You okay?"

Lucas rolled over. "Hey, Pete. What happened? What are you doing here?"

"Harriet asked me to come by, and I'm glad I did. You look like shit."

"Yeah, well, I feel like shit."

"Let's get you warmed up and in some clothes."

Pete made some coffee, and Lucas sat on the couch wrapped in a blanket. "Looks like it's over with you two," Pete said.

"Savannah? Yeah. I think I screwed it up."

Pete stared at the floor. "It'll work out. Don't you worry. She will see her mistake, or some other dame will come along."

Pete didn't understand. Lucas didn't want some other dame.

Lucas pulled himself from the couch and thanked Pete for coming by.

"I'm going to get some rest. Tell Harriet I'll see her tonight."

As the sun set, Lucas made his way to Charlie's. He parked around the back of Charlie's later in the evening and walked in the back door. For the first time, the smell of the bar made him sick to his stomach. It was a bad night followed by nothing good. After a few short hours, he told Pete to take over. He had enough for one night.

Chapter 46

Lucas abandoned his few friends, his business, and his life. Harriet would see him around the streets and try to speak with him. After a while, she gave up. The bottle became his Savannah; the nights became cold and lonely.

Days passed, then months. It seemed each day was the same, with Lucas drinking his mind into oblivion. He found himself sleeping it off either in a jail cell or a park bench.

One late evening, sitting in a local bar drowning in drinks, Lucas felt the slap of a hand on his back. He thought the usual was about to happen again—he was about to be tossed into the street—when he heard a familiar voice.

"Hey, Lucas, you rotten bastard. Where you been?"

He turned to see his old college friend standing behind him in a fancy pin-striped suit and shiny shoes. He was the last person Lucas would have expected to see, especially in this dump. You could tell by the way he dressed he didn't frequent places like this. For that matter, he didn't often see this side of town. It was not a smart thing to do, dressed as he was.

"Well, if it ain't George Robbins," Lucas said.

"What the hell has happened to you?" George asked. "You're looking pretty rough these days."

Lucas spun around on the stool, barely able to

balance, and responded, "Really? What gave it away?"

George grabbed Lucas by the shoulders. "Man, let me get you out of here!" He reached into his pocket and threw some cash to the bartender. "Here. This should cover it!"

He grabbed Lucas by the arm and helped him walk down the street to a restaurant for some strong coffee and sobering up.

"I guess we have some catching up to do," George said to his old friend.

Lucas thought to himself, perhaps for old time's sake, but was sure they no longer had much in common.

George motioned to the waitress and asked for a couple of cups of coffee.

"So, what's up with you, Lucas?"

"Just trying to make it, my friend."

"To what, an early grave? It looks like you're drinking yourself to death. What are you running from?"

Lucas rubbed his face and drank some coffee. Looking down at the floor, he said, "Me. I guess I am running from me."

Lucas told George the story of his life. How bad he had it. How rough it was growing up. The Army didn't want him, and he was just another worthless soul taking up breathing space. And when he had finally done something with himself, and he'd found Savannah, he believed their lives were so perfect. It seemed everything was perfect. What he didn't see was her becoming famous and leaving him alone. Then the drinking got worse. It took over, and feeling abandoned again, the alcohol became his companion, taking over his life as he drank himself into a stupor most every night. Lucas believed Savannah left for no good reason. He thought she was in love with the spotlight and had no time for him. She had moved on with her life, and there was nothing leftover.

"Yeah, well, look at me," George said. "Uncle Sam didn't want me either, and we all have problems."

Lucas laughed. "George, you're a great guy, but that's your comeback? You had great parents, and brothers and sisters, and the whole thing. Your hearing is bad in one ear. So, the government gave you the same answer as me?"

"Stop it, Lucas. Just stop making excuses. You know, Lucas, ever since I've known you, you've complained about one thing or another. It was always someone else's fault, or you were pointing the blame to something out of your control. I think it's about time someone kicked you square in the ass."

"Well, personally, George, let me tell you what I think. You have no idea what I have been through. This ain't college, pal, and I think you can kiss my ass."

George leaned toward Lucas, shadowing him under his large frame. "Shut it, Lucas." George continued, "As I see, we can go one of two ways. One, I can walk out of here and let you just drown in your sorrows and your sorry-assed alcoholic binges. If I was a betting man, my bet is you will be dead within the year. On the other hand, I can help sober you up, help you get a job. I can be your friend or leave this place right now, and you will never see me again. It's up to you. What do you want to do?"

Lucas sat in silence, thinking. He was almost thirty years old and had lost everything.

"George, I have absolutely nothing to live for, and the only woman I have ever loved has walked out of my life. I don't think I could be any further down." He leaned back in the booth, looked at his old friend, and continued, "But they say, God watches out for drunks and fools, and I am both."

Lucas thought he had reached the end of his time and was just waiting for the bus to take him to the graveyard. It looked as though fate had other plans. It looked like fate had sent an angel to watch over him.

"First, you have to admit that you need help, Lucas," George said. "I can't, and I won't do anything until you ask me for help."

Lucas sat for a moment and drank his coffee. "George, I don't know what to do, but I need to get my life back on track."

"Okay. Now we are getting somewhere," George said. "I have a friend. His name is Bill Wilson. I would like for you to meet him."

"Bill Wilson? Who is he?" Lucas asked.

"An old friend of mine that has been through similar challenges," George said. "Here is his business card. I need you to call him and make an appointment. Tell him you are a friend of mine."

Lucas took the card from George and looked at it. "Alcoholics Anonymous?"

"Right," George said. "Bill has a program, and I think it can help you. Are you willing to give it a try?"

"At this point in my life, George, I am willing to try anything," Lucas said.

"Good," George responded. "We are getting someplace. Listen, you finished college, right?"

"Yeah. Somehow, I managed to finish," Lucas said.

"And you studied journalism, right?"

"Yup, that's me, the journalist."

"Lucas, I'm serious," George said. "I am the Editor

of the *Early Register*. I can help you get a job at the newspaper. It's not a prominent newspaper, but it's a start—a new direction for you and a chance to turn your life around.

Chapter 47

Lucas decided to take life one day at a time. He squandered most anything given to him and lost at love. Nonetheless, the call came in, and he figured he'd better straighten out. The old friends talked into the night, and George offered Lucas a ride back to the apartment. Lucas didn't want to go. It would just remind him of Savannah, but he accepted she was out of his life and said, "Let's go."

Lucas thought of his options as he rode with George. His life changed in the wrong direction, and his options were to pick up and move on or die alone in a gutter. Lucas had one friend left in the world, and he was willing to extend a hand. Opening the door to the apartment was difficult, for all he could see were reminders of Savannah. Looking out the window, he saw the young couples walking the streets. He sat on the couch and wept.

The following morning, he woke up hearing the sounds of the street below. The bright sun shot its rays across the room. He knew what he had to do. Lucas went to the cabinets in his apartment, removed every liquor bottle, and placed them on the counter next to the sink. He opened each bottle, and he said goodbye to the poison as it drained down the hole in the sink. He believed this was his last chance to turn his life around. As he watched the booze flow down the hole, he thought he should have done this long ago when he could have saved his marriage. It was over now, and she moved on. He telephoned Bill Wilson. His hands shook as he dialed the phone. A man's voice answered, and for a moment, he was silent.

"Hello. My name is Lucas Colby," he stuttered. "My friend, George Robbins, gave me your number."

The man on the phone said, "Hello Lucas. My name is Bill Wilson. What can I do for you?"

Lucas didn't know what to say. He had never asked for anyone's help. Working all the courage he could, he said, "I need your help. I need to stop drinking. George Robbins said you could help me."

"Only you can help yourself, Lucas," Bill Wilson said. "We, however, can guide you to your new life. Can you meet with us tonight?"

Lucas agreed to meet later that evening. He was determined to be a new man.

George met Lucas at the apartment, gave him a ride, and the support talk he needed while driving to a small church on the Eastside. Lucas arrived feeling better about the future but still unsure. As he came close to the door, it opened.

"Good evening. You must be Lucas Colby," Bill said, extending his hand.

Lucas returned the handshake and investigated the room. "I see there are others."

"Bill smiled. "Yes, Lucas. You are not alone. Come in and sit down with us."

One by one, each man stood and told his story. Each story filled Lucas' heart a bit more. This meeting wasn't how he planned his life, but he knew something held him there. Something he could feel in his heart.

After the meeting, George met Lucas in front of the church.

"How did it go?" George asked.

"Not easy," said Lucas. "It was tough listening to those stories."

"Yeah, you're right. It's not easy revealing you're your darkest fears and secrets in front of strangers. Don't worry. You will get used to it, and your sponsor will be there to support you."

"I don't have a sponsor."

"Sure, you do," George said. "Who do you think brought you here tonight?"

Lucas looked over at George. "Sure. You brought me, but you have to be in AA to be a sponsor."

George smiled at Lucas. "I know."

Chapter 48

The *Early Register* wasn't much of a newspaper. Most of the big news came off the wires, and the staff made it sound like it was their reporting. In between, the newspaper staff wrote stories of sports, life, and general junk people wanted to read.

George had assigned Lucas to the local scene. His contribution was to report on a wide range of stories covering local politics, war news, and some sports. Whatever the assignment, George kept Lucas busy, knowing he needed the distraction.

Lucas had always thought everyone should have a reason for living. His mother had hope. Lucas had nothing, but he saw Savannah had dreams. She had left him, and he was beginning to see it was his fault. She had the talent, looks, and brains. She had believed she could do better, and she proved it. He was more comfortable with a bottle of scotch and didn't understand nor express the desires or needs of marriage. His drinking had driven him to a point where he didn't care.

Despite it all, it looked like his life was getting better. Sadly, Savannah was out of his life. Lucas hadn't seen her since the Sunday morning when she slammed the door shut on their world. He wished her well and thought of her every day. Too often, they had told each other love would last forever. Those conversations and the demons would continue to torment his mind, echoing in his head when he would lie in bed alone at night. He missed having her soft cheek on his chest. He missed her auburn hair and those piercing blue eyes that penetrated his very soul with just a glance. He lay in bed at night, dreaming of her soft lips, her warm caress. He thought, *Yeah. Sure. My life is better.*

Thanks to George for his support, and Alcoholics Anonymous, liquor no longer mastered his life. He didn't know if drinking drove him to Savannah or pushed him away from her, but he did know nothing was the same without her. The passion wasn't there, no fire in his heart. He knew she was somewhere in the city, but he had damaged her plenty. He also knew he was a disappointment. He knew he let her down and ruined all their dreams.

He thought about how her first husband treated her. How her boyfriend treated her, and how he treated her. *I know how to pick them*, he remembered her saying. He thought to himself, *We all had something in common. We allowed the most incredible woman in the world to slip through our hands. Maybe she just attracted jerks like us.* He hoped and prayed she would find someone to love her, as she deserved.

The first month at the *Early* was tough. He had survived on ham sandwiches and strong coffee with his days running late into the night while interviewing. It was also a challenging weekend as it would have been their anniversary. Savannah was on his mind all day. He arrived home after work and was exhausted. Dinner would have to wait as he collapsed in bed and began to dream.

He dreamed of the lake where Savannah would swim in the summer. He heard the sounds of the songbirds and the gentle questions of the owl. He dreamt of their enjoying morning coffee on the porch overlooking the lake. He could see her skinny-dipping far from shore in the middle of the lake, the making of love under the stars at night. He dreamed of Savannah and her seeing a falling star and making a wish. *What was your wish?* he'd asked.

I have never been this happy, and I don't want it to end, she said.

Like the crack of thunder in a summer storm, Lucas felt a jolt of pain shoot across his chest, jerking him from his dream. Soaked in sweat, his chest crushing, he gasped for air. There was a devastating pain in his arm as he reached for the phone. He awoke wrapped in blankets with beeping sounds around him. He mumbled something, and with eyes barely open, he thought he saw auburn hair. He opened his eyes again. It was George, and Lucas could see the concerned look on his face.

"I thought we lost you, pal. Just relax. The doc said you would be fine," George said in a low whisper.

"What happened?" Lucas was barely able to speak.

George put his hand gently on his arm. "We first thought you had a heart attack, but the doctor said it probably wasn't. More like stress, which he said could kill you just as fast. He said he's going to keep you here a few days and check you out to be sure nothing else happens."

"How did you know I was here?" Lucas said.

"You called my place. I guess you thought you were dialing the ambulance, but it was me."

Lucas took a breath. "You're a true friend, George."

George smiled and brought Lucas water.

"Listen, get some rest. The doc said your heart looks

like it's working okay," George said.

Handing George the empty glass, Lucas said, "Thanks again, my friend."

George smiled as he took the glass from Lucas' hand and placed it on the table, "See you tomorrow."

"Hey George, before you go, tell me something."

George stopped and turned toward Lucas. "Sure, pal. What is it?"

"Did I see Savannah in here?"

George chuckled, and with an odd look on his face, he said, "I think you were dreaming. She wasn't here."

He shut the door behind him as he left, and Lucas closed his eyes.

The room was cold, and he pulled the blanket closer to his face, noticing a soft scent lingering on the blanket. A gentle scent filled his senses; sweet, subtle, and it made him feel comfortable. He drifted off to sleep, and this time, he remembered an auburn-haired beauty gazing into his eyes.

****

His eyes squinted from the brightness caused by the sun streaming brightly into the hospital room window. "Good morning, Mr. Colby. How are we feeling today?" the nurse said as she entered the room.

"A lot better than before. When can I leave?"

"Not until the doctor gives you the okay, which shouldn't be long from now," the nurse told Lucas.

The doctor arrived soon after and gave Lucas a clean bill of health, and soon afterward, Lucas was able to dress. Someone at the nurse desk called for a cab and then brought a wheelchair to the nurse station and wheeled him to the hospital's front. He limped to the cab and gave the driver his address.

Arriving back at his apartment, he was feeling good and called George.

"Hey! They released me!"

"Why would they do something like that?" George responded.

'Yeah. Funny, George. Ain't you a real buddy. The nurse said I could leave because of my good behavior."

George laughed. "It sounds like they don't know you very well."

"You're probably right. Anyhow, I will see you on Monday."

"Sounds good if you are up to it."

"I am, and I need to get back to work. "

"Yeah, pal. Monday it is."

Chapter 49

Lucas enjoyed his new life. He'd conquered his demons, and it looked like it was a smooth ride ahead. He sat on the park bench during lunch while eating a ham sandwich he had brought from home. The sun was warm on his face as he recalled his life. His last visit to this park ended with bad results. This time, he was just another worker on lunch break. His writing at the *Early Register* was good, surprising even himself; George said his work was clean and precise, and he had become a solid journalist. His regular appearances at the Alcoholics Anonymous meetings were going well. He hadn't tasted liquor for a long time, and he felt good.

He wasn't in the market for any more relationships and believed Savannah was enough to last a lifetime. The boy from Ohio built a shell of defense around his heart once again so no one would know the real Lucas Colby.

George gave him the break he needed and didn't deserve. In doing so, Lucas discovered he could do something besides drink himself to death. Throwing the crumbs to the pigeons dancing around his feet, he stood and walked back to his office. George stopped him as he passed by his door.

"Lucas. Can I see you for a minute?" George shouted.

Lucas turned around and stuck his head through the doorway. "Sure. What's up?"

"Come in. Sit down for a minute. I need to share something with you," George said.

"Okay. Shoot," Lucas replied.

"I was speaking with the boss, and he has been watching your work," George said.

"What does that mean?" Lucas asked.

"Well. In this case, it means you are doing a great job, and he sees it."

"Great. I am glad to hear that. I've been working like crazy to make a good impression."

"You have, and I am beginning to see a Senior Reporter shortly," George said.

"Guess I better keep my nose clean. Eh, boss?"

George laughed. "Get back to work before I change my mind."

Lucas walked back to his desk feeling better than ever. His life was moving forward, and a new career was ahead of him. The presses completed their run, and the office runner delivered the first edition as Lucas sat down at his desk. He had interviewed a local war veteran on the current situation in Europe and looked forward to seeing the story. It had been an arduous task to get an interview with this man. It had taken months of work, preparation, and gaining his trust in that he just did not want to relive the atrocities of the war he had survived.

He opened the fresh print to review his layout, finding an entire column of his story was missing. He crunched the paper in his hands and stormed into the copy room, screaming for the idiot that prepared his story. Every head turned, and he could see jaws drop on everyone as he approached. It wasn't the first time he lost his temper in the building, but this was probably the worst.

As their eyes met, she didn't have to say a word. Lucas knew by the look on her face. He turned in her direction with all the fury of a madman, his face red and eyes glaring.

She pulled her copy and said, "Look. It wasn't me!" Her hands trembled as tears fell from her cheeks.

"Well then, what the hell happened?" he yelled back at this innocent fawn of a woman.

He threw the paper at her feet, shouting at the incompetence of everyone in the building, and stormed out. George just sat in his office shaking his head. Lucas returned to his desk and tried to work on an upcoming series. The copy girl and her sad face consumed his thoughts. Usually, he couldn't have cared less, but this was different.

Lucas sat at his desk, preoccupied with the events of the day. He thought, for sure, this would affect his promotion. From across the room, he looked up to see the young woman enter the coffee room.

He sat back in his chair for a moment and reflected. His first thought was to continue the rampage and ask how this girl could let this happen. *It wasn't her fault,* he thought, and he ran his fingers through his hair. He walked to the water fountain splashing cold water on his face.

He turned to see her sitting in the break room wistfully gazing out the window. He decided this was as good a time as any to apologize for being a jerk. He walked across the editing floor and pulled a rose from an arrangement in the office.

"One should be properly introduced before acting like a madman," he said.

Startled, she raised her head and looked at Lucas.

"My name is Lucas Colby, and I wanted to apologize for my rude behavior."

"For what?" she responded sharply and glared at the rose.

"For being such a jerk. Will you accept this rose as a token of friendship?"

With doubt in her voice, she said, "Yeah, right, like that makes it all better."

"Honestly. I'm sorry, I was a jerk, and I overreacted."

She looked at Lucas and said, "You're always overreacting, and as far as acting like a madman, that was no act, mister! I am of the opinion you are mad and at what, I don't know, but you need to fix it before somebody pops you."

She continued talking with a specific tone of disgust in her voice. "I've heard you were temperamental about your column and pretty much an ass, so I guess I shouldn't be surprised."

Lucas thought, *Well deserved comments.* He could see tears in her eyes.

"I didn't mean to make you cry," he said.

She looked back at Lucas. "I'm not crying because of you, so would you mind leaving me alone."

"Sure. Sorry." Lucas turned to leave.

He was about out of earshot when he heard, "By the way. My name is Cindy."

Chapter 50

It had been a long time since he had been with a woman. He had not lost his charm. He believed and thought it would have been nice to meet Cindy under different circumstances. She was tall and slender, blonde, and beautiful. Of course, Lucas and beautiful women went together like salt and pepper.

He thought about going back and talking with her again, but he wasn't interested in a serious relationship, and he knew the worst kind is a working relationship. Sometimes, his mind just didn't calculate all the facts, and he did stupid things. It wasn't as if he was blind to her presence as Cindy caught his eye from time to time.

He had asked around the office and found out she had a boyfriend, perhaps almost a fiancé. They met as teenagers, growing up together in the same neighborhood. She was young. He discovered she was years younger than he, and any thoughts of anything else in his twisted little mind should have stopped right there.

She and her boyfriend lived near each other much of their lives, and both families simply believed they would be together forever. Lucas and Cindy grew up on opposite ends of the city, and their paths never crossed until they worked for the same newspaper.

She reminded Lucas of Savannah, the kinder side, not the Irish temptress of passion Savannah exhibited so well.

Cindy was different from the women he would have usually approached or even held a passing interest. She was an innocent little angel.

From the second-floor office window, he watched her arrive each morning. As she walked toward the building, she would brush her long, chestnut blonde hair away from her gentle face as her tall and slender frame would glide across the ground with such grace. Lucas would tell himself that she was off-limits. His life was finally starting to show progress. He did not need any complications, and he was not interested in a relationship.

Lucas believed Savannah had left him for a good reason. His only interest was moving forward with his life. Cindy deserved more than what he could offer, and he knew she didn't deserve his decrepit soul spoiling her innocence. With Savannah, he experienced the hottest temper one could endure, hot enough to burn you if you stood too close. Lucas had found himself closer to the heat than he should have been and had the scars to prove it.

Chapter 51

As the weeks followed, Lucas and Cindy would pass each other in the halls. There was polite conversation, and he would anticipate her arrival each morning. Occasionally, she would catch Lucas watching her from across the room. He would see Cindy watching him. Her girlfriends would giggle when he came into the copy room to check his column. He would stand just over her shoulder, checking the layout and reaching around her while pointing something out. There was nothing wrong with her work, but he would point things out just to smell her hair as it fell across her shoulders. One time, she turned, and her arm brushed his. Lucas pulled back as if shocked by a bolt of electricity. She blushed, and her friends giggled.

A few days later, Lucas was running late. He had a copy due, and he was about to miss the deadline. He sprinted across the parking lot and into the building as the elevator doors were closing.

He yelled, "Wait. Hold the door," as he entered the building. The doors kept closing, so he stuck his arm between them.

"Ouch, damn it," he said as the doors bounced open. As he entered, Cindy leaned against the back wall of the elevator, smiling.

"Nice move," she said.

"It would have been a lot easier if you would have

just held the button. I could have broken my arm."

"Yeah," she said. "But you look so cute with your hair messed up and your tie hanging across your shoulder."

She moved closer to Lucas and slipped his tie between her fingers, straightening it. "Tell me something, Lucas Colby," she said. "Are you busy this weekend?"

Lucas tried to reply as she stepped off the elevator but was at a loss for words.

He didn't think much more about the conversation after arriving at his desk. He assumed the flirting of a young girl testing the waters, and the flirtation was nothing but a problem waiting to happen. He figured Cindy did not need him in her life, and he did not need this complication in his life. No office romances, he thought, and certainly not with her.

Sitting there, he realized he needed to check his copy before it went to press. He talked to himself, under his breath, while walking to the copy room, "Nothing was meant by that little charade in the elevator. Just stay cool." He hurried into the copy room and noticed Cindy was not at her station. *Perfect*, he thought. Lucas ran over and reviewed his column. *Excellent work*, he thought. *She does a fantastic job with this*.

"Like what you see?"

"Yeah. Yes, I do. It looks like the body of the text fits nicely," he stammered as Cindy walked up behind him.

"Do you think I need to move it around a little bit?" she said.

Lucas tried to think of a way to exit gracefully.

"Uh, no," he said. "I think it looks just fine like it is."

Without looking up, Lucas turned and began to walk back to his desk.

"What are you doing for lunch, Lucas?"

Not thinking that clearly, he said, "No plans."

"Good. Let's have you and me go to the café across the street—Dutch, of course," she said.

Lucas stopped and thought for a moment. "What the heck. How about you come by in about thirty minutes?"

"Perfect," she said.

As Lucas approached his desk, his first thought was, *What are you doing? You know you should have said no. This is a nice girl and someone you certainly don't deserve or need to go to lunch with. There is no need to start something you do not plan on finishing. That's it. I'll tell her something has come up, and lunch is off. Yeah, that will work.*

He walked back to her station, but she was not there. Lucas thought, *Why not? Why can't I have a friendly lunch with someone from work? It's the least I could do, considering I berated her in front of all her friends.*

Returning to his desk, he picked up the phone and scheduled some interviews later in the week. Time passed quickly, and he lost track.

"Hey, you ready?"

He looked up, and there she was, standing and ready to go. He fumbled with the phone halfway, hanging it up, trying to gather his composure.

"Uh, sure, let's go!" he said.

Crossing the editing floor, George watched from his office with a puzzled look on his face. He was funny that way. He could express his exact thoughts without ever opening his mouth.

They walked across the street to a small café

offering a light fare for lunch. It was a lovely afternoon. The weather was superb, and there was a slight breeze. The owner set up a few tables outside, so they sat and talked. The conversation was casual, one you would have with a stranger. The difference was, Lucas was a reporter with a tendency to ask questions—too many questions. He caught himself and turned the conversation to her. He believed she didn't need to know anything more about him.

"So, how long have you been at the paper?" he asked.

"Just a couple of years," she said. "I'm studying Journalism, so it's a little tough juggling work and school, but I'm making it."

"I can understand. I'll bet all work and the school doesn't leave much time for your boyfriend?" he said.

"He's pretty busy himself. Right now, he is down in Virginia."

"Virginia? What is he doing in Virginia? I guess he travels a lot?"

"You could say that. He's in the Navy, and he's training right now. He joined up about six months ago, like a lot of the young guys are doing."

"Oh. So, I guess you don't get to see him too often?"

"Not much, and it looks like it is going to be even less. That's what was bothering me in the lunchroom the other day."

"You mean it wasn't because of me?" Lucas asked.

"No, it wasn't you, at least not all of it," she said. "Good lord, Lucas, believe it or not, the world does not revolve around you."

She continued, "I just received a letter from Mitch the day before, and he was telling me he was about to be deployed. He was concerned because he didn't know if they would let him come home before leaving. As it is, I haven't seen him in six months, and we thought he would be here soon, but I guess it's what the world hands you sometimes."

They continued to explore each other as the waiter arrived with their lunch. It was just burgers and fries, but it was nice to share lunch and conversation with someone genuine. Lucas's conversations with most women usually focused on getting them back to his apartment. This was a nice change. He found the conversation engaging, and they lost track of time. Cindy was an interesting person and had a lot to say. Mostly, he could see she was soft and gentle. She would look away thoughtfully as she reflected on life and her ambitions. The waiter handed Lucas the bill as Cindy watched.

She said, "I said Dutch!"

He looked at her, smiled, and left the money on the table.

Chapter 52

The following day, as Lucas approached his desk, he could hear his phone ringing. He grabbed the receiver with more enthusiasm than usual.

"Good morning, I have an assignment for you, and I think you will like it," George said.

"I'm ready for it, boss. What do I need to do?" Lucas had new energy. The day started well, and he had not felt this good in a long time.

George said, "There's a local war hero, Captain Thomas Peterson, returning from Germany, and I would like you to meet him at the airport. He was the American liaison working with England's Royal Air Force."

"When does his flight arrive?" Lucas asked.

"In about an hour, so you need to hustle it up," George said.

"Okay, Boss. I'm on it. I will stop by your office and pick up the details."

As Lucas walked to George's office, he remembered Cindy asking about this weekend. He didn't have much time, so he tucked the thought in the back of his head and hurried along. If he were lucky, he could make it to the airport in time. As Lucas walked past the copy area, Cindy looked up from her workstation. She waved, and Lucas returned the salutation. He was sure he would see her later in the afternoon.

Arriving at the airport, he ran to the gate to meet

Captain Peterson. Lucas saw him as he walked down the terminal dressed in civilian clothes. Easy to identify, he held a fierce look of confidence expressed on a chiseled face, short-cropped hair, and a muscular body. He expected a taller man, but his stride left little doubt of his ability as a warrior.

As he came into the open area beyond the terminal, Lucas approached him. "Lieutenant Peterson?"

He looked at Lucas. "Can I help you?"

"My name is Lucas Colby, and I'm with the *Early Register News,* and I am assigned to cover your story about Eagle Day."

They spent the next six hours reviewing every detail of his deployment.

Assigned as the American liaison working with England's Royal Air Force, he was involved with Eagle Day, marking the Luftwaffe offensive beginning against the RAF. The Germans had planned to cripple British defenses, clear the sky over southern England within four days, and eliminate RAF resistance. Because of Captain Peterson, the events of Eagle Day went strongly in favor of the RAF. The Germans lost 45 planes, the British lost only 13, and six pilots could return to their units and families.

Afterward, they bid farewell, and Lucas returned to his office. He worked on the story through the night, went home for a couple of hours of sleep, and arrived early to finish the story so he could get it to press. George reviewed the work and told him it was the best work he had seen in a long time.

Chapter 53

That afternoon, as he gathered his papers getting ready to leave, Cindy walked over to his desk.

"Trying to avoid me?" she said.

"No. Of course not. What do you mean?"

"You haven't been here, and I figured you made yourself scarce in that you are avoiding me," she said.

"No. In truth, George had me running all over town. I thought, at first, he was trying to keep me away from you, but I couldn't come up with any reason why. I figured it was just George trying to keep me busy. Anyhow, I had to interview this local war hero."

"Yeah, I know. I'm the one posting your column, remember?" she said.

"Well, yeah. So, you saw the story about Peterson?"

"Sure did. Nice work. I'll bet George was pleased."

"Yes, he was. Are you on your way out?"

"I'm out of here," she said. "But what about the weekend?"

"What about the weekend?" Lucas asked

"Are you busy?" She reminded him of the elevator ride.

"Ahh yes," he said. "So, what's up this weekend?"

"I am invited to a show with some friends. I'm the only one that doesn't have a date. I want to go, but I don't want to be the fifth wheel," she said to Lucas as they approached the elevators.

"This sounds like a date to me," Lucas said.

Cindy blushed. "Not really. I just don't want to be the only one there without someone, and you seem like such a nice person, and by yourself, so I figured we could go as friends."

"I see. I thought you had a boyfriend."

"I do, and he already knows. I talked with him last night and told him all about you and that we worked together. He's fine with it," she said. "Besides, it's not a real date. I just don't want to go alone."

"He's fine with it?" Lucas asked.

"Yes, he is fine with it."

"Okay. It's a date."

For the next couple of days, George asked Lucas to track leads and stories all over town. Friday afternoon, he arrived at the office, and as he sat down at his desk, his phone rang.

"Hey, it's me, Cindy. I was just seeing if you were here. Stay there."

Lucas watched her run down the hallway toward his desk. "In a bit of a hurry?" he asked.

"Well, yeah. Remember our date?"

"Tonight?"

"Well, no. It's for Saturday, but you need to know where I live, and I wanted to catch you before I left."

"Oh yeah. Your address," he said. "I guess that would help."

"Here. It's easy to find, and my phone number is there if you get lost. See you tomorrow!"

Lucas watched her as she hustled off to the elevator. He stood and turned to the window as she approached her car. She looked up at the window to see him watching her. She smiled.

After finishing a story, he decided that it was enough for one day, and besides, he was tired. It had been a long week. He walked past George's office toward the elevators.

"Hey, come in here for a minute," George said as Lucas passed by.

"What's up?"

"Come here for a minute. Have a seat."

Lucas sat down in the oversized chair in front of George's desk. "That was a great story about Peterson. I'm impressed, and the publisher is happy as well. He thinks it will increase circulation. I've meant to tell you, but the week got away."

"Thanks. I appreciate it," Lucas said. "Peterson is quite the hero."

George shuffled a few papers on his desk, seeming uncomfortable. "Anything wrong?" Lucas asked.

"No, not really," George said. "Well, yeah. I suppose there could be. I hear you have a date this weekend?"

"Date? I don't have a date. Damn, I don't even have a girlfriend."

"I'm talking about Cindy," George said.

"Oh, that," Lucas said. "It's not a date. She just needs someone to accompany her to a show. All of her friends are going, and it seems we have struck up a bit of a friendship. It's just something to do."

"Doesn't sound like it from what I am hearing," George said.

"George, she is just a friend, and even her boyfriend knows about this. It will be fine. Besides, I have no interest in any relationship."

"Really?" George asked. "What kind of guy would let his girl go out when he's away?"

"You know, I said the same thing but thought, what the heck. Let's get out of here, and I will buy you dinner," Lucas said.

"You? Buy dinner? I can't pass this up."

Lucas was looking forward to dinner and talking with George outside of the office. The restaurant was within walking distance of the office, and they sat at a corner booth overlooking the park.

"So, what's going on in your life, Lucas? How are the meetings going?"

"The meetings are great, George, and I have made a few friends. I am also working on a story," Lucas said.

"A story? You mean, like a book?" George asked.

"Exactly. You know, George, I have been through so much over my life, and someone at AA mentioned that writing a journal sometimes helps, releasing some of those demons tormenting the soul. I thought about it and started putting words on paper. Although some of it brings back memories I'd rather forget, afterward, it feels good that I let it out," Lucas said.

George sat back and lit his pipe. "That's interesting, Lucas. Are you working on anything else?"

"I am. I have several short stories that I have created over the past few months. Nothing serious, just things that pop into my head or I see on the street and think would be interesting. Some of it is lessons I've learned or about people I've met."

George puffed on his pipe. "Listen. Why don't you bring a few of your stories in on Monday and let me see them? I can't promise anything, but maybe I can get them into the Sunday section, sort of a human-interest type thing."

"That would be great, George," Lucas said. "Hey,

listen, I wanted to say thanks for being there for me and getting me through this. If it wasn't for you, I have no idea where I would have ended up."

George peered at Lucas over his thick glasses. "I don't want to think about where you would have ended up, Lucas. Just remember, there are people out there, and they love you."

Lucas thought about what George said. He knew of a time in his life when someone did love him. It seemed so long ago. A time when there was innocence, and everything felt right. A time where you saw past the imperfections and a time when you believed it would never end. Lucas didn't believe in much of anything anymore. Each day had its own set of rules, and each day was new. He sat preoccupied as memories of Savannah entered his mind. He thought of all things won and lost.

"You know, that reminds me, George, the bar where you found me; how did you know I was there?"

George smiled at his old friend and thought about the conversations he and Savannah had in the past.

"Let's just say a little angel told me."

Chapter 54

Lucas woke Saturday morning in his bed, not in the bed of a strange woman. He was also glad it was a bed and not an alley or a bench in the park. Life was good. He and George had a terrific night, a good dinner, and a great chat about the past and the future. Lucas was able to talk about Savannah. He said he heard she was singing somewhere in the city and had quite the following. Lucas was happy for her. It looked as though her life had turned around, and things were starting to turn around in his life.

Lucas went out and bought a new suit and headed home to get ready for the night out with Cindy. He arrived at her apartment early. He noticed she had a lovely little bungalow on the westside. It was not far from the office. He knocked on the door.

"Come on in. I'll be down in just a minute," she called from inside.

He entered her small two-floor apartment, finding it dressed in soft colors, decorated with flowers, and found a place to sit on the couch not occupied by a stuffed animal. While he waited, Lucas looked at the pictures of Cindy, her boyfriend, and family she placed on the table in front of the couch. It looked like she had a beautiful life with a lot of friends and good times. He heard her footsteps as she stepped down the stairs.

Her natural chestnut blonde hair flowed across her shoulders, framing her strong face reflecting her Eastern

European ancestry. Her green eyes and soft complexion highlighted the beauty she carried in a red gown that hugged her tall, slender figure. Lucas stood, took a deep breath, and handed her a small bouquet. This time, he bought them.

"Hey," Lucas said.

"You're too sweet, Lucas Colby," she said, looking at the flowers."

"You look smashing," Lucas said.

"You're looking good yourself, Mister," she said. "Nice suit. The tie sets off those emerald eyes of yours."

For a moment, Lucas had doubts. He wanted to turn and leave—not because he was doubtful of having a great time, but doubtful of the future. He was not ready for any relationship, and just one look at Cindy reminded him of how lonely life can be. Before he had time to think, Cindy grabbed his hand and said, "Ready to go?"

The local theater put on a play, and the proceeds would help support orphaned children. Afterward, Cindy wanted to go dancing. "There is a little place just a short way down the street, and they play great jazz. You do like jazz, don't you?" she asked.

"That would be nice."

It was a beautifully calm night. Lucas put his coat across her shoulders.

"Thanks. I was getting a little chilly," she said.

When they arrived, the place was quiet with only a few other couples. They found a small table away from the front door and ordered a light dinner. Lucas found himself running out of things to say after talking about the play, work, and general conversation.

"So, tell me about your boyfriend," he said.

"Mitch?"

"Yes, Mitch. I am having a difficult time understanding how he could let you out of his sight."

"Well, the truth is, he doesn't know. I just told him I was going out with friends."

"Ah, I see. You know—"

Cindy interrupted, "Lucas, please understand. I don't mean for this to be a big deal. If you are uncomfortable, I can understand, but I just wanted to get to know you. Let's just take it where it takes us. Okay?" She placed her hand over his and said, "It's okay."

Lucas took what she said for what it was worth. They spent the rest of the evening dancing and enjoying the music. They found much in common, and he felt comfortable talking with her. She had a gentle way about her as close to an angel as he could imagine. She was a little quiet at times but lively enough to keep you challenged and on your toes. She loved to dance. They stayed together until the place closed. The bartender had to interrupt their conversation to let them know it was time to go.

Lucas knew she had been teasing him all night with a bit of pull here and a tug there. She would dance close and hold tight when the music would slow.

"Let's walk," Lucas suggested.

He thought they should walk along Main Street in front of the shops, perhaps as a distraction. Cindy liked the idea of window-shopping. She stopped and looked in the windows at the dresses and mannequins.

They walked a little further, and she slipped her hand into his. Cindy stopped and turned toward Lucas. Stretching up as far as she could, she wrapped her arms across his shoulders and pulled Lucas closer. She kissed his soft lips with the care of a lover in secret. He returned the kiss with a pounding in his heart.

Lucas walked Cindy to her apartment door as she fumbled with her keys. After a quiet drive back to her apartment, he pulled into an open space on the street. Lucas placed his hand on her arm, and she leaned toward him with anticipation. Their heated lips met again with intention.

"I don't want this night to end." Cindy whispered.

"Cindy. We can't do this."

"But we can," she whispered.

Lucas held her for a moment. She felt good in his arms. Soft and fragrant, her body formed perfectly into his. It felt so natural, so easy. His hand slipped down her back. She kissed him as a woman would kiss her lover. He returned the passion only known once before in his life. He pulled away, leaving her wanting more. "No," he said and touched her lips with two fingers. "This is not right."

She pulled away and leaned her back against the doorframe. Her arms crossed in front of her, she turned her head. She looked deep into the eyes of Lucas with desire.

"Why does love play such tricks?" she asked.

Lucas smiled and reached for her hands. "I have learned two things. Love always surprises and, if true, will leave you thirsty for tomorrow."

"Tomorrow?"

"Tomorrow," Lucas replied.

"What are we going to do tomorrow?" Cindy asked.

"I hadn't thought about it," Lucas said. "How about I come by in the morning, and we go out for breakfast?"

"I still think it would be better if you stay tonight. Besides, it's starting to rain."

Lucas looked behind him at the street. A light mist fell, and the air was the smell of rain. "So, it has," he said as he motioned her toward her door. "Let me go, and I promise I will be here early for a wonderful day."

"That would be nice, and hurry back. My night will be lonely without you."

Chapter 55

Lucas awoke to the sounds of the street below his apartment window, hearing the neighbor yell about a barking dog. It was early, and he promised Cindy breakfast.

He arrived at her place and parked a block from her apartment. He bounded up the stairs to her apartment building, feeling like a teenager. Knocking on her door, he noticed someone in the building was already cooking breakfast. Cindy opened the door, and he found those terrific smells were coming from her kitchen.

"Hey. What's this all about? I was going to take you to breakfast."

"Yeah, I know, but I thought this would be nicer and more fun than some restaurant," she said as she wrapped her arms around Lucas and pulled him through the entryway.

"Have a seat and make yourself comfortable," she said as she walked into her kitchen. "I'll bet you are ready for some coffee."

Lucas followed her into the kitchen. "You bet I am." The bacon was cooking, and the aroma filled the air. "This smells great," he said. "Do you do this for all your friends?"

She laughed. "Sure do. Last week, I had George over."

"Did you."

She walked over to Lucas and sat on his lap. "Yup. Afterward, we made love for hours."

Lucas laughed. "Now that's funny."

"Why do you say that, Lucas Colby? Are you making fun of me? It could have happened, you know."

Lucas shook his head and continued to chuckle. "Not with George, and you better check your bacon."

"Why not? George is a very nice man."

"That he is. "

"So. Would it be so unusual that we may enjoy breakfast together?"

"You could, I suppose. But believe me, breakfast would be the only thing on his mind."

"You've known George for a long time, haven't you?"

"Yes. A very long time. George and I go back a long way."

"He's a good friend?"

"Yes. An excellent friend."

After cleaning up the dishes, they walked to the park and enjoyed the day together. It was getting late in the afternoon, and Lucas suggested perhaps they could have dinner tonight. Cindy agreed. "That's a great idea! I know the perfect place."

They walked back to the apartment, and Lucas unlocked her door. She stepped into the doorway and placed her arms on his shoulders.

"I had a great day."

"Me too," Cindy said. "Now go get dressed and be back here in an hour."

Lucas stopped by the store on the way back to his apartment and picked up a gift for Cindy. He stood at the counter of the store and looked inside the slender, black box. It contained a gold necklace with a small heart.

He returned to Cindy's place within the promised hour. As he approached her door, he thought about his future. He had given up on finding anyone to love. There were so many disappointments in his life; this just didn't seem real. He knocked at her door as the minutes passed, and he felt like it was his first date in high school.

The door opened wide, and Cindy looked him up and down. "Hey, handsome!"

"Not so bad yourself," he said. "If you are ready, we can go."

"Almost ready," Cindy said as she wrapped her arms around him. She pressed her soft lips against his. "Now, I'm ready, except I see you are hiding something."

"You got me, kiddo." Lucas handed Cindy the small box.

"For me?"

She opened the package. "Wow. That's beautiful."

She pulled the necklace from the box and turned around so Lucas could place it on her neck. She held her hair up, and he attached the clasp. Before she dropped her hair, he kissed the back of her neck.

After a night of dining and dancing, they stopped by a quiet little café across town for coffee. They walked along the river and sat on the bench at the park.

"What a beautiful evening," she said while pulling herself closer to Lucas.

"Not as beautiful as you, my love."

"Oh hush, Lucas. There's no need for you to try and sweet-talk me."

Lucas reached down to the flowers that surrounded the bench. He showed the blossom to Cindy.

"Do you know what type of flower this is?"

"I know it is pretty, and that's all a girl needs to know."

He laughed. "It's called an Amaranth. Poets say the blossom never dies. Let this flower always remind us, our love will never die."

Small conversations between two lovers with undiscovered passions; two hearts left alone in the night. Lucas drove Cindy back to her apartment, and they walked to the doorstep. Lucas placed his hand over hers, taking her keys, unlocking her door. He paused for a moment, not knowing what to say. She raised her head and gazed deeply into his eyes.

"This time," she said, "you stay."

The following day, Lucas awoke with Cindy's long, slender body lying across the bed with her head on his chest. He played with her chestnut hair as it fell around her soft shoulders.

He couldn't help but think back to the conversation he and Savannah had that first night; *if you believe the scotch is strong, wait until my shift is over*. He thought about how different Savannah was from Cindy. He remembered the time at her bar. *What are you doing here?* she had said. He thought about his heart condition. *You have a heart problem?* she had asked.

Cindy popped her head up. "I can hear your heartbeat."

Lucas, startled, said, "Well. That would be a good thing, would it not?"

"I suppose it would be." She jumped from the bed, "I'm going to take a quick shower." She paused and then added, "You can join me if you like."

Lucas admired her perfect-shaped stature and smiled as she left the room.

The water was warm and felt good as he stepped into the shower behind her. He held her across her stomach and pushed his hand gently across her soft skin. She turned, and he watched as she slowly rubbed his chest with the soft cloth. The water cascaded over her shoulders and fell between her breasts and down her flat stomach. Lucas kissed her above each eye, then her nose, and then pressed his lips against hers.

They stepped from the steamed waters, lips together in an embrace, heartbeats entwined; twisting as lover's passions rose to heights of rapture, faster and faster, until surrender, they lay together as the morning passed.

"I hate to say this," Cindy said as she turned toward Lucas.

"Say what?"

"I am hungry. Are you?"

Chapter 56

Days passed, then weeks, and it seemed like they had been together forever. His new career was moving in the right direction, and he had found a girl that may be the answer to all his questions. She was kind and giving. She was loving and strong. She was unlike anyone he had ever known.

He planned a trip to the coast to spend some time relaxing. He wanted to be away from the city and away from the newspaper. He asked Cindy to join him. They drove to a small beach cottage where they could just spend some simple time together. They walked on the beach, shared a bottle of wine, and enjoyed quiet evenings watching sunsets while holding hands.

"I think I'm falling in love with you, Lucas Colby," she said one evening as they walked the shoreline.

"Is that right," Lucas said, knowing he felt the same. He held her hands and softly kissed her lips while the water fell at their feet.

Lucas was a realist, however. He knew what was ahead, and it was Mitch. Cindy needed to decide, and she was confused.

When they returned home a week later, he dropped her off at her place. She checked her mail, and she found a new letter from Mitch in her mailbox. She sat on her couch, read the letter, picked up the phone, and called Lucas.

"Hello."

"Hey, it's me! Are you busy?"

"Not me. I'm just sitting here thinking about last week. Why? What's up?"

"Not much. I figured if you weren't busy, maybe you could stop by. I need to run some things by you."

Lucas could hear something else in her voice. "Sure, be there in about an hour." He hung up the phone and got dressed.

When Lucas arrived, she was sitting on the balcony overlooking the street. She jumped up, and before he knew it, she opened the door and gave him a big hug as if she hadn't seen him in a month.

He pulled back and said, "Hey there! It's only been a few hours! What would happen if you didn't see me all week?"

"Come in. Sit down. I need to talk to you."

He sat on the couch, and she curled up next to him.

"What's going on?"

She reached to the table to pick up an envelope and pulled out the letter from Mitch.

"Do you love me, Lucas? I mean, do you love me, Lucas?"

"More than anything," he said.

"Tell me again."

"I love you."

Cindy handed the letter to Lucas. "Mitch is coming home next week. A break before they deploy his unit."

"Oh, I see. What are you going to do?"

"That's the point. I don't know what to do. I can't very well tell him about us. I mean, I can't with his leaving and everything. It's not the right time. It's not the right thing to do. Oh my God," she said, placing her tearing face into her hands. "How can I love you both?"

Lucas knew it wasn't the right thing to do, and the timing could not have been worse. Everything seemed to be falling into place, he thought, but he could see the plight in her eyes.

He put his hand on her arm while trying to calm her fears and said, "Listen, I know this is a tough situation, but you need to spend some time with him so you know what to do."

Lucas was in love with a woman, and he knew this day would come, but he didn't care about Mitch. He didn't care about the feelings of a man he'd never met. He cared about Cindy, and he cared how he felt about her. He wanted to spend the rest of his life with her, and he remembered the conversations with George. *Leave it alone,* he had said. *Don't lead her on.* Lucas thought, *I'm playing a stupid game with someone's heart, and Cindy doesn't deserve this.*

"Listen," Lucas said. "You need to spend the time together. You need to understand where your heart is. If we are ever going to be at peace, he can't remain in some corner of your heart." He could see her decision would not come easy, and the last thing he wanted was to let her go or have her choose to stay with Mitch. "You need to know I will always be here regardless of your decision. I said I love you, Cindy, and I mean it. But if love means letting you go, then that's what I'll need to do."

Cindy couldn't look Lucas in the eyes. "I have to see him. It'll be all right. We will work this out."

Lucas could see her tremble with the burden ahead of her. Hidden secrets: lies within the heart are always the hardest, and Lucas knew this too well.

He could feel her heartbeat as she pulled him closer.

Her warm breath fell across his chest, and he stroked her soft hair.

"We'll work this out; don't worry," he said. "I'll see you Monday."

Chapter 57

The following week, Cindy decided to take a few days off from work. Lucas stopped by her apartment to check on her. Cindy greeted him at the door.

"How are we doing?"

"I'm okay, I guess," Cindy said with a slight shrug of her shoulders.

"Really? This is Lucas you're talking to."

"I decided that I am going to spend some time with Mitch while he is here."

"Sure," Lucas said, already knowing what the final answer would be. He tried to keep detached, but his heart was pounding, and he was scared, afraid of losing the one thing holding him together. Lucas wanted to hold her close. Rather than wrapping her arms around him, she folded them up across her, the embrace not returned. He kissed her forehead and told her he would always be just a call away.

"Trust your heart," he said.

As he walked away, he turned once more. She was standing in her doorway, staring downward as if in a trance. She folded her arms to her chest, and her fingers rubbed the heart on the end of the necklace. He turned and walked out of the door and to his car.

Over the next two weeks, Lucas buried himself in his column. He tried to write and keep focused. Sunday morning, he awoke to the ring of his phone. George invited him for dinner, and Lucas talked about work, old times, and most anything but Cindy.

"Hello?"

"It's just me!"

"Hey, Sunshine. What are you up to?"

"Not much. It looks like it's going to be a beautiful day, and I was thinking about a picnic at the park."

Lucas sat up in bed. "Picnic? Sure, why not? Let me get moving, and I will pick you up in a couple of hours?"

"Perfect," she said.

Lucas jumped into the shower, shaved, and blew out the door as his alarm was sounding. He stopped by the market, picked up a few things, called Cindy, and told her he would be there in ten minutes. She was waiting on the curb, basket in hand, when he arrived.

"Been waiting long?"

"Nope. I just stepped outside."

"I guess you're ready, then."

"You bet."

They drove to the park, and they spread a small blanket on the soft ground, enjoying the day while watching the Mallards on the lake and people walking their dogs. Lucas leaned back on a makeshift pillow, and Cindy sat up, looking over the lake.

"Mitch's will be gone for a while."

"I figured he would be about six months?"

"Yeah. He said he should be back in about six months."

"What are you going to do? What did you tell him?"

"He doesn't know," she said. "I think he thinks something, but he didn't say anything."

"It's best for now."

Over the next few months, Cindy and Mitch

exchanged letters. Sometimes, she would share the stories with Lucas; sometimes, she would keep them to herself. Lucas could see the torment she was going through. They would go to the shows, spend time at the beach, walk the city, and explore new places.

Monday morning, George called Lucas into his office.

"Have a seat," he said. "Listen, I know it's been a bit tough for you here, and I think you need a little time away to get your mind off of things."

"What does that mean?"

"I know about you and Cindy, and before you say something, I have known for quite some time. Don't get me wrong. I am not passing judgment. I think both of you need some time apart. She is confused right now, and neither one of you need to make a rash decision. Got that?"

"You're right, George. It has been a difficult time, and I am stuck right now. I just don't know what to do."

"Fine. Then this will be good for you."

"What's that?"

"I have an assignment I would like for you to take. It's in Hawaii. The Navy base in Pearl Harbor. Nothing is happening right now, and I think you will be safe. Our competition is sending their people over, and we need to be there as well. You know you are the right man for the job, and I can trust you will bring back the news like it is."

"Hawaii? That's a long way from home."

"Yeah, I know, but you need the space, and I need the story. Besides, it's cold and ugly here, and the weather there is warm and sunny."

"You're right. I need the space right now, and so

does Cindy."

Lucas walked to his desk, sad, yet he was surprised at the anticipation of going to Hawaii. He figured it would be good to put some space between them so they could figure this out. He called Cindy when he arrived home.

"Just me."

"Hi there, just me," she said. "What's up?"

"Oh, I don't know. Have you eaten yet?"

"Nope, just thinking about it."

"How about I swing by and pick you up. We can grab a bite a Lucille's Diner. Meet you downstairs in fifteen minutes?"

"Perfect timing, I am famished."

"Well, you're perfect. What can I say?"

"You're so silly. Get over here. I'm starving."

Arriving at Lucille's a short time later, they sat at the window. The tables were plain, holding napkins with a fork and knife. The salt and pepper stood at attention, along with a ketchup bottle at the end of the table. They sat across from each other, and Lucas looked into her eyes.

"George gave me a new assignment today."

"Really? He seems to be keeping you busy lately."

"Yeah, he likes to see me busy. This time, it's different, however."

"How's that?"

"I leave for Hawaii in two days."

"Hawaii? Why Hawaii?"

"What's wrong? What's wrong with Hawaii?"

"Nothing. You just caught me off guard, and that's so far away."

"It's not forever. I'll be back, I promise. It's only for

a couple of weeks."

"It's not that. I know you will come home. I just need you here."

"We will be fine. What happened to the happy Cindy I know and love?"

"More coffee?" The waitress stood next to them with a bored look on her face.

"Yeah, sure. Please."

She poured the black brew into their mugs and came back later with dinner.

The conversation was small as they ate their dinner. Cindy just picked at her meal, preoccupied with her thoughts. Lucas could see she was busy in reflection, and he kept quiet. During the drive back to the city, she was more subdued than usual.

Coming around the corner and arriving at Cindy's apartment, Lucas couldn't stand the silence any longer. "You okay?"

"I'm fine. I'll talk to you tomorrow. Goodnight."

Chapter 58

Arriving at his apartment, it was quiet and not lending to his mood. He readied for a night's sleep as he stretched out on his back in bed on the pillow with his arm under his head. Rest would not come, but he stayed motionless while thinking about everything they had said. Cindy's words kept running through his head. He stood to go to the kitchen as his phone rang.

"I can't sleep," she said.

"Yeah, me too."

"What are you doing?" she asked.

"Just laying here and staring at the stars outside my window."

"Listen. I'm not trying to hide anything. I wanted you to know."

"I never thought you were."

"I just didn't know what to say."

"About what?" he asked.

"Mitch is stationed in Hawaii for the next six months. I didn't know how to tell you earlier."

Lucas was surprised, and the thought made him feel uneasy.

"That's fine."

"Fine for you, perhaps, but I'm nervous about this."

"Cindy. There is no need to be nervous. Even if I see Mitch, he doesn't know anything about us other than we work together. Right?"

"No. He doesn't know anything, but you know everything."

"Don't worry. I doubt I will see him, and if I do, I will just make small talk. Okay, Sunshine?"

Cindy didn't know what to do about the situation other than to trust Lucas. "Okay. Try and get some sleep."

"I will. See you tomorrow?"

"Sure."

Lucas hung up the phone. He knew Cindy was worried, but he couldn't walk away. She couldn't walk away. He dozed off sometime later but awoke to the sound of a car door slamming shut outside his window. His first thought was Cindy, and he rose from the bed, hoping to see her coming up the walkway. She wasn't there.

He packed his bags for the long trip, arranged last-minute details with the landlord for mail, and all the other things in preparation for a long journey, while waiting for the phone to ring. That evening, he went out to eat alone. It was raining, cold, and a lousy night to be alone. He thought, *If she wanted to talk, she would have called. She knows I am leaving in the morning.*

When he returned to his apartment, he poured a glass of tea. The golden color played with his mind and replayed the warmth of scotch in his throat, but he knew just one would be one too many, and he had been through too much to step back now. He thought, *My love life may be screwed up at the moment, but I don't need to step back into a time I'd rather forget.* He sat in the chair on his balcony and watched the rain splash into the puddles below.

The next thing he heard was a horn blowing, waking

him as he sat in the same chair, still fully clothed from the night before. The airport taxi waited on the street below his window. Lucas yelled down from the balcony, "I am on my way."

He saw the driver flip the meter.

He grabbed his bags, looking at the silent phone. He shut the door behind him and ran downstairs. The trunk of the taxi was open, and he threw in his bags. Lucas said, "Concourse three."

Without words, the driver took Lucas to the airport. His mood was like the November weather, dreary and gray. He expected—hoped—to see Cindy at the airport, waiting and smiling. The girl at the ticket counter was nice and polite.

"Looks like you will be there a while, Mr. Colby," she said. "Business?"

"Yes. A couple of weeks. Business. I am going to write a story about our military base and men."

"So, you are a reporter?"

"Some people think so."

Lucas made his way down the terminal to the airplane. More people were on the plane than he expected, and George had reserved a first-class seat for him. It was going to be a long flight, and he was hoping to get a little sleep. It wasn't long after taking off before he dozed off.

Turbulence shook his seat, and he awoke to the pilot saying it would be a little rough but everything was okay. "Nothing serious," the captain reflected in his deep and comforting voice. Lucas asked the stewardess for a glass of water. He had a headache and dug into his briefcase for aspirin. When he opened the case, a paper fell out, and he picked it up. It was from Cindy. A short note, but a message just the same, and sometimes a few words are all you need.

Dearest Lucas,
I miss you already.
Love,
me.

Chapter 59

Lucas arrived at the *John Rodgers Airport* late in the afternoon. He couldn't wait to get off the plane. Entering the terminal, Lucas noticed a sailor holding a sign with his name on it. The sailor looked familiar to Lucas, and when their eyes met, Lucas remembered the pictures on Cindy's table at her apartment. He felt a pit in his stomach.

"Mr. Colby?" he said. His voice was uncompromising, as expected of one trained by the military.

"Yes, that's me."

"Mitch Ewing at your service, sir. I have your bags in the car, and we are ready to go when you are."

Lucas extended his hand and said, "Thanks for picking me up. I did not expect to see you."

"Yes, sir. The Commanding Officer of the Base, Captain Franco, asked if I wanted to volunteer."

"Do you always volunteer?"

"No, sir. I volunteered because you're Cindy's friend, and you both work for the same newspaper."

Lucas smiled. "I see. But can you do me a favor, Mitch?"

"Yes, sir. Anything you would like."

"Please, just call me Lucas. All this sir business makes me feel like an old man."

Mitch opened the door and then ran to the other side

of the car. As they drove off to the base, Lucas asked, "Do you like it here, Mitch?"

"It's not bad, sir. I mean, Lucas. The people seem nice when we are off the base and in town. But there is not a lot to do when we have any free time."

"Do you get much free time?"

"We spend most of our time just hanging out doing mostly nothing. That is until the C.O. comes up with something. We are here mostly to watch over the base."

"I see," said Lucas. Looking out the window of the car, he was preoccupied with the surrounding countryside.

The sun was bright, without a hint of clouding, not like the muted colors of the city. The ocean, azure blue with large crashing waves, pounded wide beaches.

"It is beautiful here," Lucas said. "I have never seen such beautiful water or such beautiful countryside."

Mitch agreed. "With clear skies, great surf, and the year-round sun, the beaches of Oahu are a real paradise. A lot of the guys spend liberty at the beaches surfing or snorkeling, and the water is always perfect."

Mitch explained that two volcanoes had created the island making a broad valley between them as they drove to the base, and Oahu had only two seasons: summer and summer. Lucas looked out over the land as they passed field after field of pineapple crops, but all he could think about was he was half a world away from home and Cindy.

"I guess it never snows here, eh, Mitch?"

"Not lately."

"Do the officers keep you guys busy around the base? What are you normally doing?"

"Not much. We have assigned duties, watches, and

such, but it's normally quiet. I've been able to write to Cindy and let her know what was going on. I guess that she didn't have time to write back and let me know you would be here."

"Oh, that. She knew I was going to Hawaii but didn't know you would be picking me up at the airport. She didn't even think we would meet up."

"This was a surprise for me as well. When I walked into the office this morning, the C.O. said he received a call from some guy named George with your newspaper. He asked that I meet you at the airport because we both come from the same area. I guess he felt it would make you feel more comfortable with this being your first trip to the island."

"Hmm. It's all beginning to make sense now," Lucas said.

"How's that?" Mitch asked.

"Nothing. I was just thinking out loud."

Lucas was beginning to see that George had his hand in things and meeting with Mitch was no accident. Lucas didn't want to dwell; afraid he might say something and give Mitch the idea that he and Cindy had something going on. He quickly changed the subject. "So, tell me, what made you join the Navy?" he asked.

"My dad was in the Navy and served in WWI. He was one of the fortunate ones and made it home safe. When it came my time, I didn't even think about it. I just signed up!"

"What about your dad?" Mitch asked.

"My dad?"

"I mean, did he serve?"

Lucas thought for a moment and recalled times long forgotten.

"Yeah. He served. A long time ago. He was a real hero."

"Wow. That sounds cool."

"What about high school, Mitch?"

"In high school, I was on the football team. I was the quarterback and had the chance to go onto college with a scholarship, but I chose to wait until I got back."

"How did you meet Cindy?"

"We grew up in the same neighborhood and attended the same schools. We have known each other almost all our lives. Did she tell you we are looking to get married as soon as I get out?"

"Yeah, she mentioned it. She is a nice girl."

"Yup. She sure is, and pretty, too."

Lucas agreed.

"How long will you be here?" Mitch asked.

"The plan right now is about ten days," Lucas said.

"That should be good," Mitch told him. "How about I take you on a tour of the base? I mean, if there is time, and the captain gives permission."

"That would be nice. I would like to see the island."

They arrived at the base, and Mitch took Lucas to the Headquarters building. Lucas noted the planes and ships on the base, the facilities, and the housing during the ride.

Mitch pointed to a building ahead on the left. "That's the Officers' Quarters. The Skipper asked that we put you up over there. It's a nice place and where we usually place any dignitary visiting us."

The three-story building ahead had windows on all sides and a walking path from the street that wound around a couple of outlying buildings along the front of the property. Coconut trees were abundant, and low growing foliage of local plants surrounded the building.

"It looks nice," Lucas said.

"We will go to Captain Franco's office first, and I will take your bags back and get you set up."

Not far from where Lucas would stay, he saw a building with few windows. Mitch pulled into a parking space in the front of the building.

"Here we are!"

Chapter 60

Lucas followed Mitch through the doorway and to the captain's office.

Captain Franco stood as he heard them enter the building.

"Welcome aboard, Mr. Colby."

"Thank you, sir. Thanks for having me here."

"Our pleasure. Can I get you a drink?"

"That sounds good. It's been a long trip."

"I am sure. Mitch, would you bring us some iced tea, please."

After a casual conversation, the captain suggested that Lucas head to the housing area where he would stay. Arriving at his room, he found his bags placed near the bed. Lucas unpacked his bags and put everything in the dresser's drawers at the foot of the bed. From the window, he had a good view of the base. He watched some of the maneuvers going on outside. The room was small, and the furnishing was sparse but comfortable. There was a chair in the corner and a small desk near the window. He sat by the window and wrote Cindy a short note.

Dear Cindy,

The space between us is farther than I can reach, but your heart remains in mine. How I wish this trip were over so I could once again hold you close. It is beautiful here, but nothing compares to what I am missing at home.

Love, Lucas

After Lucas finished his note to Cindy, he slipped it into a small envelope and carefully wrote her address on the front. Soon after, there was a knock, and Lucas opened the door to find one of the men with a cart.

"Captain Franco sent this over," he said.

Lucas stood back, and the man rolled the cart inside the room. He saw a bottle of wine, crackers, and assorted cheeses. There was a note from the captain. He said a car would be out front at six to take Lucas to dinner with the captain at his residence.

The sailor turned to the door to leave; Lucas picked up the envelope from the table. "Is there a place where I can mail this letter?"

The sailor looked at the envelope and said, "I will be happy to see that it is mailed for you, sir. We have a mail facility here on the base."

The following morning, Mitch arrived early to meet Lucas at the apartment. They spent time touring the *USS Arizona, Detroit,* and *California.* Lucas was impressed with the fighting men and their machines. He could see how proud they were to serve their country, and in talking to them, he could hear how they were ready to give their lives if needed to protect our freedom. He could also see how young the faces were of these boys, so far away from home. The November weather was a pleasant surprise. Back home, it was snowing and cold, but here, it was warm and balmy.

Lucas said to Mitch, "What a paradise this place is. If you have to serve your country, this is the place."

Lucas and Mitch walked along the deck of the *USS Detroit* and approached an area with a sailor viewing the horizon through a telescope.

"What are you looking at, sailor?" Lucas asked.

Without turning from the scope, he said, "Broomsticks, sir."

"Broomsticks?" Lucas asked.

Mitch chuckled and explained, "Periscopes from submarines."

"You mean enemy submarines?" Lucas asked.

"Sure do. You'd be surprised what we see," Mitch said.

During the next several days, Lucas toured the base, commissary, and housing for the troops. Lucas and Mitch returned to port that afternoon, and with a few of the other men, they went on one last liberty into Honolulu before he had to leave. The Marines were on shore patrol, and Lucas stopped to interview some of them. He could see they created makeshift foxholes along the coastline, and their machine guns were mounted and placed.

"Are the Marines planning on keeping these bunkers manned?" Lucas asked.

"No, sir," the young man responded. "We are told to set up as a normal maneuver. We will be here for about a week and then tear down."

"Good. So, you aren't doing this because you think there's a problem?" Lucas asked.

"No, sir. This is only practice."

Ten days came before Lucas knew it, and it was the end of the tour. He thanked Captain Franco for his hospitality and told Mitch he enjoyed his visit. The next morning came early, and Lucas knew it would be a long flight back. Navy pilots flew him to Hawaii, and he transferred to a civilian flight to the west coast. As he sat down in his seat and reviewed his notes, he couldn't help but think of Cindy and Mitch. Lucas enjoyed the journey and thought Mitch to be a great guy. He could see that Mitch loved Cindy very much, and the discovery weighed heavy on his mind. Still, Lucas was anxious to get back to New York and see Cindy again.

Chapter 61

The plane taxied to the runway, and the engines started to whine. As the aircraft reached a level altitude, climbing above the scattered clouds, the engines quieted. Lucas looked out the window and back over the island. From the window, he watched the coastline and the waves break against the shore. Slowly, the view turned to a deep ocean blue, and the outlook from the window appeared suspended in time as the plane climbed toward California. Soon, the flight took him above the soft white cloud cover, and all Lucas could see were puffs of cloud tops. He put his head back on the seat, and the hum of the engines lulled him to sleep.

Lucas began to dream of a time in the park with Cindy.

He pushed her on a swing, and it started to rain. They ran to a gazebo in the center of the park surrounded by trees in bloom with delicate white flowers. Soaked to the skin and cold, they huddled close to each other.

"What kind of tree is this?" she asked.

"It's a Crab Apple," Lucas answered.

"What a terrible name, but the flower smells so sweet."

"There is another name."

"What is it?"

"It is called the Tree of Love."

"Oh Lucas, you're so full of it."

"No. It's true. The ancient Celts associated the apples with a tradition of finding future lovers, and there is a poem called, Into Love's Furnace I am Cast."

Lucas stood on a stage with one hand over his heart and his arm pointing toward the sky, trying to repeat the poem.

"It goes something like this. The tree of love, its roots hath spread. Deep in my heart, and it rears its head. Rich are its fruits, the joy they dispense. Transporting my heart, with ravishing sense. In love's sweet swoon to thee, I cleave—Something, something."

In what seemed like minutes passing, Lucas awoke to the resonant sound of the captain's voice on the overhead speaker announcing they were in the final approach of the Los Angeles airport and would be landing soon. He stretched his arms and yawned, wondering how time passed so quickly. Oddly, he felt rested and comfortable.

He arrived at the gate and strolled down the terminal to catch the connecting flight. There was plenty of time before the next flight, so he called Cindy at her apartment. There was no answer. He sat near the gate and reviewed his notes for the story. He thought about Mitch. He thought about his love for Cindy and knew in his heart that it wasn't right. The guilt of the relationship was tearing at him, but he knew it had to end. He heard someone announce the plane was boarding. He climbed the steps and entered the plane. An older man sat in the seat next to him.

"Good afternoon," Lucas said. "It looks like we are partners for this flight."

The man returned the salutation and introduced himself. "My name is Henry Morgan. Are you headed home?"

"Yes, I am. I just flew in from Pearl Harbor."

"Pearl Harbor? How interesting. Hawaii is a beautiful place."

"Yes, it is," Lucas agreed. "And it's a lot warmer than New York."

The plane began to taxi, and Lucas realized he had not introduced himself. "I'm sorry. I was lost in our conversation. My name is Lucas Colby."

"Oh, that's okay," Henry Morgan said. "I'll bet you are tired from the long flight. All is forgiven."

"Thank you for understanding." With that, Lucas settled into his seat and asked the stewardess for coffee. He opened a book and tried to read, but his mind was preoccupied.

"Everything okay?" asked Henry Morgan.

"I think so."

The man reminded Lucas of Charlie Leland, and he thought back to the days at the bar. He remembered Charlie as a good man. He thought of the night he met Savannah and how their lives took a wrong turn. He thought about Cindy and everything else bringing him to this stage of his life.

"Are you from New York, Mr. Morgan?"

"No. California. Born and raised."

"I see. Is this your first time to the city?" Lucas asked.

"Yes, it is. It's my first trip outside California. My niece is getting married, and I promised to give her away. She moved many years back after her parents died. Are you married, Mr. Colby?"

"No. I was once. To a beautiful woman, but that was a long time ago."

"You seem to have a heavy mind. Would you like to talk?"

Lucas chuckled. "Now you are going to tell me you're a psychologist?"

Morgan chuckled back. "No. I am but a poor preacher. But maybe I can help."

"You're very perceptive, Mr. Morgan. I find it interesting we happen to be sitting together."

"I can tell you what I have learned in my years, Lucas Colby."

"What is that?"

"Few things happen by chance."

"How's that?" Lucas asked.

"It's like this. I have long believed we are all part of one consciousness. In other words, there is a greater power above all of us that guides our life."

"You mean God?" Lucas asked.

"Well. That's what I call it, but I have been around long enough to know people have different views. Right or wrong, sometimes that's just the way it is."

"So that is what you mean by consciousness?" Lucas asked.

"That's it. I think God, or this consciousness, lives inside each of us and brings people, situations, and things together. The challenge we have is we have to stop and listen to our inner voice inside all of us."

"An interesting theory," Lucas said. "You're telling me a man, or woman, needs to listen to their inner voice?"

"That's pretty much it. Too often, people only listen to themselves, and that is when they find themselves in trouble. Look at it this way. In tribal times, the people would listen to the advice of the elders. They had the experience and knowledge of understanding. When there was a problem, the people went to the elders, and the elders gave them the answer."

"So, people get into predicaments because they listen only to their voice," Lucas said.

"Exactly."

"That may explain how I am where I am today."

"It could," said Morgan.

"Well then, tell me, preacher. Can a woman love two men equally? I mean at the same time."

"I suppose she could, just as a man could love two women. But you can only marry one of them."

"Yes. I know."

"So, is that your quandary?"

"Well. Yes. Among other things," Lucas said. He was beginning to realize the only person he ever listened to was himself. "I know this girl back home. Her boyfriend, whom she has known since childhood, is in the Navy. I met her at work, and everything started as friends. The next thing I know, I am head over heels in love with her."

"Let me guess. Her boyfriend is in Pearl."

"Yes, and that's part of the problem. At first, I thought I had it under control, only to meet up with him and discover that he is a great guy. Now, I feel worse than ever."

"I see. This could be a problem. Here is my take on things. Mind you, I am not an expert, but maybe this will help."

"I'm willing to listen, so please move ahead."

"Does this girl love you?"

"She says she does."

"Do you love her?"

"Yes, I do."

"Then you have to do the hardest thing you will ever have to do."

"Let her go?"

"See? You were listening to that voice inside of you and didn't even know it. Letting her go and letting her make her own decision is the only way you will ever live in peace."

Lucas relaxed in his seat and thanked the preacher for the advice and for listening to his story. Mr. Morgan dozed off, and Lucas sat alone for the remaining flight. They arrived in New York shortly afterward.

Lucas wasn't in a hurry as he walked down to the baggage pick-up area. He couldn't help but wish he would find Cindy waiting. He picked up his bags and caught a cab for the ride home.

Looking out the cab window, Lucas saw a light rain falling, adding to the dismal day. He thought about the cold of late November and the warmth of Hawaii with December around the corner. He thought about Cindy and her chestnut hair, her long slender body, and the graceful way she moved when she walked. He thought about how smooth she moved when she danced in his arms and how softly she moved when they made love. The rain reminded Lucas of that time in the park and the dream he had on the plane. Cindy had laughed at the playfulness. She reached her arms up to him, and Lucas fell into the arms of her love.

"Well, it's something like that," he'd said.

"That was sweet, my love, and I believe you meant it from your heart."

"Of course I did. Where else would I pull those words from?"

It was spring, and the blossoms from the trees in the park fell around them. They kissed and laughed on a wet afternoon holding each other close, trying to stay warm.

He missed her, and his heart ached.

Chapter 62

The cab pulled up in front of his building, bringing him back to a world where he didn't know if he wanted to live any longer. He paid the driver, grabbed his bags, and carried his tired butt to the front door. Opening the entrance to the apartment, it was as he expected. The small space radiated depression, sadness, and emptiness. The white walls were dull and didn't smile as they once did. There was no joy in coming home. A layer of dust cascaded its presence over the furniture, and the drapes hung as if lonely and with their eyes shut, covering the solitary window overlooking the cold, wet street below. He dropped his suitcase on the bed and remembered his last night with Cindy. Lucas stood in front of his dresser and stared at his face through the mirror. He could see a reflected image, not of himself. This man was sullen and gray. His reflection revealed a disheveled man with dark circles laid heavily under bloodshot eyes. He was exhausted. It had been a long, lonely, and arduous trip.

He walked back to the front room and collapsed onto the couch. His hand slipped between the cushions where he found an old bottle of scotch welcoming him back to this prosaic square. The poison called to him like an old friend. He twisted the top off and put the bottle to his lips. He felt the liquid surge through his body, and it felt good. There was a warm feeling in his throat as it slid across his lips, onto his tongue, then settling in his gut like a burning fireplace on this soggy and bitter afternoon. He sat crumpled on his couch, considering his options. He reached for the telephone, changing his mind. Speaking aloud, he said, "Should I call her? Should I wait for her to call me?" Back and forth, he spoke as if someone were listening, as if he were losing his mind. He conceded, but he didn't know if he won or lost his argument. "She knew when I was coming back," he said. "If she wanted to call, then she would have called. It's as simple as that." Lucas relished the last few drops from his discovered treasure, and he fell asleep.

A ringing phone jarred him from slumber. The first thought in his foggy head was it was Cindy.

"Hello."

"Hey, Lucas. George here. You made it back, eh? Good deal! I'll bet you have some great stuff to talk about!"

George's cheery voice was not what Lucas wanted to hear. He tried to be cordial.

"Uh, yeah, George. It's good to be back, but I can tell you it's a lot warmer in Hawaii. But, yeah, I got some good stuff. I think you will like it."

"Sounds great," George said. "How about I come by, and we go get something to eat?"

"Why not."

Lucas was about to hang up the phone when he heard a knock at the door.

"Hang on, George. Someone's knocking."

Lucas opened the door, and she looked up at him. He placed the receiver back on the phone after telling George he would see him tomorrow.

"Hey," he said, wanting to hold her close.

"Can I come in?" she asked. Lucas could hear a

hesitation in her voice.

"Are you kidding? I was thinking of how nice it would have been for you to be here when I came home."

Cindy stepped through the doorway, and once inside, she held Lucas close.

"I missed you so much." She buried her head against his chest. "I can't believe we are finally standing here together again. It feels like it has been a thousand years."

Lucas pulled her closer and said, "I know what you mean. It's like it's a dream."

They sat down on the couch, and Lucas started to talk, to tell her everything. Hawaii, the flight, the stewardess, and Mitch. She placed her finger on his lips.

"Shhh. It's been a long time," she said in a whisper. "Too long."

She leaned toward Lucas and pressed her warm, soft lips to his. He closed his eyes and placed his hand around her head with his other arm tightly held across her back. Her breasts pressed softly against his chest. She pulled Lucas closer as they turned toward the bedroom. Lucas stood in front of her while she slowly unbuttoned his shirt and gently pushed him back onto the bed. They tangled their embrace as two mislaid souls gone astray united in the twilight of the evening. The moon glistened through the window, spreading a band of light across the bedroom, reflecting her silhouette against the wall. Lucas watched her in the mirror above his dresser. Her chestnut hair cascaded across her arched back as she surrendered her pleasure with each reverberation of passion.

Entwined within each other's arms, as a vine winds a tree, Cindy stroked the hair across his chest, and in a whisper, she asked, "Do you love me, Lucas Colby?"

And he held her as if his world would end.

Chapter 63

The night passed too quickly, an interlude in a life on the precipice of another abandoned heart. His confused thoughts left him puzzled, not knowing if she would stay or go. His heart knew the answer, and as the glow of the sun replaced the darkness, as morning crept through the window signaling a new day, he believed this lie he'd created within his heart was all he had left.

Lucas reached across the bed, hoping to touch the love of his life only to find emptiness and quiet. He opened his eyes to see Cindy sitting across the room on a chair next to the window. A gray blanket wrapped her shoulders, protecting her from the slight chill in the room. He could see her deep in thought as she looked through the window at the street below. He watched a single teardrop slip from the corner of her eye, downward across her delicate skin.

Is it joy this tear carries? he thought. *Please let this be a joyful tear,* he prayed. This drop of moisture held a secret as the morning sun streamed across her gentle face. The moisture on her cheek reflected the touch of the morning as she turned her head toward her lover.

"Hey," she said as she stood and stepped toward the bed.

Lucas could see she had dressed and was leaving, Knowing the answer, he asked, "Are you okay?"

"Yeah, I'm good," she said as she sat on the bed next

to Lucas. "But it's time. I have to go."

She touched his bare chest, leaned over, and kissed Lucas once more. Her eyelashes brushed his cheek; her long hair fell across him. Cindy lay motionless across his chest and wrapped within his arms one more time. He could feel her warm breath and smell the scent of her hair. He could feel his heart beating, breaking. His hand slipped from hers as she stood to walk away.

"Wait a minute," Lucas said while climbing out of bed. "Let me get up."

"No," she said. "Stay. I can't do this if you follow me."

Lucas could tell by the tone in her voice he need not move. He leaned back against the headboard and kept silent, listening to the click of the heels of her shoes as they moved across his wooden floors. He heard the latch click, then the door closed. He jumped out of bed, ran to the window, and watched her as she opened the door of her car.

"Look up, look up, please look up just once," he whispered, hoping she would look at him just once more, knowing if she did, she would be back.

The car started, and he watched her drive away as he leaned outward through the window opening until he could no longer see her car.

He turned and sat on the chair, holding her warmth and scent, breathing deep, and wrapped himself in the gray blanket. He could feel her presence in the room as he hung his head. A small envelope on the nightstand against the solitary lamp drew his attention. Inside, he found a small card with a picture of a flower.

Dearest Lucas,
Our love is like the Amaranth. Let this flower remind

us of our love. Think of me often, as I will think of you. Each time it is warm, each time it is cold, and each time it rains, our thoughts will be one. Remember our last night in your heart, and I will never forget you in mine. Our night will remain everlasting. Love, Cindy

Chapter 64

Monday came early. Lucas didn't know how he was going to handle seeing Cindy at work when he arrived. Like a schoolboy on his first day of class, he stood at the window overlooking the parking lot below, watching each car arrive, waiting for a chance to see her again. He heard someone approach him. He turned, and his heart jumped.

"What are you doing?"

"Hey, George. Good morning. Just drinking my coffee and checking the weather."

"I see," he said. "You know, she gave her notice last Friday."

"Last Friday?" Lucas replied as if he didn't know George's indication.

"You know what I mean, Colby."

Lucas lied and pretended he knew. "Oh. That. She told me she gave her notice."

George was concerned for his old friend. Lucas was never able to handle being alone very well, and George knew it.

"Are you going to be okay, pal?"

Lucas could feel his eyes beginning to well up. "No. No, I will not be okay, my friend. Nevertheless, I suppose I will get over it, and don't you worry about me, George."

Lucas knew in his heart that Cindy had made the

right choice.

The week passed like any other, and Lucas settled into the routine of reporting the news. He was looking forward to a quiet weekend to sort his thoughts. Sunday morning, Lucas awoke, walked into his kitchen, and made coffee. He flipped on the radio to start the day.

The NBC network was broadcasting Sammy Kaye's Sunday Serenade with Sammy and his Orchestra. Just as the program was about over, it was interrupted. There was a news bulletin about a Pearl Harbor air bombing.

Lucas heard Robert Eisenbach speaking with someone on the phone. It sounded like he was at the base. The person said, "There was an air raid. One of the strafing planes went by our ship, and I found myself staring at the Japanese pilot who looked right at me. I knew this wasn't normal because the planes approach slowly in practice runs when our guys do this. This plane flew by at top speed and dropped a torpedo directly at us. He then disappeared in the distance, but I could see the meatball on the side of his plane. It was a Jap for sure. Being a pointer on the 6-inch guns, my duty was to go down into the magazines to get anti-aircraft ammunition up to the machine guns. It didn't take long for us to fire back." The announcer interrupted, "With two raids already under their belt, the *Detroit* was credited with three kills."

Lucas grabbed his pants and shirt. He called Cindy, but there was no answer. He drove to her apartment. He knew she would be worried about Mitch. He knocked on the door, but there was no response. He turned and leaned on her door, wondering what to do next when the neighbor across from Cindy's apartment, Mrs. Pen, opened her door.

"You are looking for Cindy?" she asked.

"Yes, Mrs. Pen, I am. Have you seen her?" Lucas asked.

"You're Lucas, aren't you?"

"Yes, I am."

"Cindy used to talk about you all the time. She was a confused young woman. It looks like the Japanese have attacked Pearl Harbor. Did you hear about that?"

"Yes, I heard of the air attack, and it was one of the reasons why I came by."

"She asked me not to say anything. She doesn't want you to know, but she has moved to Ohio."

"Ohio?"

"I think she said she has some family there," she responded.

"I see. Well, thank you, Mrs. Pen. I appreciate your letting me know."

Lucas turned to walk away. "Doesn't she know someone in Pearl Harbor?" Mrs. Pen asked.

"Don't we all?" Lucas said.

Chapter 65

As time passed, Cindy became a distant memory. A deep ember of remembrance locked inside a heart never forgotten and never held again. Lucas thought of her often, as he thought of Savannah. Two women, two loves, both lost. He thought it odd the memories were happy when sadness and turmoil sometimes invaded his thoughts. He was alone again, and it seemed it was the hand dealt for him.

Months passed, and Lucas settled into a routine. His life was as he believed it should be. He followed Savannah's career as she traveled across the country and recorded new songs. He would listen to her on the radio.

Cindy and Mitch married not long after Lucas last saw her. He heard they had a son and moved south. He was happy for them and believed she was happy as well. His work became his life as his writing expressed his past and future. He published his first work in 1942. His recognition among his peers grew, and he found Charlie's was still there. The scenery had changed; the gambling was gone, as were the chippys, their rooms, and the culture they represented. Respectability was in order. In her wisdom, Harriet was in charge, and she expanded the operation to include dining as Charlie's became the hangout for many other writers. Lucas arrived one afternoon.

"Well, my eyes be blinded! It's Lucas Colby in the

flesh!" Pete cried out as Lucas walked into the room.

"Lucas Colby?" said Harriet. "I heard the man was dead and gone."

Lucas laughed. "Only partly true, my friends. The Lucas Colby you knew is dead and gone. The new Lucas Colby stands before you, asking for forgiveness."

Harriet swung her arms around Lucas. "There is nothing to forgive you for, Lucas. We are just happy to see you. Come and sit with me and tell us all that has happened in your life."

They sat at a booth, and Pete brought sandwiches. "Something to drink, Lucas?" Pete asked.

"Water is fine, my friend."

"Water, you say? And a wee bit of scotch?"

"Not for me, Pete. I haven't touched the stuff in a long time."

"Probably a good thing, eh Lucas?"

Lucas nodded. "Yes. A good thing."

Harriet asked a million questions, avoiding the mention of Savannah. She remained in close contact with her, and the truth was, if not for Savannah, Charlie's would have closed long ago.

"I heard you have become quite the writer," Harriet said.

"Is that what people are saying? " asked Lucas. "I do have two books published and a couple more in the works. You know, it's interesting when you think about it, Harriet."

"How's that?"

"My life and how it has worked out."

"What do you mean, Lucas?" she asked

"When I lived my life, moving through it, it never made any sense. There were things, people, put into my path to guide me and change me. But now, looking back, I see how the pieces of the puzzle fit together. All of the challenges, good times and bad, the ups and the downs, have brought me to where I am today. They are there to keep me on the right track. Can you understand what I am saying?"

"So, you're saying the past is why you are here, and everything that has occurred was supposed to happen?" Harriet asked.

"To an extent, I suppose. Savannah always said that life is a journey toward a destination; if we listened to the world around us, our providence would lead us. I have found that as humans, our minds and our souls connect in one way or another. Looking back over my life, I have concluded that people came into my life for a reason. Their visit may have been for a short while, or perhaps a lifetime. They come in and out of your life at different times, acting as a boundary, something to keep you moving in the right direction. When you come to understand this influence, you will know what to do. I have discovered that when someone comes into your life, it's for a reason and usually to meet a subconscious need."

"That's quite a discovery," Harriet said.

"I can understand your doubts, Harriet. The truth is, some people never experience this and go through life just fine. I think they are the fortunate ones, the old souls; they are our guides placed on this earth. And if you study your past, things begin to add up; to make sense."

"How's that?"

"Look at my upbringing, for example. Alcoholism killed my father, and yet I ended up working at a bar. If I had listened then, I would have heard the message.

Consider my mother's life. With all the challenges she had, she always thought of me first. I couldn't see that in my youth. My mother was always quoting her Bible, and her favorite verse was, 'In all your ways acknowledge him, and he will make your paths straight.' It took years and a lot of head pounding, but I believe I have come to understand what she meant, or should I say, what the words of the Bible meant."

"What does it mean?"

"I think it means, if one chooses not to listen, they will repeat the same mistakes; eventually, all your support is gone, leaving you to stand on your own. As a result, your inability to listen to those signs around you, you hit rock bottom. I can tell you; I have hit bottom more than I want to admit."

Lucas reflected for a moment and continued, "How did I find Charlie? I searched for work from the time I left Ohio until I reached New York. I tried the Army, they wouldn't have me, and I tried almost every place on the street until a little sign stuck on a door flapped in my face. Even though Charlie gave me work, he tried to change my job. It was because of Charlie that I finished college. Then there was Savannah, and if it weren't for finding Charlie, I would have never met her. She came into my life, and I just didn't listen. As a result, I lost her, I lost my business, I lost everything I worked for, and I hit rock bottom."

Harriet took his hand in hers and said, "And you have survived, Lucas. You have changed your life."

"I have done nothing but listen and look back over my life, Harriet. It took a long time, but the message finally got through."

"A message from God, is that what you are telling

me, Lucas?"

"I can't say it's God or what, but it is whatever you believe in that guides your journey. I think it's different for each of us. Whatever it is, it places a person, or sometimes an incident, into your life to redirect your journey. The person may assist you through a difficult time or provide you with guidance and support; they may even save your life. The critical thing to understand is, they are a vehicle guiding you physically, emotionally, or spiritually. They arrive at your life at the right time, and they are there for the reason you need them to be there. You only need to see it and surrender yourself.

It is like when George came back into my life. If it hadn't been for him, I would be dead by now."

Harriet sat back and took a deep breath. "That's a helluva story, Lucas Colby."

"I think it is more than a story, Harriet. I think Savannah and all the others were the old souls I mentioned. I guess Savannah knew, and she was my soulmate, my ultimate guide in this life.

Harriet was silent for a moment, then said, "I think you have become a philosopher."

"Perhaps," Lucas said. "What I have become is wiser in listening to life's lessons and allowing its grace to guide me rather than me trying to guide myself."

"Its grace?"

"Grace, spirit, God—it's something talking to each of us. Some call it consciousness."

"I never quite thought of life in that sense. You're telling me that you quit trying to make life what you wanted and accepted life as it is?"

"What I am saying is one has to stop and listen. Too often, we rush through life and miss important things. I have learned that your life must be a journey of learning and teaching along with giving. For too long, I thought only of Lucas Colby. I was the only one that mattered. I had everything; success, money, a beautiful wife, but I never listened. With that, I lost everything I loved. Then my life changed. Nevertheless, when I thought I had it under control, I moved back into my thoughts and tried to control my direction. I learned, once again, by losing what was dear to me, that I was not in control and life is more significant than I am."

"That's what I call a journey if there ever was one," Harriet said, leaning back in the booth. "Well, regardless. I'm glad you are back."

"Me too," said Pete, who was standing behind the bar.

"You know, Pete, you remind me of a young man that worked behind that bar at one time."

"I do, do I?"

"Yeah. I forget his name. But I do remember he was much better looking."

"Aye," Pete said. "And quite the ladies' man, and so I am if you listen to the legend."

Lucas turned to Harriet. "Speaking of a lady's man. That reminds me of a cute auburn-haired beauty I used to see around this place."

"Do you want to go there, Lucas?" Harriet asked.

"Harriet, that was a long time ago, and she is out of my life. I mean, I have followed her career, and it looks like she did precisely what she said she would do. For that, I am proud of her, but I have not spoken to her in almost three years. It's over, and I know it's over."

"You think it is?"

"Of course it is. I didn't treat Savannah right, and I

would not blame her if she never spoke my name again."

Harriet smiled at Lucas and patted his hand. Struck odd by her reaction, he didn't understand her silence.

"You've got to tell him," Pete said.

Lucas looked at Pete standing behind the bar and, for the first time, noticed a picture of Savannah on the wall behind him. He stood and walked closer to read the writing. Across the image, it read, *I know you will come back to me.*

He turned and looked at Pete, who in turn looked at Harriet.

"She's waiting," Harriet said. "She knew one day you would walk through those doors and asked me to place the picture here so you would see it."

Lucas smiled and dropped his head, staring at the worn floors he used to mop for Charlie Leland.

"My life has been so many places," he said. "I have done so many wrong things. I don't deserve her."

Harriet placed her hand onto his. "Everyone deserves a second chance."

Lucas chuckled. "Second? I wish it were only a second chance, Harriet. You don't know how often I have thought of Savannah. You don't know how much I have missed her. I just can't take the chance of destroying everything all over again."

"Lucas, you said that this grace put people in your life to guide you. Do you think you ended up at Charlie's by chance?"

"I don't think I was lead here so I could be with Savannah, if that's what you mean."

"Lucas. I told you long ago. Savannah knows you better than you know yourself. She has always known the paths you would take."

"Lucas, you don't get it, do you?" Pete interrupted.

Lucas could hear Pete's voice tone change, harsh but poignant. He was disturbed like a father would be with a stubborn child. Lucas, confused and not understanding, lashed out toward his friend.

"Don't get what?"

"Look at the picture, Lucas," Harriet said. "There is the grace. I don't know a lot, but I can tell you this: Savannah was not brought into this place all those years ago by accident. She is your grace. She has never given up on loving you and watching over you all these years."

Lucas walked around and noted the other pictures of writers and poets covering the wall.

"All of these people have been here," he said.

"Yes, and many times. That is what I am trying to tell you. This is your legacy. Look at it. Through all the trials you've been through and all the jobs you've had, what was your dream?"

"I have always wanted to be a writer," he said while looking at the walls filled with photographs.

"Exactly. And long ago, when Charlie asked you what you wanted to do with your life, what did you tell him?"

"I told him I wanted to be a writer."

"And because of your past, you were lead here and found Charlie. He brought you in and taught you the business and then handed it to you so you would stay."

"That he did."

"Look back, Lucas. All of this has happened in your life, and it has brought you here again."

"How did Savannah know?" Lucas asked.

"Maybe she just understands. Maybe she's the old soul."

Chapter 66

More went on in a life full of tragedy and misgiving, of lies kept and promises broken. Lucas had lived an imperfect but full life bringing him back to a perfect full circle. This time, however, he knew how to handle it. He wasn't sure he wanted to interrupt Savannah's life again. He decided to wait. Monday, he returned to his office, settling back into a routine. Before going to his desk, he stopped by the break room. He could smell the aroma of fresh coffee. He pulled a mug from the cabinet and poured. Leaning against the counter, he looked at the chair where Cindy had sat and thought about their first confrontation. *Madman*, he thought. Perhaps she was right, and he was crazy. He thought back to all the times, good and bad. He tried to understand why all the people he loved, all the people he had ever known, came into his life and now were gone. He found himself alone again, at a crossroad. It seemed his life had been nothing but crossroads with him having to decide which way to turn. George walked over and interrupted his thoughts.

"Good morning Mr. Colby. How are you today?"

"You're in a cheerful mood this morning."

"That I am. When you are settled, can you come by my office for a moment? I have an assignment I believe you will enjoy."

"Sure," Lucas said. "Give me about ten, and I will be over."

George walked back to his desk, picked up the telephone receiver, and made a call.

Lucas walked into George's office as he hung up the phone.

"Who was that?" Lucas asked.

"What? On the phone?"

"Yeah. On the phone."

"Oh. Just an old friend. Nothing else."

Lucas wondered at George's odd behavior but said, "Okay. What's up, boss?" He sat in the oversized chair in front of George's desk.

"There is this guy, W.T. Grogan. I would like you to interview him this week. Give him a call and see what you can arrange. I was thinking of doing a special feature sometime next week. He has an apartment at the hotel on Broadway and Second Street. So, give him a call as soon as you can and make the arrangements."

"Sure. What is the background on this guy?"

"Seems Mr. Willard Tucker Grogan lost everything in 1932 but somehow miraculously survived and became even wealthier than ever before. My guess is, he took advantage of old widows and others having no choice but to sell all their belongings when the Depression about killed all of us."

"So, you want a human interest slant on this, or should I tear the guy up?"

"Just a simple story will do. I am told his doctor said he was dying and didn't have much time left. Since he doesn't have any family, old W.T. has decided to donate all his money to charities. I figured this is his way of making apologies to all the people he screwed to make his millions, but who knows."

"Hey, George. Maybe if I am nice to the old codger,

he will put us in his will."

"Yeah. Sure. Just get the story."

"I'll give him a call."

"By the way. Happy Birthday."

"Birthday?" Lucas responded. "I had forgotten all about that."

Lucas walked back to his desk and considered how this was a change of pace. He needed something to keep his mind occupied. George wanted to do a human-interest story. Lucas had a genuine dislike for these self-righteous piglets like Grogan. He made the working man look like he was begging in line for bread while this fat cat enjoyed the good life. He picked up the telephone and dialed.

Lucas scheduled a time with Grogan and told him he would ring his room on arrival and then meet him in the hotel lobby where he lived in the Penthouse floor apartment. The hotel also had a Supper Club attached, and Grogan suggested drinks and dinner.

He arrived early, and Grogan was sitting on the edge of his seat in the lobby waiting for him as if Lucas were the only person in the world. As he approached, Grogan stood and introduced himself. He was a dapper gentleman with a long handlebar mustache and dressed in a plaid suit and vest. *Interesting looking fellow,* Lucas thought. He extended his hand, expecting a firm grip from the millionaire; however, it felt more like a limp, dead fish than a handshake.

"Mr. Grogan. I'm Lucas Colby with the *Early Register.*"

"Yes, Mr. Colby," he acknowledged. "It is my distinct pleasure to meet you."

After some simple introductory conversation,

Grogan suggested they move to the bar for a couple of drinks. Lucas wanted a drink desperately but said no thanks and accepted a glass of water. He followed Grogan across the lobby and watched as Grogan tripped over a floor marquee. Lucas turned and helped him up as the Bell Hop picked up the marquee and pushed it to the side out of the way. Lucas saw the sign that said something about special engagement with somebody's big band something. He figured they would probably get most of the interview out of the way before the band started and he could head back to his apartment.

Lucas and Grogan were seated at a table overlooking the street below near the entrance to the Club. Grogan's back was against the window, and Lucas, bored out of his mind, listened to him talk about how great he was and all the things he had done.

"I made my first million when I was just nineteen years old."

Lucas thought, *I was riding a freight train to New York City when I was nineteen.*

"My parents were both farmers, and I figured out a way to improve the crop which tripled production across the state." Grogan continued about how he sold the patent to farmers across the country, making millions of dollars when the Depression hit. He invested in the market and then lost everything.

Lucas was trying to pay attention to Grogan; the drone of his voice was putting him to sleep. The skies were a dull gray, and the weather began to turn. A mist of rain fell on the large picture window as his mind wandered beyond Grogan at the street outside the window. He watched as people passed with their umbrellas open. The taxicabs waited for fares as the slow, rhythmic pace of their wipers kept the windshields clear. A long, black, stretch limousine pulled up and parked in front of the hotel. The driver exited and ran around the car while opening a large umbrella. There was a crowd gathering. From where Lucas sat, he could see the umbrella as someone stepped from the vehicle. He saw a woman only because she waved to the crowd and he could see her hand. He strained to see beyond the blocking umbrella but could see little else. He thought about Savannah for a moment.

"Did you hear what I said, Mr. Colby?"

Grogan tapped the table with his finger and brought Lucas back to the droning of the old chap.

"Yes. Got it, Mr. Grogan." Lucas reviewed his notes, rattling off facts like a grocery list. "Made millions, lost it, Depression, planning on supporting a children's adoption fund, starting a trust fund for the local college." He paused for a moment and then added, "Very admirable of you, sir."

By the time Lucas looked beyond Grogan once again, the crowd had moved on. They continued the interview for the next hour, with Lucas trying every excuse to end the torment when he heard the band warming up. Lucas took this as his queue to wrap up the interview.

"Well, Mr. Grogan, that was some great stuff, and I am sure we will have a great story about you in the coming weeks."

"Oh, but I have so much more to talk about, Mr. Colby."

"I am sure, sir, we could go on all night, and I would love to, but for now, it seems I have more than enough to tell your story."

"Well, I suppose," Grogan said. "But if you need anything else, don't hesitate to call me."

"Absolutely, sir. It would be my pleasure to be able to speak with you again." Lucas politely shook Grogan's hand and bolted for the door.

The band was playing, and the sounds of the Ray Carter orchestra permeated the lobby. As Lucas approached the door, the music subsided, and Lucas pushed the revolving door forward. He stopped as he heard, "Ladies and Gentlemen. A warm welcome for the lovely and talented seductress of the evening, Miss Savannah Vaughn."

Lucas turned and said aloud to no one in particular, "Seductress of the evening? What is this?" He walked back into the lobby and saw the marquee standing in the corner. The picture of the auburn-haired beauty with ocean blue eyes demanded attention; standing, dressed in a skintight, sequenced gown in the center of the poster, was Savannah Vaughn. Lucas stared at the marquee and could not believe his eyes.

"My Savannah?" he thought.

He rushed to the doors of the Supper Club and pushed them open. The band cranked up the sound as Savannah began to sing. Lucas watched her on stage singing as sweet, as seductive, as sexy, and as warm as he could remember. Savannah looked to the back of the room. She saw Lucas. She looked to her left and down at a table in front. Lucas could see three seats. Two were empty, but in one sat a man. He looked back at Savannah and pointed to the table. She continued to belt out a tune and shook her head back and forth, and again pointed. Lucas walked to the front of the room. He could now clearly see the man at the table.

Chapter 67

The man seated at the front row table was balding, a little heavy, and didn't appear to be Savannah's type. Then again, Lucas thought, it has been a while. Maybe her taste in men changed. Lucas cautiously approached the table as the man turned around. The man, hearing Lucas as he approached the table, turned around and stood.

"Hey, Lucas," George said. He pulled Lucas close. "Here's your birthday present. " He pointed toward the stage.

"George? What are you doing here? What's going on?"

The conversation drifted away as Savannah's voice filled the room and filled his heart with memories. Anyone could see she was the desire of every man in the room and the envy of every woman. He sat and watched. George sat back and smiled, knowing his plan was well on its way.

After a crowd-pleasing performance, Savannah walked over to the table to sit with Lucas and George. As she approached, Lucas stood up and pulled out a chair for her.

"Wow! Is this the same Lucas Colby I know so well?" she said with a smile.

Lucas looked at George and said to Savannah, "No. This is not the old Lucas Colby you knew so well."

At that moment, George mumbled something about a telephone call he needed to make and abruptly stood, announcing he was leaving the table. Lucas and Savannah absently glanced in his direction and smiled. George picked up his hat and walked away, leaving the evening to them.

"Where have you been?" Savannah asked.

"You mean all your life?" Lucas added.

She laughed once again at his silly joke.

Her radiance filled the room. She had become everything she said. Lucas looked at Savannah, knowing she was now out of his reach, and said, "More beautiful than I remember."

With a coy look of seduction, a look reminding him of everything he missed, she said, "You know, I have missed you terribly."

Lucas, somewhat embarrassed, paused. He could feel his blood rushing up his neck and across his face.

"Oh my, Lucas," she said. "You're blushing? I don't think I have ever seen you blush."

Savannah reached over, held his hand, pressed it against her face, and said, "I'm sorry. Now I have embarrassed you."

Lucas smiled at Savannah and gazed into her eyes, remembering only the good. "No. I am not embarrassed, but I think I am falling in love all over again."

"Is that right?" Savannah said. "Now I'm turning red." She paused for a moment. "Well, it just so happens, I have nothing to do for a few weeks after this show, so maybe you can tell me more?"

The band started playing, and she moved closer to Lucas. "Listen, I know it's been a long time, and I want to talk. Please say you'll stay."

"Stay? Not a chance, doll face."

Savannah laughed, held his hand, and said, "Cut the doll face chatter."

Lucas laughed at her response.

"You didn't think I remembered, did you?" she said.

Savannah leaned over to kiss Lucas before heading back to the stage, and Lucas blocked her with his hand. "Not on the first date, please."

"Cute," she said. "I'll remember that for later tonight when you take me home."

Savannah walked across the stage and picked up the microphone. Any fool could see every guy in the joint wanted her. Lucas thought how beautiful she had become and watched her long hair flow across her soft shoulders, her sultry eyes as they watched him, and her voice—the voice of an angel. Lucas felt as if wrapped in a warm blanket while sitting in front of a burning fireplace. He was warm and comfortable, but this time, it would be different. This time, it had to be different.

As the sound of the music grew, Savannah welcomed the crowd, and they applauded.

"Hey everybody! I have a special friend in the audience tonight. He's a novelist and a columnist for the *Early Register News*, so watch what you say or do, or you might end up in the papers tomorrow—or maybe one of his novels."

There was loud applause as she walked over to the table, and Lucas gazed up at her. "This is for old times and new times to come."

She began singing *Night and Day*, a tune familiar to them both, and Lucas watched her parade across the stage. Mesmerized, he thought about all the good times they had seen. The bad times were behind them, no more sorrow, and both had come a long way down a dirty and dusty road. He was falling in love all over again.

After her night ended, they met backstage. They sat in the bar until the bartender tapped a glass, letting them know it was time to leave.

Lucas drove her home and tried to think of what to say as they approached her door. She turned and gazed into his eyes.

At a loss for words, Lucas said, "The Giants and the Dodgers play tomorrow at two o'clock."

She laughed. "So what?"

"Do you want to go? It's supposed to be a great game."

"Well, yeah, sure if you want to. But I thought you weren't interested in sporting events?"

"Uh, well, uh, yeah, sporting events can be fun."

She reached up and put her arms around his shoulders. "Let's do this. Let's sleep on it and make a decision in the morning."

Lucas took her keys into his hand and unlocked the door. She nudged the door with her shoulder and stepped into the foyer. With her arms firmly wrapped about his neck, she said, "Don't mind the kitchen. I'm still not much for cleaning up."

When Lucas awoke, he realized it was late morning. He was alone. "She's gone," he said quietly. He rose from the bed and realized he was not at his apartment. He grabbed his pants off the floor, slipped them on, and walked into the front room. Savannah was wearing his shirt from the previous evening and sitting at her table drinking coffee.

"Good morning, my little goddess from heaven," he said. "I was wondering what happened to my shirt."

Savannah smiled. "It smells of your cologne and reminded me of last night." She stood and wrapped her arms around his waist, stood on her toes, and kissed him. "Would you like some coffee?"

"Great idea, and then let's hop over to that café on the corner and grab some breakfast."

"You've got my vote! I'm going to jump in for a quick shower while you drink your coffee."

Savannah left the room, and Lucas called George.

"Hey, George. It's Lucas."

"How was last night?"

"About last night, George," Lucas paused. "It was perfect."

"Excellent!"

"I just wanted to call and let you know that Savannah and I are going to take a couple of weeks and get to know each other again."

"Call me when you get back in town," George said.

Savannah walked from the bedroom and saw Lucas place the receiver on the telephone. "Did you call George?"

"I did. How did you know?"

"I was only guessing." She walked up to Lucas and kissed him once again. "You know, George is a good friend."

"Yes, he is."

After breakfast, they walked along the river's edge along a stone pathway and stopped at a park. "Where do we go from here?" Lucas asked.

"Where do you want to go, Lucas?" she asked.

Chapter 68

The month of renewal with Savannah was going well. They had dinner at Mark's, and afterward, Lucas invited Savannah on a carriage ride through Central Park.

"Do you still have the cabin?" Lucas asked.

"Of course I do, darling. I will always keep the place. Are you thinking about going up there?"

"That's exactly what I was thinking. How about next week, before it gets too chilly?"

They arrived just before sunset, and Lucas asked her out to the porch to watch the sunset. He lit a candle and poured a glass of wine for each. She came from inside the cabin and joined him. As the sun disappeared below the mountains, he turned to her and dropped to his knees.

"Do you forgive me, my love?" Lucas asked.

She smiled, held his hand, and said, "Of course I forgive you." She leaned over, wrapping herself around his head, holding Lucas close in the comfort of her arms. "I forgave you the moment I saw you.

"Can you love me again?" Lucas asked.

"I never stopped loving you, Lucas."

Lucas built a fire in the hearth, and they spent the evening together in each other's arms, planning their future.

When Lucas arrived at his apartment the following day, he called Harriet.

"What do you think about me renting Charlie's for the evening?"

"That's a silly question, Lucas."

"What do you mean, silly?"

"You still own the bar, so I suppose you can do as you please."

"Point taken. I guess I should get used to that again, eh?"

"Not a bad idea, as long as I can still have a job here," Harriet said.

He told her of his plan, and she thought he was crazy but agreed. He arranged to have a dinner catered and a small quartet to play music in the background. After making plans with Harriet, he stopped by Savannah's apartment.

"Hey, handsome! I was hoping you would stop by." Without words, Lucas kissed her with all the passion of the past.

She pulled back. "What was that all about?"

"I am in love with the most beautiful woman in the world."

Savannah laughed at his antics.

"Listen, Savannah. Before we get too deep again, I need to tell you something."

Her smile fell from her face as her expression became solemn. "Lucas. Please—"

"It's not what you think, baby." He interrupted. "I just need to get this out."

She moved to the couch and sat down. "Come sit by me and talk."

"Okay. Here goes. I have discovered perfection doesn't exist. I'm not a perfect person, and there are so many things I wish I hadn't done. If only I could live my life again."

"Oh God, Lucas," Savannah said. "Do I want to hear this?"

"I think you should. I think you need to know that throughout all of this, I have continued to learn. I never meant to do those things to you, Savannah, and I just want you to know this; I've found out a reason for me to change the man I used to be. I have discovered a reason to start over."

"And what is that reason, darling?"

"It's simple. The reason is you."

"Me?"

"Something told me it was you in the background, and I would have seen it if I hadn't been so blind. You saved my life, and for doing so, I am forever grateful. Moreover, I know I must live each day for the rest of my life with the knowledge of all the pain I put you through. I wish I could take it away, and I wish I could have been there to catch your tears and lock them away in my heart.

That is what I needed you to hear and what I needed to confess."

Savannah sat for a moment in silence, thinking about her life, which wasn't perfect as well.

"Lucas. We have all made mistakes, and through all of this, I think we have learned that neither one is perfect. The only thing that matters is you have found your way home and back to me. Now we can be together forever."

"Listen. I have an idea."

"Savannah rolled her eyes. "Here it comes."

"No. I'm serious. How about dinner Sunday night?

"Sunday?"

"Yeah. I have a little place I would like for you and me to visit."

She pretended to think for a moment. "You know, I can't think of anything else I would rather be doing."

"Then it's a date. I will give you the instructions Sunday afternoon."

She looked at him, puzzled. "Instructions? For a date?"

"You'll see. It's a surprise." Lucas jumped up and ran back to his car. He turned and said, "I have something to do. I will call you later!"

Lucas stopped by the jeweler and chose the best diamond ring that money could buy. He contacted the local cab company and gave them instructions on what they needed to do. He sent a courier to Savannah's apartment on Sunday afternoon with a note and three red roses.

You are the guest of Lucas Colby for an evening of dinner, dancing, and delight. A taxicab will pick you up in front of your apartment at precisely four o'clock on Sunday evening, December 12th. Please enter the cab but say nothing to the driver. He knows the exact location.

Sunday afternoon arrived, and Lucas, in grand anticipation, felt like a schoolboy at his first dance. He could barely contain himself with the excitement. He'd asked the driver to wait ten minutes in front of the window after Savannah walked into Charlie's.

Constant checking of his watch showed the time was near, and he looked up to see the cab stop in front of the bar window. He took his position behind the bar and waited.

The cab arrived, and Savannah exited from the back seat and shut the door. Lucas watched her smile as she shook her head and proceeded through the front door. He felt the cold night air blow across the floor and slap him in the face as the door opened and there she was, headed straight for him.

Once again, the answer to his dreams, a goddess blessed him with her presence. She was tall, slender, and beautiful. She had long, auburn hair. Spectacular, one would say. Her blue eyes cut through the darkness of the bar as she approached. She looked like she meant business, and she was coming at him with purpose. Lucas stood his ground, and this time, he knew exactly what to say to her.

Acting as if he couldn't have cared less as she approached the bar, he said, "If you need a phone to call a cab, you can use this one." He pulled the telephone from under the counter.

She looked down at the telephone and said, "Thanks, but I'll just have a cup of coffee."

Her skin was soft and perfect, like a doll. She was flawless. He moved over, standing in front of her. He was quick to notice she wasn't wearing a wedding ring.

She sipped her coffee. Her eyes never left his when he said, "That for you?" He pointed toward the window and the taxicab out in front.

She turned and looked out the window. "I won't need a cab tonight."

He looked deep into her eyes, realizing this life was where he wanted to be. From his pocket, he placed a small black velvet box on the bar in front of her.

"Well. If you don't want a cab tonight, then how about this?"

Savannah opened a small card tucked inside, and a handwritten note said,

To the only woman I have ever honestly loved and

the only woman that has ever honestly loved me, my heart is yours forever.

She looked up into the eyes of the man she had always loved and smiled.

"Marry me," he said.

And they came to know love for what it was supposed to be.

Chapter 69

Lucas quit his job at the *Early Register* and became Savannah's full-time agent. They traveled the country with the band and did shows for the troops. During her performances, Savannah would read out messages from loved ones. She became the *Sweetheart of Armed Services* and one of the most popular female entertainers on the circuit. While in the U.S., she would go into hospitals to interview new mothers and send messages to their husbands overseas.

She hosted the Tuesday and Thursday broadcasts of an NBC musical variety radio program and had a million-seller with their version of *Night and Day,* their favorite song. She left Capitol for Columbia Records and soon after returned to Capitol. At Columbia, she was the first recording artist to sell ten million records. She had a string of popular hits, six of which charted. Her last song was Savannah's biggest hit, topping the United States and the United Kingdom charts.

In 1946, Savannah began a series of programs bringing her international recognition. In Hollywood, she had a weekly one-hour show called the *Voices of America*.

Soon, she added another weekly half-hour musical show and broadcasted to *Radio America*. The public demand for her appearances took her across Europe, where she headlined at all the major clubs.

In 1952, traveling and tours began to take a toll. Lucas, seeing how easily Savannah was tired, suggested she should visit a friend. A doctor Lucas knew.

After some tests and blood work-up, he called them in for another visit.

"It doesn't appear to be anything serious, but I think it looks a lot like simple exhaustion," he said.

"So, what am I to do?" she asked. "I'm an entertainer, and this is our life."

Lucas suggested a short break, and Savannah ultimately agreed.

"It will give you some time to start that book you want to write," she said.

"Honestly, Savannah? It will give us some time to be together, alone, and let you recuperate."

They closed the apartment in New York and decided to spend some time at the cabin. Savannah and Lucas sat by the lake at the cabin. She reminisced about their past, their life where they had been, and how everything changed. As the day closed on a warm summer evening, Savannah looked at Lucas and said, "This is not the life I expected."

Lucas held Savannah close, and she placed her head on his shoulder. He wrapped his arm around her and said, "It never is."

At night, Savannah and Lucas would sleep when tired, and if one woke, the other would rise so neither would be alone. There were times in the past when each wanted to be alone, but those days had passed. They discovered loneliness and being alone were not the same. People fear loneliness, but together they were never lonely, never afraid. Lucas knew the night could be a dreadful time. His thoughts were echoing his past, the memories haunting every corner. But with her there with him, there was no haunting, and he wasn't afraid any longer. He thought, if one person can bring so much courage to the other, you know it cannot last. Good things don't last forever, and soon, everything changes back to the way it was. He knew this, and he had seen it many times before. It's as though something has to come and take the person and put their goodness somewhere else. As if there are not enough good people to go around. And then, they are gone, and you miss them terribly. The love, the experience you have shared, should live within you and build you, making you stronger, but the truth is that it hurts deeply, and you wish you could take their place and let them stay where you are now.

Chapter 70

After a month of relaxing and rediscovering their love, Savannah signed for one last tour. However, the performing had started to grow weary, and they decided it was time to look for other pleasures.

After almost twenty years on the road, they both needed a change. During tours in Europe, Savannah and Lucas would stop in France for vacation. They fell in love with the people and the beauty and magic of this countryside. It had always been a dream, and Savannah spoke the language. Lucas knew enough to get by with the locals. They had thoughts of a large family, but it was never their blessing, so the decision came easy. One morning, Lucas had just finished a telephone call when Savannah walked in.

"Who was that?" she asked.

"Remember Louis Rousseau?"

"Rousseau," she paused, tilting her head as if trying to recall the name. "The man from Paris that accompanied us while in France?"

"Yes. That Rousseau," Lucas told her. "I had contacted him last year knowing you wanted to move to France. I had hoped the villa we'd visited was for sale."

"Wouldn't that have been nice," Savannah said.

"Well. At the time when we spoke, it wasn't."

Savannah looked at Lucas with surprise. "You mean, it is now?"

He took Savannah into his arms and said, "Yes. I just wired him the money. Happy Anniversary."

The idyllic landscape and picturesque village were the perfect settings for the villa. Beautiful, romantic with red brick shutters and poetic gardens, they could walk and view the natural forest line running across the back of the property. Savannah always wanted a garden to grow beautiful flowers. In Brantôme, it felt as though time had stopped, and they had an eternity to be with each other. To the east was a naturally wooded site with a crescent-shaped cliff jutting from the treetops. At the base, the villa and the river Dronne curled around, surrounding the town.

The overlook near the villa contained the remnants of an old church and the enigmatic bas-relief sculpting from the 15th century. The area was rich in history.

Savannah and Lucas would walk for hours, hand in hand, and at the end of the route, they would relax by the water's side. Lucas caught trout in the river while Savannah would relax under a tree, reading or perhaps napping. Every day was a new day, and they would never run out of things to discover. Lucas could never understand why Savannah loved him so much, but he was happy she did.

From the balcony at the villa, they could see the five stone bridges connecting the village. Following the right-angle bridge that spanned the Dronne, they discovered the Monks Garden. The garden retained remnants of three altars with fluted columns and Corinthian capitals. They would spend hours sitting on the park benches along the river and enjoying the perfect day. Sometimes, they would take the bridge facing the abbey and visit the village. The ancient town had retained all of its medieval distinction, and every day was an adventure. On the calm days, they would sit on the terrace with an unrestricted view of the river. The ducks would come around the tables to gather up their offspring, and giant white swans would sleep peacefully just in front of the arches of the next bridge.

While in the village, they would stop at Porte des Réformés and gather their bread and cheeses supplies. During autumn, as the weather would start to cool, they would watch the flocks of geese in the fields set in a perfect country scene with apple trees all around. Savannah enjoyed the autumn raspberries.

As 1967 passed quickly. Lucas continued to work on his latest novel along with a journal of their life and travels. Savannah worked in her garden and tended her ever-growing flowers as their soft and fragrant scent filled the air drifting through the open windows of the villa.

Lucas watched Savannah each day from the window in his writing room overlooking the garden. As her garden continued to prosper, his love for her grew every day. Each season, the roses and the tulips, along with other beautiful things, would come from her tender hands.

On this afternoon, as Lucas peered into the garden from his writing room window, he could see Savannah sitting on her bench surrounded by everything she had created. Across the courtyard, he saw the land that spread to the mountains beyond. The sun sat just above the peaks of the snowcaps in the distance, and he longed to travel again, to take her with him, and discover new and different things. And then he remembered: their life had been complete, and they were together. They slept in a large bed and stayed warm in winter intertwined within each other's arms. When Lucas would sleep, she would sleep, and when he rose, she would follow. And when she walked, he would walk with her, and they would be together. She would talk of things, he would listen, and he would read to her in the evening by the fireplace. In the summer and spring, they would travel the village and beyond. Lucas would fish in the streams while Savannah made sandwiches for a picnic lunch. They would sip lemonade while sitting on the riverbanks and feed the ducks with crumbs of bread. Life was good, and it was complete.

While watching her tend her garden, he listened to the water from the river splash on the grinding wheel. He listened to the sounds of the birds as they chirped in the trees. Savannah looked up at him as he stood at the window. He gazed down at the love of his life as she nurtured her garden, and he thought of how she looked after him and how he came to realize she was the angel watching him all this time and how she had saved him and never left, never stopped loving him.

The years had taken the luster from her auburn locks that peeked from beneath the straw bonnet she wore on the head. Still, he could see her striking, soulful blue eyes, as bright as the night she walked into his life. She waved and threw him a kiss and held up a rose.

She motioned toward him, waving her slender hand and pointing to the bench in the garden where they would always sit and watch the sunset each evening. It had been a long day, and he knew she was tired, but it was a proposition Lucas could not refuse. He hurried down the stairs, stopping only to collect a small pitcher of lemonade so they could enjoy the afternoon weather and their company together. He walked briskly into her garden. As he approached the bench where she sat, he watched the rose fall from her soft hands and onto the ground.

Lucas said goodbye to his Savannah on a quiet afternoon surrounded by the things she loved so much. She knew she had legions of adoring fans, and she traveled the world in search of happiness. Together and ultimately, they discovered the perfect love between two imperfect people.

Savannah had requested to have her ashes spread among the River Dronne. She had said, "In doing so, my soul will spread across the waters and touch the distant shores, so no matter where you are, my darling, you will be by my side forever."

Lucas walked to the waterside holding the container of his angel Savannah and released her soul into the waters of the Dronne.

He sat at the side of the river, and he wept.

Chapter 71

As the years passed, Lucas lived in Brantôme and worked on his journal and other writings. He had hired a gardener to keep up the garden, spending each afternoon sitting on the bench.

One afternoon, he sat where he had said goodbye to Savannah seemingly so long ago. Each day was a painful and yet wonderful memory of a life shared and lost. He had enjoyed a long and prosperous life and could not understand why fate would allow him to outlive everyone he had loved so much.

He thought about Savannah's gentle touch, lessons she so lovingly taught him. He thought about how she watched over him when he thought he was alone. He recalled the memories of his friend Charlie and how Charlie became the father Lucas never had. He thought about how George was always there for him. Lucas thought about all the people in his life and mostly how blessed he had been.

Children were never part of their life. Lucas often wondered why fate would test him all these years. Life had given him so much wisdom without giving him someone to pass it on.

Sitting on their favorite bench, Lucas heard his telephone ring. He walked to the villa to answer the call, and it stopped ringing the moment his hand picked up the receiver. He began to walk away, and the telephone rang again.

"Hello, Lucas? Bill Lansing from Horizon Publishing.

"Hi, Bill. What's up?"

"We received your latest manuscript, and we are going to publish it. I will, however, need to fly you to New York for some reviews and final touches."

"I can be there next week."

Lucas decided to spend a few weeks in New York. It had been a long time since he had been there, and he wanted to see George. In their last conversation, George mentioned he had planned to retire soon and Lucas should be there for the party, so the timing couldn't have been more perfect.

The following morning, he packed some things and, while doing so, considered it was probably time to move back home. It had been a long time since he lived in the states.

Lucas closed the villa, met with the caretakers, and gave them instructions and contact numbers. He stopped by the waterside once again before he left Brantôme.

He took a taxicab to the small airport, connected again in Paris, and flew directly to New York. Once he arrived at the hotel, he called George finding that he was about to retire from the *Early Register*.

"It's still a few weeks away, and I had planned on calling you this week. It sure is a coincidence you have arrived here," George said during their telephone conversation.

"Stranger things have happened over the years," Lucas responded. "I can extend my stay here. I want to be sure that I don't miss the party."

"You won't my friend. I have a special table just for

you."

"Where do you plan on having the celebration," Lucas asked.

"Charlie's. Where else?" George said.

"Are you kidding?" Lucas said, surprised. "I didn't think Charlie's was still open after all these years."

"Really?" George responded. "You know, you are famous."

"Famous? What makes you say that?"

"There is a picture above the bar of you and Savannah dancing, and above the picture is the book you wrote about her life."

"Well then, count me in. I will be there!"

"Tell you what, Lucas. Why don't you meet me at my office?"

Lucas thought about the offer for a moment and said, "Tell you what. Why don't I meet you at the café where we always had lunch? I don't want all the office chatter and such. You understand. Don't you?"

"I understand, and that's fine. I will see you about five."

After Lucas met with his publisher and agreed to the new deal, he grabbed a taxicab and headed for the *Early Register*. He arrived at the café at about four o'clock, figuring he would get something to eat before the long night ahead. Over the years, he and George had visited each other and kept in constant touch through phone and mail, but he had not seen him since he came to France when Savannah passed to help Lucas through a tough time. Lucas believed George was always and would always be his friend. Lucas thought perhaps he would join George in the celebration with a glass of wine, but certainly not like the old days. The taxicab stopped in front of the café, and Lucas walked inside, like stepping back in time. He picked up a newspaper left casually on the table. It was the Early Register's. He took a booth near the window to watch for George. He ordered a sandwich, his favorite, ham on rye with mayo on both sides, and black coffee. While waiting for his order, he read the paper to help pass the time and catch up on the local gossip.

He heard a couple of women come into the café and sit In the booth behind him. He couldn't hear much of what they were saying, but the laughing and carrying on began to bother his concentration. He had grown accustomed to the quiet solitude of the villa, and the noise felt like an intrusion. He knew it would have been easier just to leave, but then he wouldn't have anywhere to go, and it was at least forty-five minutes before George would arrive. He tried to ignore the prattle but could not stand it any longer. He stood and turned toward the booth, directing his comments more to the table rather than to the occupants.

"Ladies, if you could hold it down just a bit, I would appreciate it. Your chatter is beginning to disrupt my thoughts, making it impossible to stay here"

He returned to his seat, satisfied, and thinking it was quieter now.

A few moments passed after opening the newspaper as he noticed a woman's voice. This time it was louder in that she was standing over him at his booth.

"You're always overreacting, and as far as behaving like a madman, that was no act, mister! I am of the opinion you are mad. At what, I don't know, but you need to fix it before somebody pops you" She continued with a certain tone of disgust in her voice. "I have heard you were temperamental and pretty much an ass, so I guess I shouldn't be surprised"

Lucas lowered the paper held in front of him and responded, "Excuse me?"

She was tall and slender, and then he noticed a soft fragrance, an incredible smile. Her chestnut hair held silver strands now, but her eyes could still stop him in mid-sentence.

"Hey, handsome" she said.

"Hey, Cindy."

She sat at his booth. The conversation they had before she left all those years ago came back to him.

"I was talking to my mom about us, and I asked her what she thought I should do" Cindy said.

"What did she have to say?"

"Well, it was about you and Mitch. I couldn't make up my mind because, as odd as it sounds, I loved you both. My mom said that I will always love both of you, but I must choose. That's okay because sometimes, a girl is fortunate to have two true loves in her life. Eventually, I will have to decide but, if fate decides, maybe one day, I may end up with the one I walked away from"

Chapter 72

Lucas loved Savannah with all his heart, but he never forgot Cindy. He thought about her and Mitch off and on for the past thirty years. He had conversations with George during their talks over the years, and he told him Cindy was doing well and settled near Atlanta. There were three children, and Mitch had his own business of some sort. Most importantly, they were happy.

As with lost love, Lucas thought about what could have happened if he and Cindy had married. He often thought about what it could be like to see her one more time, just once again to say farewell. Now, nearing the final chapter after they had their first lunch date together in this very place, their paths cross once again—both a little older and perhaps a little wiser.

"Where have you been? What have you been doing?"

The questions kept coming from both as fast as they could speak, a whirlwind of conversation between two old friends, between two lovers.

"I am in town to meet with my publisher, and George told me he was retiring. The group is having a party at Charlie's this evening."

"That is why I came back to the city! My girlfriend called me last month and said she wanted me to be here. I never in my dreams would have thought you would be here!"

As the conversation calmed and both began to see clearly, Cindy asked, "Any children?"

"No. It wasn't in the cards for us. We tried, but it just never worked out. It was best, though. Savannah and I traveled extensively with her touring, and it just would not have been fair to have children dragged along or worse, staying at home but having absent parents. Besides, Savannah was enough for me to handle without kids."

Cindy told Lucas she followed Savannah's career and owned some of her albums. "She had such a beautiful voice," Cindy recalled.

"I have also followed your career, Lucas Colby."

"My career?"

"Sure. And I have read your books. Even the one about Savannah, and I couldn't believe it when I saw my name. At least you didn't tell all of our secrets."

"I was planning on leaving those secrets for my next book," he said.

There was a pause in the conversation, and Lucas looked again into the lovely face of love lost. "I return the question, how about you? I heard three little ones were running around the house! I would assume they are all grown by now?"

Cindy laughed. "Yes. Grown and married, and with children of their own." She paused for a moment. "Mitch and I have three wonderful children."

She hesitated for a moment, and Lucas could see her soft skin blush. "What's wrong?" he asked.

"Our first child. His name is Luke," she paused as only Cindy could. She glanced away and then looked into Lucas' eyes.

"You named him after me?"

"Well. You could say that."

"Really? Why would you do that? You know, with Mitch and—Oh, my God. Cindy, tell me it's not—I mean. Really?"

Cindy just smiled. "It's okay."

"I didn't know. I should have been there for you."

"No. Really. It's okay," she repeated. "That's how we wanted it to be." She reached across the table, holding his hand. "You see, before Mitch and I married, I told him everything about us. I needed to have a life with a clear conscience, and if I didn't tell him, I would have felt guilty all my life, and it would not have been fair to him or you. I knew it was a dangerous thing to do, but I had to trust love. I was perplexed at best. If I had gone to you, I ran the chance of you feeling guilty, and worse, wanting to marry me and make me an honest woman. I also knew Mitch could have walked out of my life, never wanting to see me again, but it was a chance I had to take. Mitch looked at me after I spilled all my guilt and said, "I know." I said to him, "No, Mitch, you don't know." He held me close and said, "I mean, I know about you and Lucas. I always have."

Cindy touched her eyes with a soft handkerchief pulled from her purse. "I told Mitch, and he said it was nothing we couldn't survive as long as we were together. And being together is all that matters," Cindy said. "He loved me unconditionally, and I could never have asked for more than that."

Lucas could see her eyes begin to well up, and she held his hand tightly. "It was Mitch deciding to raise Luke as our child. We agreed there was no need to complicate matters. To be honest, I think I will never know or understand why he thought as much about you as I did. We had an open and honest relationship during our entire marriage. He was quite a guy, and I have no regrets. When Mitch died about five years ago, I thought about talking to Luke but decided it was best we kept it our secret."

For the first time in his life, Lucas had no idea what to say.

He watched as Cindy's disposition changed. She waved at someone just coming through the door. Figuring it was George, Lucas turned to exit the booth and stand up to greet his old friend. A young man walked toward them, dark brown hair with a slight wave and emerald green eyes. He was tall, and he stopped at the booth as he approached Cindy and Lucas. He smiled at Cindy with a wink and said, "Hey, mom."

"Lucas Colby, I would you like to meet my son, Luke."

He extended his hand and, with a firm handshake, replied, "How do you do sir? My parents have spoken of you quite often. I hear you are a writer?"

Lucas smiled. "Yes, I am, and a good friend of your parents."

"Lucas will see I get back to the hotel tonight, Cindy said.

Cindy and Lucas left the café arm in arm and met up with the crowd at Charlie's. Just before they walked in, she stopped and said, "Are you sure you want to go inside? I know this place holds a lot of memories for you."

"I only bring the girls I am in love with to this place."

They pushed open the doors, and the old crowd was

gathering around George. Lucas walked up to his old friend, and George stood up.

"You lucky dog. You're finally getting to retire after all these years," Lucas said.

George laughed and looked over Lucas' shoulder. "I think you are the lucky one, my friend. It is hard enough to find one love in your life. You, my friend, have had two. I believe you are the luckiest man in the world."

As the evening began to quiet, Lucas asked Cindy if she wanted to leave. They walked the boulevard where they shared a kiss in remembrance of so many years passed. Lucas continued to live in New York and visit the villa in France from time to time. He and Cindy would visit throughout the year and would always enjoy each other's company.

One year later, Cindy and Lucas were visiting England. It had been a long day, and they were both tired but decided to go out to an early dinner.

Afterward, they walked the portico surrounding the building and then along the path near the water to enjoy the cool evening. They stopped and sat on a bench and pondered love's fate returning to an undeserved soul.

"I recall a conversation from many years ago," he said. "You were a confused young lady caught in a dilemma. You sat down with your mom and asked her for advice. She said that you would always love them both, but you couldn't marry both of them, and that was okay because sometimes, a girl will have two true loves in her life. Some girls are just lucky. However, if fate decides, one day you may end up with the one you walked away from."

Cindy looked into his eyes, and Lucas could see the dampness in them. She whispered, "I remember."

As their hands entwined, he said, "Look around. Do you recognize the flowers surrounding you?" Lucas paraphrased a note Cindy had sent to him many years ago.

"Our love is like the Amaranth. Poets say the blossom never dies. Let this flower always remind us of our love for each other. Each time it is warm, each time it is cold, and each time it rains, our thoughts will be one. I will love you, like the blossom of the Amaranth, forever."

****

They lived as one and enjoyed all the times they missed while apart. Fate had brought them full circle, giving Lucas the family he thought he would never have. He recalled when he asked why fate let him live for so long. He thought he'd outlived everyone he had ever loved, and yet fate knew his destiny all along.

She died that spring, and Lucas said his final goodbyes to a love lost and rediscovered. He and my mother had attended a beautiful church in New York not far from the streets that held so many memories for them in Greenwich Village. All the children and grandchildren were there, and he made sure their Amaranth was with her on her final journey, placing the flower in her hands as he said his last goodbye.

As we arrived at the cemetery, a stirring breeze caused the blossoms from the surrounding apple trees to fall like snow flurries in winter. Lucas could smell the sweet aroma of the blossoms as they created a blanket around his feet.

With a clear and perfect sky, the preacher spoke of deeds and remembrances, of love and life. Without warning, misty rain fell. Some ran for their umbrellas while others huddled under trees. Lucas simply remained on a bent knee with his love.

He inhaled deeply, hoping to stop the tears but could not as he drew in the sweet scent of the blossoms that had fallen around him. Cindy could still touch his heart, and only Cindy could make something good out of a rainy day. He could feel her presence on his shoulder, and he remembered a time so long ago.

They kissed in the afternoon, never wanting the day to end.

Chapter 73

Lucas believed we live through pieces of each other's life. Like a puzzle, those pieces fit together and create the whole picture. He believed life held no regrets, sorrows, or mistakes. There were no boundaries with love. Like a puzzle, if you remove one piece, there is nothing left but emptiness. It's that emptiness in your heart that will forever remain and shape your life. As different as all their lives were, and as much as they were the same. Their lives needed to be complete. Throughout the years, each life touched another life. These seemingly unrelated themes were creating the path of the river as it flowed to its destination.

Walking the streets of Greenwich Village one last time, his travel brought him to Washington Square Park, where he'd spent the night long ago, alone and without hope. He stood at the large archway, reading the inscription once again. *Let us raise a standard to which the wise and honest can repair. The event is in the hand of God.* The message he needed had been there for him all this time.

Years of denial and years wasted in trying to find his way, Lucas finally understood. Do what is right and leave the event in the hand of God.

Boarding the plane in the afternoon, he returned to Brantôme. He spent his final days with memories of Savannah while sitting in her rose garden or at the waterside with her spirit.

Each summer, my wife and I, along with the children and grandchildren, visit the villa. We would talk about the old days, the Depression, the rough times, the good times. Lucas told the children stories about how Charlie, a tough man with a gentle undercurrent, taught him character, integrity, and respect. How he gave Lucas a chance when no one else would. He talked about his friend George and how he saved him from certain death, and how George was always there watching him.

Lucas told stories about Mitch and his heroism at Pearl Harbor, how he survived the war. He told us what Cindy meant to him, her gentleness and kindness, and Savannah and how she lit up a room by just walking in. We listened to her music, and we danced on the veranda. Lucas Colby never wrote another word.

After a quiet night with his family in 1992, my father fell into a deep sleep. He dreamt once again. "*He heard the click of the cylinder lock on the door. She placed her hand around his belt buckle, and with a light tug, she said, "By the way, handsome, you're not going anywhere.*"

A word about the author...

Steven first published short stories of personal adventures through a national magazine. A South Florida native, he prefers hot weather and has a full wardrobe of cargo shorts, and T-shirts to prove it. He believes art imitates life as much as life imitates art and it is those experiences that allow the crafting of true writing. His first novel exposes human frailty, the reality of truth, and life experiences. He creates an imaginary world of intrigue, desire, and humor reflecting the perfectly imperfect. He is a weaver of stories and understands the simplicity of people; how they act and talk in everyday life. His characters are unpretentious, fallible, quirky, and honest. Human nature drives his characters, curiosity drives his story. www.stevenlabree.com

Thank you for purchasing
this publication of The Wild Rose Press, Inc.

For questions or more information
contact us at
info@thewildrosepress.com.

The Wild Rose Press, Inc.
www.thewildrosepress.com